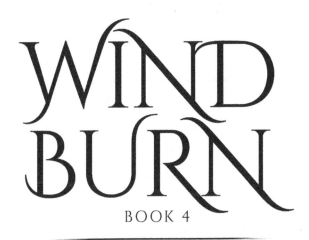

WIND BURN

BOOK 4

THE ELEMENTAL SERIES

PRAISE FOR THE ELEMENTAL SERIES

"I love Shannon's Rylee Adamson series . . . and I was wonderfully surprised that I loved her Elemental Series even more!"

-Denise Grover Swank
USAT & NYT Bestselling Author of the "Chosen Series"

"I could not put it down and greedily consumed it in one sitting!"

-Books In Veins

"I think Larkspur aka Lark is the new heroine to watch out for . . ."

-Coffee Book Mom Reviews

"What a fantastic start to a new fantasy series! I love a strong female lead and we were delivered that in spades with Larkspur . . . This story is fast paced and exciting right from the start. I can't wait to see what comes next!"

-Boundless Book Reviews

Copyright
Windburn (The Elemental Series, Book 4)

Copyright © Shannon Mayer 2016
Copyright © HiJinks Ink Publishing, Ltd. 2016
All rights reserved

Published by HiJinks Ink LTD.
www.shannonmayer.com

This is a work of fiction. Names, characters, places and incidents are either the product of the author's imagination or are used fictitiously, and any resemblance to actual persons living or dead, business establishments, events or locales is entirely coincidental. Or deliberately on purpose, depending on whether or not you have been nice to the author.

Original Cover Art by Damon Za
Mayer, Shannon

WINDBURN

BOOK 4

THE ELEMENTAL SERIES

SHANNON MAYER

USA TODAY BESTSELLING AUTHOR OF *RECURVE*

ALSO BY SHANNON MAYER

THE RYLEE ADAMSON NOVELS

THE ELEMENTAL SERIES

Recurve (Book 1)
Breakwater (Book 2)
Firestorm (Book 3)
Windburn (Book 4)
Rootbound (Book 5)

THE BLOOD BORNE SERIES

(Written with Denise Grover Swank)
Recombinant (Book 1)
Replica (Book 2)

THE NEVERMORE TRILOGY

The Nevermore Trilogy
Sundered (Book 1)
Bound (Book 2)
Dauntless (Book 3)

A CELTIC LEGACY

A Celtic Legacy
Dark Waters (Book 1)
Dark Isle (Book 2)
Dark Fae (Book 3)

THE RISK SERIES

(Written as S.J. Mayer)
High Risk Love (Book 1)

CONTEMPORARY ROMANCES

(Written as S.J. Mayer)
Of The Heart

CHAPTER 1

Defiance is not a word Elementals use lightly; not when it can see us banished from the very places where we draw our strength and feed our soul. Yet the word was one I was beginning to know all too well, in theory as well as in practice.

I stared across the table at my younger brother, Raven. He stared right back, concern knitting his thick dark brows.

"Lark, please say you will change your mind and stay here. Stay out of the human world. The more you stray from the tenets of our father and the mother goddess—"

I waved a hand, cutting him off as I leaned forward

with a grimace. My body was still sore from the battles within the Pit, and my muscles protested even that slight movement. "You would rather we leave the king to fend for himself when we all know he isn't in his right mind? He must name an heir . . . something he has yet to do."

That was one reason I needed to go after Father. While little love was lost between him and me, our people needed an heir. How each elemental family replaced their ruler was different, and this was ours. It had to be someone the previous ruler chose with the guidance of the mother goddess.

As far as we knew, Father hadn't chosen anyone. Which meant if he died, there could easily be civil war. Already lines were drawn within the Rim as to which sibling our people would back if it came to war.

Worse, Cassava could return and *technically,* as the first wife of the king, could take over. As strong as she was, that scenario was a distinct possibility. On my lap, Peta stirred and looked up at me, her green eyes clear as emeralds.

"You must tell me about her sometime, Lark. I sense great pain in you when you think of her name." Her words were soft enough I didn't think Raven heard. Most likely he didn't realize Peta was my familiar. No one in the Rim had ever been handed a feline as a companion. Ever.

Most of my elemental family thought she was a cat I'd picked up. A stray. And for the most part, I hoped to keep it that way.

SHANNON MAYER

Peta made an excellent spy when people didn't know she could comprehend.

My brother tipped his head back, and his throat bobbed as he seemed to struggle for words. I, on the other hand, did not suffer that particular ailment.

"Raven, I appreciate your concern, I do. But there really is no other choice. We all know it, but—"

Lifting his left hand, he waved it once between us, and for a moment, I caught a glimmer of green as lines of power trickled up his arms. I could see when another elemental was about to use their power, and the intent behind the usage. A gift—as far as I knew—only I had. Rather handy in a fight. Which, the way my last few months had been going, was almost a daily issue.

On the loaded table in front of us, a vine shot up through the cracks. A creeping larkspur vine flowered violet blue blossoms as he reached out and touched it.

"You are stronger than we all knew, Lark. And deadly, I am beginning to think, not unlike your namesake. Do you know our siblings talk about you when they gather?"

Snagging an overripe peach from the table, I took a bite out of the flesh. The juices—sweet with the last rays of the summer sun—dripped down my chin and onto Peta's head. She flicked her ears and glared at me before jumping from my lap to my shoulder where she groomed herself.

I swallowed, making him wait for my answer. "When are they not talking about me? I'm the half-breed bastard turned Ender. I'm the blemish and blight on our family tree, if you recall."

Raven shook his head, reached across the table and took a hunk of fresh cheese off my plate. I glowered at him in mock anger.

"That was before what happened with Keeda." He popped the cheese into his mouth and chewed while his words settled around me.

The sweet taste of the peach's juice turned to dust in my mouth, and I struggled with the second bite. Guilt roared through me like a lion unleashed on unsuspecting prey. "What are you talking about?"

He leaned forward, his blue eyes intense as they bored into mine. "They know what you did to her. They don't know how, I don't know how. But they know the way she is . . . you did it. And it scares them. Elementals do stupid things when scared, you know that."

The peach rolled out of my suddenly numb fingers, and dropped to the table. I lowered my hands to my thighs, gripping the fabric of my pants. "What . . . are they saying exactly?"

"That you broke her mind. That you are some sort of freak because of your half-breed status. There are rumors coming from the Pit that maybe . . . maybe you aren't half human like we always thought. Maybe your mom was a—" His mouth clicked shut and his face paled at a rather alarming rate. Perspiration beaded his upper lip as he gripped the edge of the table.

Raven was afraid of me.

"What do you think she was? A goblin?" The

words were light, but the tension between us was anything but.

"A Spirit Elemental," he breathed out.

There, the words were finally in the open. I didn't deny them, seeing as my mother was exactly what he thought.

"Are you talking to the others? To Vetch and Briar?" I made myself say the words, and to not cringe as I spoke them. Raven was one of two siblings I was close with. He was of an age that Bramley—my brother, who Cassava had killed—would have been. Raven always stood with me, tried to help soften the cruelty of his mother and our other siblings. With the recent changes in Bella's relationship with me, he was no longer the only one I could truly call a friend as well as a sibling. But the thought that he was afraid of me burned a hole straight through my heart. "Raven, please tell me you aren't afraid, too."

Clutching the table, he slowly shook his head. "I don't know what to believe. Vetch says the information about Keeda came from someone he trusted. Someone who had no reason to lie to him. And now your reaction confirms the truth in it. If you would hurt her, one of the weakest siblings, what would you try to do to the rest of us?"

Goose shit and green sticks, I was my own worst enemy. "So Vetch, Briar, and you have been discussing whether I'm dangerous to you?"

"And Bella," he said softly, his eyes flicking downward.

If he had taken one of the carving knives and

jammed it into my stomach, I'm not sure it would have hurt any more than the sharp pain his words cut into me.

"Bella wouldn't," I spat out, pushing back from the table. Whatever appetite I had was gone.

"It's not like that, Lark. She . . . she's the ruler right now; she has to know the mood of her people. And like it or not, any of our siblings could be in line for the throne. Bella is being smart; she needs to keep her fingers in every discussion she can. Particularly when it comes to our siblings."

I didn't want her to be smart. I wanted her to tell them they were horrible and that she trusted me even though I had to make tough choices. She of all the people in my life knew the truth of what happened to Keeda in the Pit.

Thinking she was about to become the new queen of the Pit, Keeda had attacked me. Wearing a disguise, I'd thought her to be my stepmother, Cassava. I'd used everything at my disposal to stop her, including my untrained, and wildly unpredictable, ability with Spirit.

In doing so, I'd burned out my sister's mind, taking away her personality and memories, along with most of her ability to speak—everything that made her an Elemental. The grief and horror of my actions were raw, oozing like an infection I couldn't heal.

Anger cut through the weaker emotions. Belladonna knew I had had no choice but to stop Keeda the way I had. Damn her for turning on me.

Peta dug into my bare shoulder, jabbing me with

her tiny—yet ridiculously sharp—claws. "Don't be a fool. They are wary with reason."

The anger slid out of me with a slow exhale. She was right, as was so often the case. "Please don't be afraid of me. Please. I promise I would never hurt you. You're my favorite brother."

A tentative smile crept over his lips, curling up more on one side than the other. "I believe you. I'll try to sway Vetch and Briar, but they are scared. Terrified, actually, if I am honest."

"Fear makes people do stupid things," I said, repeating his words. "What do you think they are planning?"

He shrugged. "Nothing yet. A lot of talk about how horrible you are. How much Vetch hates you and wishes you'd died along with your mom and brother."

"Right. So nothing new there."

"Nope, sorry, sis. You still suck rotten apples even though you've saved the Deep and the Pit. In the Rim, you're still nothing but a dirty little Planter." He winked to soften the words, but there was for the first time a feeling of discord in him I'd never sensed before.

Almost like he believed what he was saying. The urge to use Spirit to discern how truthful he was snaked through me. I tamped it down. Every time I used Spirit, I lost a part of myself.

Eventually, if I kept using it, I would end up like Cassava. A twisted, cruel version of the person I'd once been. Besides, this was Raven. Like Bella, I knew he had my back. Wasn't he proving it by giving me the heads-up on my siblings? Yes and yes.

"Raven, stay out of trouble while I'm gone, will you?" I stepped away from the table. A part of me wanted to hug him goodbye, but after our conversation, I wasn't sure he'd let me touch him. Better to not reach for him and be rejected.

He stood. "What, no hug?"

So I wrapped my arms around him, gratitude flowing down my cheeks. I brushed the tears away with one hand. "Thanks."

He rubbed my back in a slow circle with one hand as he squeezed me tightly. "Nothing to it. Figured if you were going to do me in, it would have been when I filched the cheese from your plate."

Do him in . . . was that how my siblings thought of me? As a rampant killer out to annihilate my own family? I didn't realize I was out of the kitchen until I was on the stairs that led up and out of the Spiral, my emotions and Raven's words chasing me like hounds on a fox.

Peta swayed on my shoulder. "Where are we going? To see Bella?"

Much as I wanted to see my sister and have her reassure me, I needed to be strong.

"To the Enders Barracks. You're right about Bella. She's doing her job and I have to do mine; I don't need to bother her with silly insecurities." I stepped out of the Spiral and looked into the swaying branches of the redwoods around us. Filtering between the trees, the morning fog rolled in as if a living entity. This was home, and no matter how far I went, no matter how long I was forced away, my heart belonged here. Hopefully the search for Father would be the last excursion I had for a long while.

"Did you mean what you said to Raven about finding your father?" she asked.

"I promised Bella I would go after him," I said as I trotted down the steps, "and that's exactly what I'm going to do."

CHAPTER 2

 gaggle of children ran by me, laughing and squealing as they chased one another. Peta's eyes followed them. "What I would give to be oblivious to the responsibilities of the world and be a kitten once more."

Her words triggered a thought that had been burrowing for some time in my brain. I had responsibilities I needed to check in on.

I was in the possession of not one, but two precious stone rings. Long before I'd ever been born, the Elementals had been a bit naughty. To remind them of their place, the mother goddess went to the five nations of man. For each, she fashioned a powerful stone to be held in times of need to help rule a portion of the elemental world and keep humans safe.

The humans with the stones helped keep the world in balance.

Those stones were supposed to be legend, yet I'd found four of the five. They weren't all rings, but they were all powerful. The two I still had in my possession controlled Spirit and Air. I'd hidden them away so those who would abuse their power would not get their hands on them. And I needed to make sure both stones were hidden still.

I couldn't allow that much power to fall into the wrong hands.

Twisting on my heel, I changed direction and headed out to the Planters' fields. As early as it was, the Planters were already doing their job, tending to the seedlings, bringing water from the ravine and working the soil for late fall planting.

I'd spent most of my life here, struggling to make a plant even sprout. For so long I'd been blocked from my connection to the earth, but the Planters, for the most part, had accepted me as one of their own. Yet as I walked past them, not one lifted their eyes to me. I looked for Simmy, my old friend, and saw her one daughter. Waving, I caught her attention.

"Petal, where is your mother?"

"She died when the lung burrowers spread," she said, her tone more than a little frosty.

I closed my eyes and whispered a prayer to the mother goddess for Simmy's soul. "I'm sorry."

"You should be."

I was more than a little dumbfounded. "Excuse me?"

"I said you *should* be." She poked at my chest with her hard, soil-blackened finger. "Cassava wouldn't have done that with them burrowers if there was no interference. She would have been a strong queen. And now what do we have? A king who's gone on a walkabout with no one to rule but his useless wife, or worse, his untested, pregnant daughter. Pregnant with an *Undine's* baby. Yet another half-breed to pollute our world."

I took a step back. Not out of fear. At least not in the conventional sense. I was afraid I'd wrap my hands around her neck and squeeze until either she retracted her venomous words or she stopped speaking altogether. "That is your soon to be queen. I'd watch your tongue if I were you."

"I doubt it, half-breed." She spat at my feet.

Peta's tail flicked around my neck and her cold, damp nose shoved into my ear, hiding the fact she spoke. "You can do nothing right now, and fighting would only prove them right. Ignore them and keep walking, Dirt Girl."

Forcing my feet to move, I walked toward Petal, forcing her either to step out of my way or get trampled.

She moved at the last second, so I ended up thumping my shoulder into hers.

"Half-breed freak," Petal said before she spat at my feet a second time. The two pieces of my spear hanging at my side beckoned me with a deadly whisper. One quick twist and the weapon would be whole. I could hold the blade to her throat and force her to apologize.

Before Peta could say anything, I'd already tamped the anger down. We were clear of the planting fields now. "Peta, how can they be so blind? Cassava was the one who brought the lung burrowers, then held our family hostage with the cure."

Peta was quiet for a moment. "The humans have a funny saying I heard once, and I didn't understand it at the time as I was very young. But more and more I see it to be true. 'The devil you know is better than the devil you don't.' They knew Cassava, knew she was horrible and out of her mind."

Slowly I nodded, understanding what she was getting at. "And so they would rather deal with Cassava than an unknown factor. Even if it's Bella."

"Or your father." She shook her head. "From what I've gleaned in the last few days, he didn't rule much. Cassava ruled through him. In his own way, he is an unknown factor to his own people."

"Damn." I breathed the word out. She was right.

"So bringing him back doesn't really give them a measure of peace, because in their minds, you are bringing back a puppet."

Her words didn't have long to echo in my ears before a new problem arose, one I'd been dreading. The blasted field section of the Rim was where the earth had died. A plague long before I'd been born had eaten away at the dirt and now nothing was left. No power to draw, no nutrients for plants and animals. And it was where I had hidden the two gemstones.

The gray earth had footprints all around, crisscrossing back and forth.

"Oh, this is bad, Peta," I whispered. "How in the seven hells did anyone figure out where I'd hidden them?"

"Hidden what?" She leapt from my shoulder and sniffed the ground. "I smell nothing. I see footprints but there is no scent. There is only one Elemental I know who can do that."

"Blackbird."

Him wanting the two gemstones didn't make sense. Blackbird was the only elemental who carried all five elements. He was the child Requiem had been trying to breed in the Deep. A monstrosity of power and destruction.

"Explain what is hidden and why Blackbird wants it." Peta trotted in front of me, her gray fur blending with the ashen earth, creating a strange camouflage where moment to moment she almost disappeared.

"I have two of the stones from the legend of the five."

She stopped with her paw mid-air, and her head swivelled to look at me. "Come again."

"I have the pink diamond and the smoky diamond. Spirit and Air."

Carefully she lowered her paw and sat. "And someone knows where they are hidden besides you?"

"I told no one." I headed for the boulder I'd buried them under, far deeper than I needed to, probably. At least that was what I thought when I'd done it. Now I wasn't so sure.

I dropped to my knees and buried my hands into the loose, dead soil. I dug down through the layers of the blasted earth with my power. Peta stood beside me with her front paws on my thighs. "You know, you should not be able to do that."

"What do you mean?"

"The soil is dead, Lark. Nothing can grow here. There is nothing left to be manipulated. There is no power in it."

It took a full minute for the bag I'd buried to be pulled up through the ground. "Must be another quirk of mine." I gave her a grin and she shook her head.

"Quirk? You're just plain weird, Dirt Girl. You do supposedly impossible things without any problem."

I shrugged. "Spirit boosts my power with the earth. We know that."

"But this much?"

I had no answer. I didn't know why I could do what I could do. Maybe because I was the mother goddess's chosen one.

Or maybe I was a freak, as Petal had said.

Under my fingers rolled the pliable leather bag I'd put the two gemstones in. With a quick look around, I pulled the bag out and peered inside.

"Drop them into your hand. Someone could have switched them," Peta said. Goddess, I hoped she was wrong.

I spilled the stones onto my palm. They glittered. Swirls of power glimmered and flickered from their depths, sending a scattering of rainbow flecks over my arms. I had no doubt these were the originals.

I sighed, relief washing over me. I stuffed them

back into the leather bag and then inside my vest. "I have to hide them again, but where?"

"May I make a rather bold suggestion?" Peta asked.

I couldn't help but roll my eyes. "Please. When do you ask if you can be bold?"

"You are going on a rather dangerous journey in search of your father. What are the chances we run into Blackbird? Or Cassava? Or some new threat?" She paused, but before I could formulate words she went on. "Don't bother answering. The chances are high; Spirit Elementals draw trouble to them, and we are going to add a Tracker to the mix which will cause a duplication of said trouble."

I folded my arms over my chest. "All those words, and no actual suggestion yet."

Her lips twitched. "Keep the smoky diamond close to you in case you need it; hide the pink since you already carry Spirit."

Her idea held merit, but it bothered me. An Air Elemental had been the one to kill my mother and little brother. I did not want anything to do with that particular element. "Perhaps. I will think on it."

The crack of a twig spun me around. A fleeting figure was all I could see dashing off into the distance.

"Peta, go!"

From one beat to the next, she was a tiny gray housecat, then a bounding gray and white snow leopard tearing through the forest after the spy. Now was my chance. I took off in the other direction, heading toward the northern lines of the Rim. There was only one place safer for the stones than the blasted fields.

Mind you, there was one person who wasn't going to be happy about my solution.

The trees and bushes, animals and birds blurred as I ran. I tapped into the strength of the earth and used it to boost my speed and agility. The power allowed me to cover the distance between the blasted fields and Griffin's home in no time.

As a wolf shifter, he was not allowed to live within the Rim with us. But he was welcome to the edge, which was where he stayed. I wasn't sure if I could call him a friend, but he had helped me more than once.

Skidding to a stop at his door, I didn't hesitate, but let myself into the rounded hut that was his abode. "Griffin, I'm sorry to barge in on you." I spoke swiftly, recalling all too clearly his method of teaching someone a lesson.

My eyes adjusted to the dim light; I was alone. Maybe this was better. I strode to the center of the room and went to my knees. At my urging, the hard dirt floor opened a hole big enough for the leather bag that held the two diamonds. I paused, thinking about what Peta had said. If she was right, and I needed the extra help but left the smoky diamond behind, I would be furious with myself. And if I didn't need it, the stone was as safe with me as anywhere else.

I reached into the leather bag and pulled the smoky diamond out. One quick knot on the bag and I dropped it into the hole. Fifteen feet deep and in the middle of Griffin's home . . . that had to be safe enough. "Mother goddess, keep it safe."

Smoothing the dirt over, I took a moment and let my curiosity lead me through the room.

Griffin led a sparse life, with little in the way of knickknacks or personal items. The table held a few clay dishes, leftovers of his last meal. A shirt hung over the single chair. What caught my attention, though, was a single book on the bed. The rumpled bed sheets camouflaged it so I almost missed it. The cover was black with no title, no author's name. Using one finger, I flipped it open.

Images stared up at me, startling me. I stepped back, then forward again.

These were what the humans called . . . photos . . . . I'd heard of them, but never seen them. Like a painting, only clearer and crisper. Crouching, I flipped through the book. Some of the pictures were black and white, others were in color. The ones that stopped me were those of Griffin with his arms around a petite blonde woman, a young boy sitting in front of them. The child was maybe ten or so, and was Griffin's son without a doubt. They could have been duplicates of one another. A child then . . . perhaps he'd lost his family . . . maybe that was why he hid in the woods.

Feeling like I'd seen something intimate I shouldn't have, I backed away and slipped out the door. Drawing on the power of the earth once more, I raced to the center of the Rim. I wove my way, deliberately backtracking and changing direction several times.

Just in case more than one person was watching me.

I reached the Enders Barracks when the sun hung mid-sky, beating down on my head as it burned off the last of the morning fog.

Stepping inside the building that had so quickly

and naturally become my refuge, I took a deep breath. The smell of leather, oil, and sweat permeated the air. My room was through the main exercise area, and near the far end of the sleeping quarters. I hurried there, wanting nothing more than the quiet of my own space. Once inside my room, I leaned against the door and finally let the task ahead of me crash down.

Finding my father would be an arduous process. I had to nail down a Tracker first, and from what I understood, they could be tricky and temperamental on the best of days. Then I had to persuade the Tracker to help me. Then convince my father to come home.

But worst of all . . . once he was home, I needed to make my father see that not only did he need to name an heir . . . for the sake of our family, he needed to step down as king.

The final topper? I was afraid to see him again. To have him tell me once more how useless I was. That I was the mistake he regretted more than any other. I put a hand over my eyes.

A task I had to do out of duty.

A task I dreaded with all my heart and soul.

 I leaned my head against the door. "Mother goddess, help me not screw this up."

knock on my door snapped me out of my half-hearted prayer. I turned and opened the door. Honey gold eyes locked on mine, and my tongue seemed to tangle on his name. "Ash."

"Lark, we need to talk about you going after your father." His eyes softened with concern. For me. My heart warmed more than a few degrees.

"Do you have an idea of where he might have gone?" I stepped back so he could come into my tiny room. I could have lain down twice in either direction, which gave me room for a small bed, desk, and chair, and that was it. I sat on the bed.

Ash didn't sit. He tucked one thumb into the edge of his belt and ran the other hand through his short blond hair. "I don't think you should be going after him."

"What?" That was not what I'd expected—at least not from him. Cactus maybe, or even Niah. But not Ash. As an Ender, he had taken vows to protect and obey the king at all costs.

Somehow those vows had slipped by me during my Ender testing, but I tried not to worry too much.

"Your father left of his own accord, Lark. The Rim guards reported he spoke to several of them. Told them he needed to clear his head and think about his next step in dealing with those who would try to steal his throne."

I gripped the edge of the bed, the mattress creaking. "And did he give names of those he was concerned about usurping him?"

"Your name came up. So did Raven's and Belladonna's."

"So now, of course, this information is all over the Rim because the damn guards gossip like a bunch of old ladies," I snapped.

He shrugged. "Like always, some things never change." His eyes softened. "Lark, he wanted to leave. No one forced him."

"You don't know that," I said. "The power of Spirit is tricky. Cassava—"

"No longer has the ring. And it's still hidden, right?"

I nodded. He was right, Cassava didn't control Spirit anymore. That didn't mean we were out of the woods in that respect. "Blackbird could have done it."

"But why? You're grasping, Lark. I know you don't want to believe ill of your father. He is my king, I don't want to think he'd abandon us. But it's obvious he has."

"Then we need to get him back. We need him to take his place and name his heir."

Ash cleared his throat and looked at his feet. A pit grew in the center of my belly and spread outward with fear.

"Mother goddess, tell me he didn't name someone before he left. Or if he did, that it was Bella."

"Documents were brought to me this morning . . . they look like your father's handwriting."

"Who did he name?" Bella, Raven, or even Briar would be reasonable.

Ash shook his head as he spoke. "He named your eldest brother, Vetch."

Whatever hope I'd held out for my father's mind disintegrated. Vetch was Cassava's son through and through. There was no doubt in my mind she was behind this. The only choice I had now was to bring my father home so we could keep Vetch off the throne as long as possible.

"Even more reason for me to go. That has to be wrong." I refused to believe my father was working within all his capacities if he had named Vetch as heir.

Ash crouched in front of me and placed a hand on each of my thighs. "We can weather this storm, Lark. We've managed well until now. This is another squall we need to hunker down and ride out." His hands warmed my legs through my pants as he squeezed my thighs gently.

"I don't want to lose you, Lark. I feel like this time we might not make it if you leave. If you go after your father—"

"Don't say that," I whispered, finding myself leaning toward him. He took a crouched step closer so my legs were on either side of him and he could slide his hands around my waist.

"Your father would not look for you, Lark, and I cannot bear the thought of him taking another piece of your heart and smashing it in front of you." His hands slid up my back to my shoulders and then down again.

I bent forward and pressed my lips against his, a tiny moan slipping out of me as I whispered his name. My whole life he'd watched over me, tried to protect me and keep me from harm even when Cassava controlled him with the ring. He'd trained me to be an Ender, helped me grow as a fighter and pushed me to my limits at times.

Under all that was this truth: I loved him because he pushed me to be my best. He never let me wallow in my self-doubt.

Tangling my hands into the short strands of his hair, I held him to me as our hands and mouths began a hungry perusal of one another. He tugged at my vest, then slid my thin undershirt over my head, before shedding his own top.

I slid back onto the bed, the sheets soft against my bare skin. "The door."

He spun, locked the door, and was on me in the space of perhaps a single heartbeat. A laugh slipped out of me. "Eager much?"

"You have no idea," he whispered into my ear. His teeth grazed its edge as his hands explored my body and I returned the favor. I helped him remove his pants and then mine. Our bodies were hard with muscle, scarred and bruised, yet I felt none of that as he slid into my warmth.

Home. This was home.

Our hearts beat in time with one another, our mouths breathed as one, our bodies tangled until there was no telling where one of us began and the other ended.

In all my years, even with Coal, nothing had prepared me for this feeling of unity. Of knowing the person I was with would always stand with me. Even when he didn't agree with me. Maybe even more so in those moments.

Trust. Love. Faith. They were all bound in the heat between us.

Ash was one of the few people in my life who *knew* me, and my secrets, and loved me still.

I linked my fingers with his, reached above our heads and pressed our joined hands against the wall. "Don't stop." The words from my mouth in a whispered plea.

The cadence of our joining never faltered, never became frantic as we stared into each other's eyes. A glimmer of possibility spun in front of me, and I knew it for what it was, even if I didn't understand it wholly.

Spirit wove through us, showing me what could be if I stayed. If I forsook my father and stayed here, with Ash.

Laughter, love, a home.

A child with golden eyes and blond hair who carried his father's smile as he held my fingertip with his tiny hand.

Ash's hands . . . he would fight for me, hold me tight when I fell, lift me in the dark hours. A companion who would never turn from me, or the battles I chose.

The Rim, empty of life, desolate and barren. Our family wiped out.

That last confused me. What would happen if I didn't stay? If I went after my father? The question spun out another possibility.

Blood pooled on the dead soil, the tip of my spear buried in it to the wooden haft.

Bodies littered the ground.

My father's face twisted with anger.

Standing alone in the middle of the Rim.

My people alive, battered and bruised, but alive.

Survival for my world even while I lost all I held dear.

I closed my eyes, but the images were there. They started a flood of tears I couldn't hold back as I reached my peak. Climax of the body, and a piercing of the soul at the same time tore a cry from my lips. I untangled my hands from Ash's and wrapped my arms around him, clinging to him as I sobbed. He spoke, but his words were the buzzing of a bee's nest in my ears as Spirit throbbed through me, ebbing as though a tide receding on the sand.

"Larkspur, look at me." Ash's voice was hard and finally cut through the emotional storm raging inside.

I blinked several times and did as he asked. He'd rolled us to our sides, his right arm tucked under us as he kept me pulled tightly to him. "I'm sorry, it . . . it was Spirit."

His turn to blink several times, confusion clouding his eyes. "What do you mean?"

"It showed me a possibility." I made as if to move away from him and he tightened his arm around me.

"No. Talk to me, Lark. Any problems we've had have been because of piss-poor communication."

Mother goddess, how could I tell him what I saw? It would only reinforce that he was right and I should stay. The problem? I saw all too clearly the child with his father's smile and golden eyes. Yet that path would lead to the destruction of the Rim.

As would the second; though it at least left life to start again.

"I think I saw what would happen if I stayed. And if I left." I paused and he touched the side of my face.

"Tell me."

"Neither option ended well." I trailed a hand down the side of his face.

This. I wanted this and I wanted him. I wanted the little boy who would call me mama. My heart felt as though it would burst. Ash dropped his lips to mine.

"I don't want to lose this, Lark."

"We won't." I had to believe I could have it. To

believe I could go after my father and have the fairy tale of Ash at my side and a future together.

A soft scratching at the door turned my head.

Peta spoke as though she had her mouth pressed against the wood. "Lark, you and Ash better get your clothes on. Cactus is on his way."

Cactus.

His name shot through me, reminding me that my heart was torn in two, even if at the moment it leaned precipitously toward Ash. Scrambling to get my clothes on, I noticed Ash lying on the bed, stretched out like some sort of languorous cat who'd filled his belly with warm milk. Almost like he wanted Cactus to catch him.

Damn man. Damn me for sleeping with him.

No. I would not regret Ash. But I couldn't stop the guilt that cascaded through me. I couldn't tell Cactus. Not yet. Maybe not ever, if I wanted to remain friends with him.

But it wasn't fair to string him along either.

Still, I knew I wasn't ready to let him go.

"Get your clothes on!" I threw Ash's pants at him.

He laughed and shook his head. "You think I don't know you have feelings for Cactus? I would share you, if you asked it of me. But he won't, Larkspur. We both know that. He has too much Salamander in him. Jealous bastards that they are."

I pulled the last of my clothes on and turned my back as he laughed softly. There wasn't an ounce of meanness in it. That wasn't his way. He didn't hide once he'd set his mind on something.

In this case, he'd clearly set his mind and heart on me. I jerked the door open. Peta sat on her haunches in her housecat form and stared up at me with large, too-innocent green eyes.

"Have fun?"

Heat flushed my face. "How much do you sense when I . . ." I waved my hand behind me to encompass the bedroom and a still-lounging Ash.

"Enough to know not to find you right away. I've been through this a time or two, Lark. Trust me to know what I'm doing." She trotted away. "Perhaps you should follow me, Dirt Girl."

I took her advice and hurried after the twitching white tip of her tail as she led the way back into the main hall where the training room was situated. In the minute it took to get there, I calmed myself.

I'd done nothing wrong. I'd never promised Cactus anything.

As I stepped into the main room, the door across from me swung open, and Cactus strode in. Whatever calm I'd gathered fled. My heart did a funny little jump followed by a spurt of guilt.

"Lark, you should have come and woken me." He grinned, his bright green eyes glittering with good humor. We'd been back in the Rim for only a few days, but already he'd gained strength and health. He jogged toward me, grabbed my hand and lifted it to his mouth, kissing the back of it.

"Mmm. A bit sweaty. Been working out already?" He lifted his eyes to mine and I jerked my hand away. A rush of heat climbed my neck and I fought to get my emotions under control. I did not want to hurt him. He had been my best friend when we were children, and he'd helped me both times I had to enter the Pit as an adult even though it had been years since I'd seen him last.

Peta put herself between us, her tail twitching spastically. "What do you want, Cactus? Lark is an Ender and has duties that have nothing to do with you."

He crouched and ran a hand backward along her fur, messing it up in a single swoosh. "Easy, Peta. I want to see if I can help find her father."

She swatted at him, hissing a word that made my eyes pop.

"You two knock it off." I bent and scooped Peta up, and placed her on my shoulder. "I'm going to see Bella, then I'm leaving the Rim." The words slid out of me. As always, the timing seemed to be against me.

"That's your decision?" Ash said behind us. His voice ghosted over my skin, bringing a rather delicious shiver of remembered pleasure. I held my ground, afraid if I turned he would be naked still. Cactus looked past me, his eyes narrowing ever so slightly.

"You think you can make her stay?"

"I'm trying. Her father is not the king he once was. I don't believe he is worth the danger she would put herself in by going after him. I think you would agree, Cactus. Her life is more important than his." Ash drew closer as he spoke, his voice gaining in increments.

Cactus straightened. "I'll support her in whatever decision she makes. I always have."

Before they could say anything else, I strode forward, putting distance between both men and myself. Peta gripped my vest to keep her balance. Her words, though, surprised me. "To think they both love you like that. A blessing, I should say."

"Easy for you to say. You aren't the one stuck between them."

She laughed. "True enough. True enough. But can you imagine *that* fun if you could convince them to share you?"

My lips twitched and I let the sad smile spread over them, knowing it for the dream it was. "All too easily."

CHAPTER 4

 left the men behind, and went looking for Bella.

"Who listened in on us at the blasted field?"

Peta shivered. "A Rim guard."

"And?"

"I lost him in a crush of people. He was wearing a helmet. I never saw his face, but he was missing a hand."

Coal. My ex-lover was the only one I knew who was missing a hand, and he was a Rim guard. Why had he been spying on me?

"That's Coal." I rubbed the back of my neck. Damn. It was possible he'd been manipulated by Blackbird. Coal had been one of Cassava's pawns too.

"You're sure?"

"He was my lover. I took his hand, and now he's struggling to live without it. If we have time we'll talk to him."

I didn't want to talk to Coal, though. The last time I'd seen him things had gotten ugly between us. His mind was not stable, a side effect of losing his hand.

As we walked, I told Peta about Cassava and the things she'd done. How she controlled everyone using the Spirit gemstone, how she killed my mother and baby brother, Bramley, and how in the end, I'd fought her and saved our family from the lung burrowers.

Peta swayed on my shoulder, shaking her head. "It is hard to believe one person could cause so much pain."

I stepped around a downed log and pushed through a small patch of huckleberry bushes. "She's still alive, Peta. I doubt she's done causing pain."

We found Bella in the forest on the west side toward the ocean. She sat with her hands in her lap, carefully holding her belly. Though she was not far along, her tiny waist gave truth to her condition already.

She smiled when she saw me but her lips trembled. "Lark. You heard the news about Vetch?"

I nodded. "Yes. He's booted you out already?"

Bowing her head, she put a hand to her eyes. "He threatened my baby, Lark. Said all half-breeds should be slaughtered as the curs they are."

Peta hissed, low and long. I had to agree. I sat on the log beside Bella. "You shouldn't stay then, Bella. It isn't safe."

"Where would I go?"

I took her hand, squeezing her fingers gently. "Finley would take you in until we can straighten this out."

Bella's jaw twitched. "You think I could go back there after what Requiem did to me?"

Tightening my grip on her hand, I stared her down. "For the safety of your child, what would you suffer? *A light in the darkness* was what the mother goddess said. That light will be snuffed if Vetch has his way."

A sob escaped her. "How could Father do this to us? How could he leave Vetch as his heir?"

I wrapped an arm around her. "I don't think he did. I know he was not in his right mind—"

"That's just it. He seemed to be back to his usual self. There were no bouts of anger, no unreasonable demands. No silly frivolities. Fern even said he'd spoken to her about hunting for Cassava. About finally dealing with her. It was the last thing he said before he disappeared." Sniffling, she lifted her head. "It makes no sense that he would leave us like this."

Maybe he'd gone to hunt Cassava. But that would mean he was in grave danger, both his mind and body.

"His leaving may not have been his doing," Peta said. "The power of Spirit can mask much, Bella. If Cassava did as I understand and controlled so many of you, surely you remember the inability to fight her power. The thoughts made you believe the choices were your own."

Bella closed her eyes, tears trickling down

her cheeks to drip onto the edge of her dress. "I remember."

"Then you know your father very well may have left under compulsion." The tip of her left ear twitched as she spoke.

"Peta," I said, "how can that be? Cassava no longer has the ring."

Peta's eyes flicked to mine. "There is another who can manipulate Spirit. And his actions thus far have put him solidly in her camp."

Blackbird. "He had to be here in the Rim, then, to manipulate Father."

"Wait, what are you talking about?" Bella tugged on my hand.

"Blackbird, he's the one in the cloak. The one who worked with Keeda. He carries all five elements, Bella." I paused and let the words sink in, seeing it in her eyes as they did.

"All five? Are you sure?"

"Yes. He always wears a cloak weaved with his power and so remains hidden. Have there been reports of anyone like that?"

She shook her head. "No, nothing. And I've read every report since Father left."

I stood and held my hand out to her. "We need to get you out of here. And Cactus too."

"What about you, Lark? You're a half-breed, and I have no doubt Vetch means to see you dead." Her words shouldn't have shocked me. Maybe a small part of me had still hoped my siblings and I could get along. That we could truly be a family one day. Silly Dirt Girl, a family isn't for you.

Peta leapt from my shoulder and hit the ground in front of us, shifting into her leopard form. "He will have to come through me first."

"Excellent," a voice boomed from the left of us. "I never liked cats."

We spun and I jerked Bella behind me. Vetch stood with his hands on his hips. He was a younger version of our father, stocky and muscular with dark brown hair and green eyes. I suppose he was handsome, but the cruel twist of his mouth made him ugly to me. He had two familiars ranging to either side of him. One was a small brown bear and the other was a husky dog. They were two of my father's three familiars. The third was a hawk I hadn't seen in years. Four Rim guards stood behind them with weapons pulled and visors over their mouths.

Peta snarled, baring her teeth. "A dog? *That* is your familiar? I see why the Rim is thought to be a breeding ground for the weak."

The husky let out a howl and took a step forward. Vetch kicked to the side with his boot, catching the dog in the ribs. "I told you to wait."

"Bella." I reached behind me and she took my hand. "The necklace and the Traveling room. Don't stop for anyone."

"I'm not leaving you, Lark."

Vetch began to draw on his power to the earth, the lines of green running up his arms, a perfect signature of what he planned. The ground would soften below us in less than a few seconds.

"You saved me in the Pit with your strengths. Now it is my turn to save you with mine." I let her go and pulled my spear, snapping the two pieces into a single long weapon. "Now!"

A whoosh of skirts and Bella was off. One guard broke away to follow her and Vetch snapped his fingers. "We'll get her later. She'll be easy. That's her style. How do you think she got knocked up with an Undine's brat?"

The guards laughed and anger swelled through my chest. Slimy bastards. Vetch focused again and the power ran through him into the ground.

"Quicksand." The words barely left my lips as the ground shifted. Peta leapt to the side as I leapt toward Vetch. His eyebrows shot up and his mouth dropped open as I slammed the haft of my spear into the center of his chest and drove him to the ground. Ribs cracked under the blow, the snap of bone clearly ringing through the air. He writhed as he struggled to catch his breath.

The Rim guards stepped up, surrounding me. The one on my left came at me first, his sword pointed at my chest. "Half-breed slut."

I knocked his sword to the right, then slid my spear down the blade and sliced into his hand. He dropped his weapon with a cry. Spinning, I slammed the haft of my spear into his head, dropping him next to Vetch. The second Rim guard grabbed me from behind. "I'll hold her. You two boys cut her open."

His arms encircled me and tightened like a noose being slowly twisted. I didn't fight his grip, but instead lifted my feet so he carried my whole weight. He stumbled forward—I was no tiny flower of a girl—and I spun my weight to the side. We slammed into the ground, me on top of him. A gust of air exploded out of him. One of his buddies lunged at me, sword aimed at my head. I jerked out of the way. The sword cut through the air where I'd been a quarter-beat before.

The crunch of bone and flesh being cracked told me all I needed to know; I didn't turn to look at what had happened. The remaining two guards backed up as I stood. "You two sure you want to finish this dance?"

They looked at one another, shook their heads and took off.

"I didn't think so."

Before I had a chance to celebrate my victory, a blur of brown fur and the heavy scent of musk slammed into me. I tumbled through the ferns and bushes before coming to a stop against the side of a redwood. I tapped into the power of the earth and brought it up to me, prepping myself to use it. Vetch stood once more, panting with a hand clutched to his sternum.

He glared at me, and then pointed a shaking finger. "Kill her."

"Vetch, this is a mistake." I still wanted to believe he could be reasoned with. "Your mother was wrong; the half-breeds have a place in this world too."

The bear rushed me, his fur rippling in the spots of sunshine that cut through the trees. His name was Karhu.

I sidestepped the first swipe of the brown bear. Barely. He roared, his lips rippling with the force of his battle cry.

I could fight him, wound him, and take him from Vetch. I could cut him apart and Peta would help me; I knew it in my gut. My eyes and his met.

Pain. Shame. Fear.

I swung the spear around and planted the haft into the ground, going to my knees in a choice that could spell my end. But I believed Spirit when it recognized the emotions flowing from the bear.

"Karhu, he does not deserve either of you." I held his gaze. "He has forgotten you are a companion, a mentor, the one he should turn to as a friend and confidant. Just as my father forgot."

The bear stopped and let out a grunt, his nose twitching. "What do you know of familiars?"

"Do you not know Peta? She has been assigned to me." A part of me had assumed all familiars knew each other, seeing as how few there were.

The bear turned his head to look at where Peta and the husky circled one another. "A cat?"

"A long story," I said.

The bear backed away. "This time, I will spare you. For the truth you speak. Hercules. Let's go. Leave Vetch to his stupidity. The girl is right, he needs to learn our value."

The husky turned his head and lifted his dark

eyebrows. Peta swatted his ass with his attention off her, and sent him tumbling toward the bear. "Do as you're told, mutt."

Hercules bared his teeth, but followed Karhu into the forest.

Vetch shook with rage. "Then I will kill you myself." He lifted his hand, lines of power coursing along his skin.

"Not this time." Peta leapt at him, taking him down in a single blow. Her mouth clamped around his neck, her long canines breaking the skin. The thought in my head was crystal clear. Let her kill him. End that trial. Bella could take over as she had and we wouldn't need Father at all.

A strange urge came over me to do that. Blood lust roared through me and I struggled to push it down, to keep myself in check.

No, that wasn't me. Fear trickled with the blood lust. I knew what was happening. This was the result of using Spirit. This was the beginning of the price I would pay for using an Element destructive in its very nature.

"Don't," I said. "I have to believe he's being manipulated by Cassava."

Peta spat him out. "Doesn't make him any less dangerous to you or the other half-breeds."

Vetch lay panting on the ground. His green eyes widened as if he suddenly realized he'd been outmatched. "What are you going to do to me?"

That was the question of the day. "The dungeons will block him from his power, and from whatever manipulation laid on him. We could stick him there. Someone would find him eventually."

I didn't think his eyes could widen further. I was wrong.

"You wouldn't dare. I am the heir to the throne!" he spluttered as he scooted away. Peta snarled.

"Shut up, this isn't up to you, worm."

Worm. Yes, that was what he was. The fact that he'd attacked me using the power of the earth said it all. He was not playing by the rules. We could try and drag him back to the dungeons, but he'd fight us and fight dirty.

I swung my spear, aiming for his head. He screamed like a child, shrieking at a pitch I was surprised he could manage at his age. At the last second, I spun the spear so the haft caught him in the side of the head, the momentum knocking him out.

"What a baby." Peta snorted. I bent and picked him up, slinging him over my shoulder. The dead Rim guard though . . . would prove a problem if he was found. I flicked my hand over his body and let the ground suck him down.

"They will think you killed him."

"Of course. Might as well put off the inevitable as long as possible." I adjusted Vetch on my shoulder and started back to the Rim. Keeping to the edges of the homes and buildings, I made it to the Barracks before someone stopped me.

Thank the goddess it was Ash. He met me on the steps of the Enders Barracks. "Usurping thrones again, are we?"

"No. Just putting him in a safe place for a bit. Did Bella make it to the Traveling room?"

Ash nodded. I followed him through the main hall and down the long stairwell that took us to the dungeon. As if this was something we did every day.

"She said to tell you she would wait on your word to come home. What happened?"

As we hurried toward the dungeon, I filled him in on Vetch's plan to wipe out half-breeds in the Rim. Starting with Bella and me. Ash shook his head as he held the cell door open. "He's always been cruel. But even for him this is a new level."

The cellblock was one of the few places that truly barred an elemental from using their power. Or from having another elemental's power used on them.

If Cassava had any influence on Vetch, it would be gone while he was in the dungeon.

Maybe all hope wasn't lost for him yet. I dumped him into the cell and stepped back, locking the door behind me. More than ever, my heart was twisted about going after our father. Whether he was in his right mind or not, he was the only one who could set to right the problems with who he'd named as heir. Yet with him gone and Vetch locked up, perhaps Bella could rule.

No, I had to see if Vetch was himself or not. I still had hope he could be saved.

Like Bella. There had been a time I'd believed her to be an enemy, and now we were closer than I was with any of my other siblings.

Minutes ticked by and Vetch finally let out a groan. "What the hell have I been drinking?"

"Vetch, do you remember the last hour?" I gripped the bars of the dungeon. "Do you remember coming to kill me and Bella?"

He slowly sat up, blinking as though the light hurt his eyes. "Kill Bella?"

"Yes. And me."

Vetch took a breath and rubbed his chest where I'd slammed him. "I was dreaming. How could it be you know what I dream?"

I backed away. "Ash will explain it to you. I have to go, I have to get Father and bring him home. Whatever you do, stay in the cell, Vetch." Mother goddess, what a mess of redwood proportions this was.

Two steps and I was out of the room, but a hand on my arm stopped me.

"Be careful, Lark. I can't come with you if you go this time. Someone has to stay here and keep things running with Bella gone." Ash tipped his head forward and pressed it against mine. "Come back to me."

With a gentle tug from him, I was in his arms, kissing him as he held onto me as though it would be the last time. I didn't care that Vetch could see. I kissed Ash back with everything I had before pulling back for a breath. "I will always come back to you."

"You just want that pedicure I promised."

Laughing, I stepped away. "Yes, that too. We've put it off too long."

His golden eyes followed me as I backed the first

few steps up the stairs, unable to look away from him. A heavy sense of longing followed me. As if perhaps our moment had passed and I would never be able to regain it.

But that couldn't be.

I wouldn't let it.

CHAPTER 5

eta and I ran up the stairs and out of the Enders Barracks.

"Where to?"

I stumbled to a stop. Peta's question was more than loaded. I had no idea where to start looking for a Tracker. I needed a damn Tracker to find a Tracker. "Worm shit, I don't know."

"Is there no one you can ask? Is the mother goddess's consort not here?"

I blinked several times. "Excuse me?"

"Griffin. He's the . . . I thought you knew?" Peta looked up at me and then away, her eyes darting to the side. "Perhaps I was not supposed to tell you."

In some ways, that explained a lot about Griffin. Except for the picture of the woman and the little boy. Who were they? Call it a hunch, but I had a feeling the mother goddess wasn't much into sharing her consort with other women. "I won't spill the can of beans. But he is not our only option. Niah can help. I think."

Niah had a home in the southern edge of the Rim and I hurried that way. As our storyteller, she spun all the old tales. But she seemed to have a Reader's knack for knowing what was coming and what was needed.

Crossing the main road of the Rim, the sun caught the tips of a head of bright red hair bent over a redwood seedling. My heart clenched at the sight of Cactus. "Peta, loving them both is going to kill me."

"Don't be melodramatic. It doesn't suit you. Take Cactus with you on this journey. He's powerful in his two elements, and he needs to be away from Vetch. Perhaps some time with him will show you he's not the one for you."

Her words stopped me. "What do you mean, not the one for me? How can you know?"

"I've said enough. You need to figure the rest out on your own." She trotted ahead of me, stopping beside Cactus. "Prick, are you coming with us or staying here to play with the seedlings?"

I opened my mouth, words on the tip of my tongue. But she was right. I snapped my mouth shut. Cactus stood, saw me, and grinned. His love for life was contagious. I smiled back, but the smile faltered, as I understood what Ash had meant about not being able to share.

I could never tell Cactus I slept with Ash. Until I could tell him I'd picked Ash over him without a question in my mind. And I wasn't sure I would ever do that.

Damn my heart for its ability to love more than one person at a time. Apparently my father's blood ran truer than I'd previously believed. The royal lines of the Terralings were littered with mistresses and children born out of the monarch's official marriage. That wasn't unusual to us; it was normal as far as we were concerned. But I'd thought I was above that, only ever bedding Coal.

I grimaced at the thought of being anything like my father.

Cactus stepped beside me and slung an arm over my shoulders as we walked. "Wanderers like us, we never really settle down, Lark. So where do you think your pop is?"

"I don't know." I brushed his arm off, feeling the traitorous desire to leave it there. "We're going to Niah's to speak with her."

"The old storyteller? Is she still alive?"

"She's not that old." I laughed, but the laughter died as I thought about Ash having to deal with Vetch. "Come on, I don't want to waste time."

We jogged to Niah's, silence between us. Peta bounded through the forest, her pleasure flowing through the bond between her and me. Stopping suddenly, she pounced on something that squeaked, then let it go. She turned a sheepish face up to me. "Sorry."

"Don't apologize. I'm glad you like it here."

We came to a stop at the edge of the Rim. Niah's house was built into a redwood not unlike my previous home. Only instead of being fifty feet in the air as mine had been, the entrance to her home was on the ground. If I remembered correctly, she had a bear as a familiar that didn't look a whole lot different than Karhu. Tangling with one bear was enough for me. I didn't go to the door, but instead called out.

"Niah, are you here?"

There was silence for a moment, then the door swung open on well-greased hinges. Niah peered out, her long gray hair hanging in braids to either side of her face. "Larkspur?"

"Yes. I was hoping for some guidance."

She peered at Cactus. "Why have you got a lizard with you?"

"This is my friend, Cactus. He's a half-breed like me. He used to live here in the Rim as a child."

She snorted. "Ain't nobody like you, Lark. Come on in, bring your cat with you."

"Your familiar won't mind?"

That stopped her. "Why would my familiar mind yours?"

I closed the distance between us and held the edge of the door. "Vetch has been named the heir and has two of Father's familiars. They attacked us."

Niah gasped and put a hand to her throat. "Fool boy, what does he think he's doing?"

"I think Cassava still has some hold on him." I didn't want to explain about Blackbird. We didn't have time for a long story, and that was what Niah loved more than anything. Eating and storytelling.

The three of us stepped into her home. I had to

blink several times to adjust to the dimmer light. The room cooked with heat from a fire roaring on one side of the room and a kettle squalling on the stove. Being late summer, it wasn't exactly cold outside. Sweat popped out on my brow immediately.

More surprising than the fire was Griffin sitting in a chair, his long legs stretched out in front of him. His dark eyes swept over me as he gave me a toothy grin reminiscent of his wolf form. "Larkspur, keeping out of trouble yet?"

"Not yet," I muttered, as I took a seat. Niah brought me a mug of tea without asking and I let out sigh. This would not be a quick visit. I wasn't sure if that pleased me. A part of me wanted to hurry, to find my father and bring him home to straighten out Vetch. The other part didn't want to find him at all. With my father gone, though, we would have to battle Vetch, and I didn't want to start a civil war. . . but that would settle things. I was not so sure my father would be able to rule if his mind was broken as badly as we thought.

Peta jumped onto my lap and curled up so her tail wrapped over her nose. "Griffin." Her voice was muffled through her fur.

"Kitten. What are you doing here?" He leaned forward and ran a single finger down her spine. She shivered, but she wasn't bothered by his touch, or I would have pushed his hand away.

Her green eyes blinked up at me, then back at Griffin. "Long story. Your consort said I was needed, so I am here."

His eyebrows shot up. "With Larkspur? Shit, she must be in for a wild ride then, yeah?"

I lifted my tea and took a sip, choosing not to respond. Niah waved her hands, fluttering them like bird wings. "Not a word until the boy sits down. His red hair makes me nervous." She winked to soften the words, though I felt a thin string of truth running through them.

The distrust between our families ran deep and long.

Cactus laughed and sat beside me. "Nah, I'm not really a redhead. This is a new shade of brown."

She grinned at him, and the tension broke.

"Niah, I need to find a Tracker." I spit the words out before we could get sidetracked again. Or maybe before I decided to sit there and let my father rot wherever he was. "Can you help me? Or you, Griffin, if she can't?"

The two of them looked at each other.

"I don't know if we should help her," Niah said as if I wasn't even there. "She'd be breaking the rules again and that's going to catch up to her at some point. She hasn't even drank half her tea and she's demanding answers."

"I know, yeah? Kids these days, always wanting an answer quick." Griffin folded his hands on the table. "But what happens if we don't help her? Viv is playing games again, and I don't like it. The least we can do is throw our weight behind the player we want to succeed, yeah?"

I glanced at Cactus, who shrugged and mouthed "old people."

Peta snickered, her tiny body shaking on my lap.

Forcing myself to sit and wait was, to say the least, difficult. Patience was something I was learning. Rushing into this journey would not help me find my father.

I leaned back in my chair and closed my eyes.

"Where's the best place to send them?" Niah asked.

Griffin gave a low grunt. "A Reader would be best, easier to find than a prickly Tracker, yeah? They move around like the wind."

A teacup clinked as it was set down, the shifting of chairs and the succeeding creak of wood. Smoke from the fire tickled my nose and I breathed in, holding it in my lungs.

An irrational fear began in the soles of my feet that once I left the Rim this time, nothing would ever be the same in my life. That the things I saw through Spirit would be a sure thing. Yet another reason to take my time with this journey. To make sure I didn't rush into anything I shouldn't.

I opened my eyes to see Niah staring at me. I ran a finger along the rim of my teacup. "Have you decided, then?"

She nodded. "We will tell you where a young Reader lives. She was trained by a banished elemental and is quite good at what she does despite her age."

Griffin tapped his fingers on the table, drawing my attention to him. "Her name is Giselle."

They stared at me like her name should mean

something, so I nodded. "Okay. Giselle. And the elemental who trained her?"

Peta sat up in my lap. As she did so, Niah trained her pale violet eyes on the cat. "Someone Peta knows rather well. But I don't think you're quite ready to meet him yet. Is she, cat?"

Peta stiffened slowly. "I don't know what you're talking about."

Griffin barked out a laugh and slapped his hands on the table. "Fun. This is going to be fun, I think, yeah?"

"Do you know where Giselle is? Knowing her name is one thing, but I am no Tracker. I need more than a name to find someone." There was no point in following the tangent they had gone off on. Things happened or they didn't; either way, I would deal with them at the time.

Standing, Niah beckoned for me to follow her. I did so, and we headed deeper into the hollowed-out tree. She spoke softly over her shoulder as we walked. "She's in the human city of Bismarck. North Dakota. The land there is empty of magic in many ways, but it is because of what is coming for the place in the future."

A chill swept through me. "You aren't going to tell me, are you?"

"No. Right now you need to find Giselle and find her quickly, because you are not the only one looking for the Tracker. Nor are you the only one looking for a true Reader. Giselle is one of few who can truly give a glimpse into what is coming, and already her talents are being noticed." She took my hand and pressed it between both of hers. When she took her fingers away from mine I turned my hand up. Two items were in my palm. One was a fishhook earring, identical to the one she'd given me before I'd headed to the Deep. I'd lost the first one in a fight for my life against Requiem.

"Why do I need this?"

"It is magic that belongs in the Deep, Lark," she said. I frowned. We knew my father wasn't in the Deep. Finley had scoured her home for him, and I trusted her to tell the truth. The other item was far closer to my heart. The seed of a moringa plant. I rolled it in my hand. It would grow in poor soil with almost no water, and was edible, but it was not native to the redwoods, or North America for that matter.

"No point in asking what I need this for, is there?"

Smiling, she shook her head. Her eyes twinkled. "You'll know when the time comes. I'm no Reader, Lark, but I listen when the promptings of the soul of the earth come to me. I suggest you do the same."

She tipped her head. "The white stone you took from the Pit. Do you still have it?"

My eyebrows shot up. "Yes."

"You'll need it, Lark. When you least expect, that stone will save your life, I think."

How a stone could save my life, I had no idea. But I trusted her.

Bending, I pulled her into a hug. "Thank you."

With great care she pushed me away from her. "Don't thank me, Lark. I am encouraging you to break rules. Rules that have been in place since the mother goddess first birthed our forbearers."

I shifted my shoulders, then tucked the two items into my side pouch. "Yes, I know."

"And you realize taboo, when broken, will bring you a punishment you will not be able to stave off?"

There was only one thing for me to say. "Yes. I know."

"Good." She tapped me on the arm. "It's about time someone shook up our world. I'm glad it's you."

Her words caught me by surprise and I laughed. "Thank you?"

She pushed me toward where the men waited. "Pshaw. Be off with you now. You have a long journey ahead with several stops along the way. Do not rush, let the journey lead you where it will."

Her words echoed my own desire and so I clung to them. I would not rush after my father, but go carefully.

At least, that was the plan.

Taking our leave of Niah and Griffin, we headed toward the Enders Barracks.

"I overheard what she said about this being a long journey," Cactus said.

"And?"

"I mean, how hard can it be? We go to this Bismarck place, talk to a Reader, Travel to where she directs us . . ." He looked at me, but I said nothing. Peta swung a paw at him from my shoulder.

"Prick, you are a fool. The Reader is not going to simply give us directions. More likely some silly game we have to play and maybe require some form of payment. Readers don't hand out their knowledge for nothing."

Cactus's face fell, and with the dimming of his smile, it was as if the light around us dimmed too. I lifted a hand to touch Peta's side. "Go easy. Cactus could be right, we could end up finding the journey to be as straight as an arrow, and as quick."

Peta's mouth dropped open and incredulity flowed from her to me. I pressed a little harder against her, wanting her to understand. Part of what made Cactus Cactus was the joy he gave so freely to others. He grinned at me.

"That's the spirit."

Indeed.

I didn't want him to lose that spark so early in the journey. Because I had a feeling I was going to be the one to take it from him at some point. Most likely when he found out about Ash and me.

Under my hand, Peta softened as if she heard the words in my mind, though she would pick up on only emotions. "Fine."

The Rim hummed with energy when we returned. People flowed through the main thoroughfare, stopping and talking more so than usual. I grabbed the first person I recognized.

"Blossom, did something happen?"

The girl who'd been an Ender in training with me stopped and spun, a surprised look on her face. "Lark, you'd better get out of here. He's looking for you. Go!"

I didn't have to ask who or why. Vetch had to have

broken free of the dungeon. I grabbed Cactus's arm and bolted toward the barracks. Behind us, shouting erupted as someone spotted us. Not like we were hard to spot. At six feet, I was a good four inches taller than most of the men of the Rim with the exception of Ash, and Cactus with his red hair . . . we were easy to pinpoint.

Peta leapt from my shoulder. "I'll slow them down."

"I'm not going without you!" I said.

"Of course not."

She let out a snarl as she shifted, covering our backs. Cactus and I raced into the barracks, though it was a struggle not to stop and face those who came for us. Could I have fought off the guards? Yes. But it wasn't their fault Vetch was an idiot slug of a man. They didn't deserve to be hurt because of the choices he made.

Too many had already died because of Cassava and her machinations. I didn't want to add to the list.

Bursting through the barracks' main doors, I stumbled to a halt when I saw what waited for us. Ash stood in the middle of the room, arms loaded with human clothes.

"You two don't have a lot of time." He threw jeans and a white T-shirt at Cactus. "Those should fit you. They're from the last time I went into the human world."

Cactus caught the clothes and quickly changed. Ash held out a tall pair of boots to me. "I think if you wear these, you should be okay. With your looks, the humans will forgive strange clothing." He gave me a quick wink.

I took the boots and slipped them on. They laced all the way up to my knee, the soft leather cupping my calves. Made of a deep brown deerskin, they complimented my darker leather vest. Not that I was looking to be fashionable. I only needed to fit in enough so the humans didn't notice me.

Ash crouched in front of me and helped me lace up the boots, his hands lingering on my legs. "Be careful, Lark."

"I will." I touched his head, running my fingers through his hair, forgetting for a moment we were not alone. Behind us the door burst open and Peta fell through. Her white and gray coat was flecked with blood.

Horror ripped through me. How could I have not felt her injuries? "Peta!"

"I'm fine, it isn't my blood," she panted. Cactus ran to the door and slid a bar through it.

"Time to go." Ash grabbed me and spun me toward him. I knew a kiss when I saw it coming and I turned my head. It was one thing to love him, another to rub it in Cactus's face. His lips caught my cheek and the surprise, then laughter in his eyes made me smile.

Cactus grabbed my hand and dragged me away toward the stairs and the Traveling room. I let him, but couldn't take my eyes from Ash as we moved out. How had Cactus not noticed?

The boom of something heavy hitting the main

doors snapped me out of my fog. I shook off Cactus's hand and stepped into the lead. Stopping at my bedroom door, I grabbed a small leather bag I could tie to my belt. I looped it through and stuffed the trinkets Niah had given me in beside the smoky diamond that controlled air. The last thing to go in the bag was the white stone from the Pit. I didn't hesitate, just stuffed it in knowing I could trust Niah.

I took a knife and tucked it into the top of my boot, then backed out and led the way down the hall again. Through it all, the silence from Cactus was as damning as if he'd screamed at me. Apparently he *had* noticed.

Beside me, Peta lent me her support, her furred body against my leg. I dropped a hand to touch the back of her neck. What a mess my heart was. Almost as bad as the mess my father had left in the Rim.

The doors to the Traveling room were wide open. I stepped inside and as always was for a moment awed by what was laid out in front of me. Situated like a globe, the room was completely round. It was as if we stood inside the world, and looked out toward the land and seas.

"Get that armband off the wall," I said to Cactus as I reached up and touched the hovering image of the world. Flexing and tightening my fingers, I brought the image of North America closer and closer until I'd zeroed in on the badlands of North Dakota, and then tightened it further to the main, glowing city of Bismarck. Adjusting it ever so slightly, I held out a hand. Cactus set the armband on it and I slid it onto my other arm. Made of highly polished cedar wood, it resonated on my bicep, like a tuning fork. "Hang onto me."

"You sure your boyfriend will be okay with this?" Cactus asked.

I turned my head to look at him. Okay, maybe glare was a more accurate term. "Seriously? You want to have that conversation right now?"

His jaw flexed. "Is he your boyfriend?"

"No. Now stop being a fool, Prick, and hang onto me." I used Peta's nickname for him and she snickered beside me as she wrapped a big paw around my calf.

He did as told and I reached up to touch the map over Bismarck with one finger, twisting the armband with my other hand. The world around us slipped away and I was tossed into a memory not my own.

Mother goddess, I kept forgetting about this hiccup of Traveling. As an added perk of having Spirit as one of my elements, whenever I Traveled with another person I was plunged into one of their memories.

I hoped for something from Peta.

I got a memory from Cactus.

The Rim was not as he remembered it. Beautiful, and flowing with plants and green things, that was the same. But the undercurrent reminded him more of the Pit. The feeling that people were afraid, that they didn't see their home as safe anymore.

He frowned and ran a hand through his hair.

Catching a glimpse of long blonde hair and gently curved hips, he stopped in his tracks. A grin spread over his face. The rest of the world didn't matter as long as

Lark was here with him. Jogging, he tried to catch up with her, but in seconds she was gone.

The barracks. That had to be where she was headed. He made his way there, nodding to the Terralings who looked his way.

"Cactus, I need to speak with you."

He spun, surprised to see Peta sitting on a log at eye level at the entrance to the barracks. "Bad luck cat, what do you want?"

She grimaced. "That is not my name, Prick."

"Well, until you stop calling me Prick, that's what I'm calling you." Childish, he knew, but he couldn't seem to help himself.

"You don't love her the way she needs," Peta said, shocking him.

"What do you mean? I love her. What else is there?"

Peta shook her head. "You love her, but love isn't enough. Not with her life. Love is strong, Prick. But your love will not be what her heart needs. And certainly not the love you want to put on her. With expectations and rules and how you want her to be. I see it in you. She is not the woman who will settle down and give you a brood of children."

He grinned at her, even as he struggled not to let her words affect him. "You don't know that."

"You see, you do not even deny my words."

"Why would I? Of course, I would want to have children with her. That is what you do when you love someone."

She snorted and started to groom her left paw, wiping it over her ear. "I'm her familiar, Prick. I can feel her heart and her needs. She doesn't need you."

Leaning toward her, he lowered his voice. "I don't want her to need me. I want her to want me."

Peta put her face so close to his he could feel the breath from her mouth. "Desire is not enough. Love is not enough. She will chose the mate who understands her and can help her through the trials she will face. You are not that one."

Anger snapped through him and with it the Fire in his blood heated. "I am."

"You're not." She let out a sigh and shook her head. "Go away, Prick. You are not needed here."

The desire to lash out curled through him and he stepped back toward the forest and away from the barracks. Having Lark see him like this, angry and on the verge of losing control, was not what he wanted. All because of a few words that scared him, and made him think perhaps Peta was right.

He strode away from the barracks. "Stupid cat. You're wrong. I know you are."

Yet, he doubted, and in the doubt he wondered if he was chasing a ghost of the girl he'd known. A memory he'd let grow into a fantasy that didn't mesh with reality.

What if Peta was right?

What if Lark didn't love him?

CHAPTER 6

 jerked out of his memory as we popped through to Bismarck, but the emotions it stirred in me would not leave. Breathing hard, I fought the desperation and loneliness that bled through his memory into my heart. I closed my eyes and tried not to think, tried not to feel the guilt of not loving him the way he wanted me to.

"Hey, you okay there, princess?" He leaned over me, far closer than he should have. I opened my eyes and the blue sky was replaced with green eyes and his trademark grin.

"Yes, I'm fine. And don't call me that. I've never been a princess, and wouldn't want the title even if it were offered to me." I pushed on his chest and he gave me some room. In his white T-shirt, jeans, and dark shoes he looked . . . human. I, on the other hand, looked like what I was—an Ender. But I trusted Ash. If he thought I could get away with looking a little different, then that's what I was doing.

Thoughts of Ash brought the guilt back up in a roll not unlike nausea. I forced the guilt away and stood. I would not feel bad for loving Ash. Peta gave me a nod of approval.

"Why did you really come with me?" I stared at Cactus and he stared back. His face softened.

"I know you love him. I know you love me. I want to show you I fit in your life, Lark. That I'm good for you. The only way to do that is to be here. To be where I should have been all these years. At your side."

My throat tightened, my ears rang, and I knew he was telling the truth as he saw it. I didn't think, though, that he'd be happy with what the end result was going to be.

Peta broke the moment. "Let's find this Reader. Do you know where in Bismarck she is?"

I shook my head as Cactus nodded. "How do you know?"

He grinned. "Griffin gave me something call an add-dress." He held up a slip of paper.

I took it from him. "He wasn't supposed to, was he?"

"No. But he pointed out we'd probably waste a lot of time looking for the Reader, and apparently he thinks you might try to stall for some reason."

Embarrassed, I stared at the paper.

"Are you stalling?" His words were soft and gentler than I thought I deserved.

I looked up from the paper and made myself hold his gaze. "I don't know. I . . . my father needs us to find him. The Rim needs us to find him. Bella needs us to find him." I paused, took a breath and spit the rest out. "But I don't know what I want."

Oh, those words were hard to admit. Cactus nodded. "So we take our time. I don't mind in the least." He reached out, took my hand, and wove his fingers through mine.

Exactly as I'd done with Ash. I didn't pull away, though. I stared at our locked hands. "Cactus, I don't want to hurt you."

"You won't. I trust you to make the right choice."

Worm shit. I did pull my hand away then, and looked again to the paper with the add-dress.

The words really meant nothing to me—some numbers, 569—with a single word, Smith. To a human they probably made sense. I looked around. Where was a human when you needed one? They were usually like ants, swarming about and all but climbing over one another, there were so many.

We were at the edge of a large square building with a pole in front with a flag on top. The flag was covered in stripes and stars in the corner. I rather liked the look of it.

"Maybe someone lives in this box." I took a few steps toward a double set of doors set into the box, and an alarm went off, screeching through the air like a flock of harpies gone mental. I slapped a hand to my side for my spear.

Peta leapt to my shoulder. "Nothing is wrong. This is a way for the humans to tell time."

The shrieking ended as suddenly as it had begun and I lowered my hands. "Why do they not look at the sun's passage? Why do they need a shrieking siren to tell them the time?"

What was wrong with them?

"Lazy," she muttered.

The doors to the big building burst open and a flood of humans rushed out, laughing and yelling at each other, shoving and milling.

It took me a minute to zero in on what I was seeing. They were all teenagers, to the last one. Their life forces hummed around them like a buzzing beehive; they were like bees, not ants. Not unlike a beehive, they kept pouring out of the large boxed building.

I backed up a few steps until my back was pressed against a large tree that shaded a portion of the road we stood near. "How will we ever find her in this mess?"

Cactus took the paper from me. "I'll see if any of them know what this means."

Before I could tell him to wait, he ran into the crush of humanity. He wove between them with ease, and with a shock I realized in some ways he fit here. There was no fear in him. But for me the place was overwhelming. "Peta, why is it so hard for me to stand here? I feel like I have all these emotions, and—"

"That is Spirit. Human teenagers are rolling with emotions: angst, fear, hope, love and hate. You're getting a rather large dose of it all." Peta pressed her cheek against mine and some of the anxiety flowed away from me. Having her there was enough to help calm the emotions.

"I could never live among them, even if I were banished."

"Do not even joke about banishment," she said. "It isn't funny."

"Well, I'd still have you."

Her silence was enough to send a chill through me. "Peta, if I was banished, would you not still be with me?"

"No. Banishment from the elemental world strips you of all your rights and familiars." Her voice dropped. "I had one charge who was banished, Lark. You do not want that to happen. The madness would take you and then you would end up killing yourself one way or another."

"What did he do?" I wasn't sure I really wanted to know, but the talking helped keep the emotions of the humans at bay. Helped me pretend I wasn't feeling the press of hundreds of teenagers' fluctuating feelings swirling through me.

"He was an assassin of Fiametta's predecessor."

"How successful was he?" I didn't recall ever hearing about an assassination attempt that had actually succeeded.

She snorted. "He was banished and Fiametta became the queen. What does that tell you?"

Cactus spoke with a trio of girls who even at a distance I could see he'd charmed. They giggled and flipped their hair this way and that as they batted their eyes up at him. My mind, though, was still on the conversation with Peta, about her charge who had been banished.

"Did you know what he was going to do?"

Peta let out a hiss. "I did not."

"Don't get your tail in a knot. I ask only because I know you. If you'd known, you would have tried to stop him. Right?"

"Of course."

But there was a hesitation in her; she wasn't sure. Her loyalty ran deep to her charges even when they were idiots. "I will do my best not to put you in that kind of position."

Another snort, but she said nothing more. Cactus jogged back to us. "You won't believe it, this add-dress is right here. This is a school, which means Giselle is somewhere in this madness." He waved a hand behind him. "The three girls didn't know her, though. I did ask."

Peta's head swiveled back and forth. "Look for her aura. It will glow like fireflies."

I scanned the crowd. "There has been nothing that looks even remotely supernatural."

"It's not like she's going to have wings and be speaking in tongues, Lark," Peta said.

We stood there scanning the crowd for many minutes. Two older humans in suits approached. The one in the lead had mostly gray hair and a bit of a gut. "Can I help you two?"

"We're looking for someone, a friend of ours," Cactus said, his smooth talking coming into play.

Perhaps he was the best companion for this journey. Ash would have glared at them and expected them to go away.

The two human adults raised their eyebrows. "A friend? Do you have a name? This is private property."

Something in their tone, the way they held themselves, made me reach out and touch Cactus on the arm. "We'll catch up with her later. Let's go."

I knew a territorial stance when I saw one. Either of us could have forced the men to their knees and made them beg for mercy, but that was not our way when dealing with humans.

Cactus gave me a questioning look and I tipped my head. We walked away, but the feeling of being watched lay heavy across my shoulders. "Peta, can they see you?"

"Yes."

"But they can't hear you."

"That is correct. Unless I want them to. And I most certainly do not."

We walked away from the school. The crowds thinned, along with the feeling of eyes on us. I glanced back. The two men were gone. I slowed beside a fence that surrounded a large green space behind the building. An open field of perfectly manicured grass but no fruit trees. No garden or flowers. How very strange to have grass, but nothing grazing on it. What was the point?

A figure darted out of the building, her body ablaze as if she were lit from within. "There." I pointed as she ran into the center of the wide field. I grabbed the edge of the metal fence and vaulted it, Cactus right behind me, while Peta leapt ahead of us, racing toward the girl.

But we weren't the only ones closing in on her.

A swirl of a black cloak ran after her from the building. Blackbird would reach her before us if I didn't do something. Niah was right: we were not the only ones looking to chat with Giselle.

I flipped my hand at him, bucking the earth under his feet, but he used the momentum to leap forward.

"Damn!" I tapped into the earth and redoubled my speed. I had to get to her first.

Whatever Blackbird wanted with her, it couldn't be good.

Whether he was there to take Giselle for his own uses or only to slow me in my search for my father, it didn't matter. Either way, I had to stop him. A fireball shot past me and slammed into Blackbird, sending him backward in a tumble ass over teakettle. The girl cried out and fell to her knees. Peta reached her first and curled her body around her.

The Reader was barely into her teens, if her size was any indication. A child. Niah had sent us to a child.

I went to my knees in front of the Reader, facing Blackbird. "Stay down, Giselle."

"Who are you?"

"Friends."

"Friends don't shoot fire at each other," she said.

I didn't dare look back at her. "True, but he is not our friend."

Blackbird strode toward us as though he hadn't been slammed with a fireball. Then again, he carried all five elements . . . it was hard to imagine what would hurt him. Maybe nothing but cold hard steel.

"Larkspur, you are really beginning to be a pain in my ass." Blackbird came to a stop twenty feet from us.

"Consider the feeling mutual." I stood and pulled my spear from my side, twisting the two halves together. I pointed it at him. "Time to leave, boy."

His whole body jerked as if I'd hit him. A sore point, then? He had to be young; being called a boy would only bother a young man trying to prove himself.

With a grin I whipped the spear forward. "Tell me something: what do you want with Giselle?"

"I do believe that is none of your business."

Needing him to make a mistake, I poked at him. "I'm making it my business, brat."

A snarl escaped him, giving more evidence to what I believed. He had a temper and didn't like people thinking he was too young.

"My lover wants to speak with her." He spat the words out as though they cost him.

"You mean Cassava, don't you?"

Blackbird lifted his hands and the wind around us picked up, a gust slamming into me and flipping me backward before I could anchor myself into the ground. I flew through the air, catching glimpses of the scene around me. Peta clawing the ground to hold Giselle firm. Cactus out of sight.

The ground rushed up and I hit it hard, landing

on my hip and shoulder. Rolling, I was on my hands and knees in a flash. Forty feet away, Peta's fur rippled as the wind hammered her. Giselle screamed as she slipped, her arms wrapped around Peta's neck.

"Don't let him take me!"

Propelled by the need to protect them both, I ran straight for Blackbird. He saw me coming and I watched the power lines climb his arms. At the last possible second I arced my arm back and threw my spear at him. It flew true straight for his heart.

He threw himself to the side, catching the blade in his shoulder. Crying out, he touched his arm and twisted his hand over it.

With a pop of air, he was gone, my spear buried in the ground behind where he'd been. The wind eased immediately, and I stood there, panting with adrenaline as much as exertion.

"He's got a Traveling band," Peta said as I approached them.

"Yes. Why would he use it now? Not that I wish he'd stayed, but it makes no sense."

"Perhaps, he is a coward?" Giselle said softly. "My mentor told me cowards always run when they are first injured."

Though her words were true, I doubted that was the case. I didn't know what the reason was and that bothered me.

"What's a Traveling band?" Giselle asked as she sat up. Her tawny hair was in disarray and her pale blue eyes seemed almost transparent as she took me in.

"Wait." I crouched in front of her. "Did you hear Peta?"

"Yes. I'm a Reader. The rules don't apply to me." She gave me a tentative smile.

I held my hand out. "My name is Larkspur. And I am an elemental."

She put her hand in mine. "My name is Giselle. I knew you were coming. You have a big job ahead of you. Maybe bigger than you even realize. But . . . the boy in the black cloak. Do you know him?"

Cactus jogged up beside us, panting. He had blood running down the side of his face. "That bastard threw me against the wall." The wall was a good three hundred feet away.

"We were lucky this time." I looked around, knowing I was right. We were in an open space, with humans on the fringes. Even now a few watched us. Blackbird wasn't stupid, even if he was young. He was waiting for me to be weak and alone before he took me on.

"He will fight you soon. You will do something that will enrage him and it will push him over the edge. You'll hurt someone he loves," Giselle whispered, her eyes unfocused. "He knows you, though, Lark. He knows you better than you know him."

Helping her to her feet, I chose not to say anything. Silence was often a virtue overlooked by those in a hurry to get their answers. Something I'd learned from my mother.

Peta shifted to her housecat form and I scooped her up. Cactus grabbed my spear from the ground where it had lodged and cleaned the tip off before handing it to me. "Where to now?"

I looked at Giselle. "Do you have somewhere we could talk?"

Giselle looked from me to Cactus and back again. "Yes, I think so."

Without another word, she walked toward the trees backing the green space.

I put myself beside her, wondering how such a small supernatural would survive in a world with so much violence and death. "You were trained by an elemental, correct?"

She blushed. "Yes. Since I was ten."

Five years.

Most banished elementals didn't last long outside of their home before they lost their minds. During the second year the longing for home overrode any other need.

I glanced at Cactus, wanting to ask him who he knew who had been banished in the last five years. He shook his head, already knowing the question. "None I can think of."

None, there had been none. I knew it; I'd wanted him to confirm for me, though. But that meant it was someone before. Yet . . . that was impossible.

"What was the name of the one who trained you?"

She cleared her throat. "His name is Talan."

Again I looked at Cactus, who shook his head. The name didn't ring a bell for him either.

"Peta, any clue—"

"No." My cat leapt from my shoulder and

proceeded to trot far enough ahead that there was no way I could speak to her without hurrying. So Peta knew the name, and it obviously meant something to her.

I twisted my lips and chewed on the bottom one while I thought. "You live with your parents, then?"

The blush deepened. "No. I'm an orphan. But I have my own place, Talan helped me get it. But . . . please don't tell the school. They would put me in a home for children and I can't . . . I can't do that again. It's hell." She looked at me, pleading with her eyes.

"I won't tell anyone."

Her shoulders sagged and once more the silence thickened. Yet within it were all the questions swirling. Who was Talan, how did Peta know him, and how was such a young Reader going to help me find a Tracker?

CHAPTER 7

iselle's home was in the middle of an undeveloped area. To either side of the human house were empty lots with signs in front of them. For Sale. Sold. Sold. For Sale.

I knew the concept around buying a piece of the earth, but it made little sense to me. How did one buy a piece of a living entity and then call it theirs? Stupid humans.

Inside the house was very little furniture. A few chairs, a kitchen table, and a fur rug in the middle of the floor that Peta promptly went to and sniffed. "Smells funny."

"Oh, it's fake. I would never have a real fur rug," Giselle said.

I did a slow turn, taking the home in.

There was something off about the place, and it took me a moment to peg it.

"Can you feel them too?" Giselle asked. I turned to her.

"Feel who?"

"The spirits." She spoke simply and without fear. I raised an eyebrow and held a hand out to the air between us.

A whisper of wind ghosted between my fingers. "Yes. I wondered what that was." Spirits of the dead, particularly those attached to a Reader because of love or responsibility, were often found in the home of the Reader they followed. Waiting for them.

Giselle smiled. "I have a book I've been working with. I would like to use it to help you. Talan said I need to always be stretching my abilities, trying new ways to Read what is coming so I can see clearly."

Without waiting for me to answer she ran up the stairs, her feet clumping like a herd of buffalo on a rampage. I shook my head and Cactus laughed. "Notice how quickly she blows off the fact we were attacked?"

Peta nodded. "That is the great part of being young. You quickly forget how close you come to death time and again."

I lowered myself onto the rug beside her, sitting cross-legged. She curled into my lap and put her chin on my thigh. I ran a hand over her head, but said nothing about Talan. Whoever he was, she wasn't ready to tell me.

When she was, I would be ready, but I had learned

to trust her judgment. She let out a contented purr. "I will tell you soon enough."

Smiling, I looked up at the sound of the buffalo herd rushing down the stairs. The kid would never sneak up on anyone.

Giselle stepped into the doorway with a book almost as big as her torso. The leather was cracked and moldy in parts, the spine broken away and the binding frayed. The pattern in the leather was familiar, but I couldn't quite place it. Like I'd seen it before, but with so much of it missing and covered in rot it was hard to decipher. More than that, though, the cover drew my eye. The heavy pentagram carved into it was still clearly visible. The hairs along the back of my neck slowly rose to attention.

"A grimoire," I said, fighting the urge to grab the thing and toss it into the nearest flame.

Giselle smiled. "Yes, you know what it is?"

"Did Talan give it to you?"

Her face paled. "No, he . . . he left and then I found it in the attic."

Slug slime would not be slicker than the slope she stood on. I held my hand out. "May I see it?"

Her jaw ticked and a funny light came into her eyes. "It's mine. I found it." She stepped back.

Peta growled under her breath. "He would not want this for her."

The young Reader frowned. "You don't want me to have it. It's MINE!" She turned to run.

I leapt forward from my knees, tackling her while

she writhed. The book bent backward and wrapped itself around me, the leather tightening like a python.

Python, that was the skin the cover was made of. Tighter and tighter it squeezed while I fought for breath. Blackbird I could fight, but this? The book let out a long low hiss as it slowly crushed my body.

Cactus dropped to my side and put his hands on the book. I stared at his fingers as they lit up, the heat crisping the leather. The book reacted, jerking off me. Gasping for air, I reached for it, but Cactus beat me to it.

"I got this one," he said. As soon as he had a hold on the book it tried to turn on him, lengthening and flattening out as it attempted to wrap around him. The lines of power ran up his arms and the flames that erupted from his hands were a deep blue. The book flipped over backward and Giselle let out a scream, her hands going to her face. "NO, no, I don't want to be alone!"

The wind in the house picked up, fanning the flames Cactus set, urging them forward. So the spirits in the house were not the same as the ones in the book.

"She is ours, she is ours." A warbling voice snaked out of the book. Cactus held onto the leather and the flames raced up and down his arms as he battled.

Stepping around him, I reached for Giselle. I pulled her into my arms, protecting her with my body. "She is not yours. No child belongs to the spirit of evil."

My own connection with Spirit flared and I shrank

from it. The last time I'd actively used it, I wiped out my own sister's mind.

But I could see the lines of Spirit in Giselle already made, road maps through her mind and heart created by another elemental. I followed them, allowing Spirit to calm her heart, and show her she was loved. Show her I would do my best to protect her.

Around us, the air crackled with static electricity, sharp against my skin and hair. The light dimmed until there was nothing but a pinprick around Giselle and me.

"Lark! I can't see you!" Cactus sounded far off in the distance, even though he was not even on the other side of the room.

I ignored him as the air pressed in tightly, squeezing us as though it were now a constrictor. Giselle gasped, her thin arms clinging to me.

"Peta, help me!" I could barely get the words out, the crushing darkness forced me to my knees. Giselle trembled as I tried to keep her from whatever was attacking us.

My familiar put her nose tight against my ear and even then her voice was tinny and small. "Use Spirit, you have to. Your heart against the darkness here, it is the only thing that will protect her."

"I don't want to hurt her." I couldn't control Spirit, I had no idea what I was doing. There had to be another way around this.

Giselle cried out and was yanked from my hands, her body sucked into the shadows that encompassed us. I shot to my feet. No choice. There was no choice if I were to save her. I opened myself to Spirit and it flared inside my heart, pulsing like it had a life of its own.

I held my arms out to the side and the darkness shrank from my fingertips. Two steps forward and Giselle was there, huddled on the floor at the foot of the stairs. The shadows writhed around her, diving into her body and back out as she jerked and moaned.

"Please." Her mouth made the word but there was no sound. Cactus may have burned the grimoire, but the spirits that resided in it . . . they needed to be burned as surely as the pages they encompassed.

"You have to let them into you, Lark," Peta said. "I saw my other charge do this once. Let them in, then destroy them with Spirit."

The spirits laughed and slowly pulled away from Giselle. Giselle flung herself back, away from the spinning sparkles that gathered into a pulsating orb. How bad could a bunch of fae-looking sparkles be?

"*YEs. LeT Us iN. HAhahAHa.*" They called out as tendrils of the spirits lashed at me, their voices rising and falling in a spine-tingling cadence.

Well, that was reassuring. I let go of my hold on my element and tipped my head back. "Come on, then, let's see if you like tangling with someone your own size."

The innocuous sparkling orb slammed into me so hard it picked me up off the floor. A hair-raising screech exploded out of Peta. I closed my eyes as my body was spun around. This was not a fight of the flesh, I didn't need to see where I was going.

My feet touched the floor again and I went to my knees. The darkness . . . it blinked up at me from inside my head, like we were standing face to face. A child not much older than Giselle grinned with sharpened teeth and eyes of solid black like a night of no moon. "You should never have let me in. The girl fought me and you saw how she did as I wanted. She would even fight you, though she had no desire to do so. And here you are, letting me in. You are not stronger than me. You are useless."

Useless. The word wrapped around my throat like a noose, cutting off my life as surely as a woven rope. She grinned at me, her sharpened teeth flashing. "Words. They have such power over those weak of heart."

No. I would not let this happen.

I lurched forward, tackling her to the ground. She screeched and flailed at me, the darkness tightening further over my entire body. I clung to her. We would all die if I didn't do something—fast. I opened myself to Spirit and the girl stiffened under me.

"No. He was to be the last! There was not supposed to be more!" She slapped at me as I drove Spirit into her, pushing hard to fill her with its deadly, pulsating light.

"You will not end me! Astrid cannot die!"

Her body began to glow, fissures and cracks breaking along her face and skin. Her fingers dug into mine as she tried to pry them off. I tucked my head down and hunched my back.

"You will not beat me," she snarled. My fingers

slipped, and Astrid skittered from me, her black eyes wide. "Bitch. I will destroy your soul."

Every breath I took felt like fire in my lungs and sweat dripped from every part of me. Spirit flickered on the edges of me. I was running out of juice.

Astrid took a step toward me, and held a hand out. Those miniscule sparkles surrounded her fingers. If I couldn't get my hands on her, I wasn't sure I could fight her off.

A single tear escaped me and I blinked it away. "Then I'm taking you with me."

I opened to both Spirit and Earth. The power of the earth flooded through me, and Spirit tangled with it, like lovers long parted.

Astrid snarled, "No. You won't."

With a burst of speed, I leapt at her. She dodged to the left, her black eyes narrowed as she glared, the sparkling lights darkening to shadows that thrived and danced. I snaked a hand out and grabbed her shoulder. I dug my fingers in until she screamed.

Last chance. We tumbled to the ground and I wrapped my legs and arms around her and held her tightly to my chest.

She clawed and screamed, writhed and fought. The shadows drove through my body, filling my nose and mouth until I couldn't breathe. Spirit and Earth, that was all I had left. I released myself to them, let them pour through me into her.

She stiffened in my arms. "No. NO!"

I opened my eyes. Face to face, I saw her eyes fade,

the black shadows retreating until there was a pair of everyday normal green eyes looking at me.

"No," she whispered.

Once more her face cracked, tiny fissures running under the skin. They opened, and light poured out of her in rays as though she'd swallowed the sun. Sorrow flowed from her to me. A pain so intense, I couldn't help but grieve for what I was doing to her.

That I was the one causing her pain even though I had to. Her green eyes blinked once. "Thank you."

"I'm sorry," I said as I ripped her essence apart. Astrid's soul, and the darkness that had been in her scattered, first through my mind, and then into the world once more. Only this time she was so small, so miniscule there would be no infection of another grimoire, or person.

Panting, I realized I was on my hands and knees. Across from me, Giselle sat on the edge of the stairs, her eyes wide. "What happened?"

"I . . . pulled her apart. Broke her into tiny pieces."

"I didn't know you could do that."

"Neither did I." My voice cracked as though I'd been running in the desert.

Cactus.

I turned my head to see him staring at me with eyes nearly as wide as the kid's. "I didn't know you could do that either."

With a shrug, I pushed to my feet. I shouldn't have felt embarrassed, yet I did. Like being strong was a sin. Giselle wobbled to me and touched the back of my hand.

"You feel like him."

I felt like him. Like Talan, the one who'd taught her to use her abilities.

Understanding flowed over me. He had to be a Spirit Elemental. Or maybe a half-breed like me. "Mother goddess, I am not alone." The words escaped before I could catch them.

In front of us, Cactus stood over the ashes of the book, his hands still flickering with firelight. "You got a dust pan?" Yeah, those were not the heroic words I'd expected out of him. Yet that was Cactus for you.

Giselle shook her head.

"Open the door," I said, pointing at the back door. He walked over, opened the door, and the wind in the house picked up, blowing out the ashes of the grimoire, and along with it, the feeling in the house settled.

I touched Giselle's head. "You understand why we burned it and destroyed the spirit in it?"

"Yes." Her voice was barely audible. "Ask your questions."

"Are you up to it?" I held her out from me so I could look her in the eye.

She drew in a deep breath and nodded while Cactus grumbled about me pushing her too fast. I glared at him. In some ways he was still the wild child I'd known in my youth. Quick to find a game, slow to do what he was asked to do. "This is her job. She will be pushed every day for the rest of her life as she tries to balance what she is with who she wants to be." He frowned at me. "Do not give me that look, Cactus."

Giselle stood. "I can do it. I . . . I thought the grimoire would help me be stronger. At least," she put a hand to her head, "that's what it felt like when I read it. What she told me."

"Grimoires are the journals of witches and Readers gone bad." Peta wove herself between Giselle's legs. "They hold evil spirits like a honey holds flies. You are not the first to be fooled, nor will you be the last. You are lucky we came along when we did. Pray the madness hasn't taken seed in you."

The kid nodded, swallowed hard, went to the middle of the room and sat on the rug. "Larkspur, can you sit in front of me?"

To business it was, then. It made me like her even more to see her put herself back together with such speed.

Only the strong of heart could pull that off.

"Do you not want to discuss payment?" I asked.

She lifted an eyebrow. "You saved my soul. That is payment enough."

I moved to the rug and sat across from her. She reached out and took my left hand first. Her fingers trailed lightly over my skin, pressing here and there, turning my hand from side to side while she squinted at things only she could see.

"Is she going to marry soon?" Cactus blurted out behind me. I startled with the sound of his voice, and then glared at him over my shoulder.

"No. I don't see a marriage for a long time, if at all," Giselle said, her voice a bit dreamy. "Love. Lust.

Sex. She sees marriage as a yoke that will bind her wings and break her."

"That is not my question." I bit the words out, silently cursing Cactus for butting in.

"I can handle those three," he said as he crouched behind me. I whipped my head around and stared hard at Giselle.

"Are you ready for me to ask my question?"

She shook her head. "Not yet. I'm following your life line." She trailed a finger across my palm. "It's too interesting not to Read."

I closed my hand over hers. "I am not here for my own life, Reader. I am here to save another."

"Your father, I know. I see that. But you need help to find him because he is in the shadows of his own madness. I cannot see him clearly; he is cloaked from me."

I didn't like how she put that. It made me think of Blackbird. If my father had been caught by Cassava and her lover, they could in theory put that cloaking spell on him. Giselle went on. "Someone doesn't want you to find him." Her eyes flickered ever so slightly. "Am I right?"

I was relieved. Another step in the journey, one that would take time. A quick nod was all I gave her.

"You need a Tracker then," she said. "That is a bit harder than doing a Reading of your palm, or answering a question like 'will she marry?'"

She stood and went to the kitchen. The sound of a drawer opening and closing and then she was back with me. In her hand was a deck of cards. She held them out to me. "Think of your question, then choose a card."

"Why don't I say it out loud?"

"That's not how this works." Giselle looked at me, her face serious. I on the other hand struggled not to laugh. Niah had sent me to a child who had no idea of her own abilities. Sighing, I pulled a card and handed it to her. She flipped it over and laid it in front of me.

The picture was of a large black tower with flames curling out of the windows. A smell of burning flesh tickled my nose and I clenched my teeth to keep from gasping. The picture on the deck moved as figures ran to put the flames out.

"The Tower," Giselle said, her voice aging as she spoke, leaving behind the girlish tones. "Violent and destructive change comes your way, Larkspur of the Rim."

Her words echoed my own vision that Spirit had shown me. "I know. But that does not answer the question I asked."

Giselle put her finger on the Tower. "This is a picture of the Tower of London. I think that is a clue as to where you will find the Tracker."

The air tensed around us and for a moment I thought the dark spirit was back, but it was not that one. Giselle's guides whispered around us.

The lion and the unicorn
Were fighting not to drown
The lion saved the unicorn
When they hid in Shire town.
Some struck them on the rump,

And some just frowned;
Some gave them magic
While drumming out of town

Cactus let out a low whistle. "Damn, my skin is trying to crawl right off my body."

I didn't take my eyes from Giselle. The song was twisted from the version most people knew, but it had originated in England, giving credence to her suggestion of the Tracker being there.

"I want to ask another question." What I wanted to know was if there was anything else she could tell us about the journey. Anything helpful.

"Pick a card." She held the deck out to me again. I paused, letting my hand hover over the cards before picking the one on the far edge. I gave it to her and she flipped it over. A gruesome creature looked back at us, blinking up at me with tiny pig eyes. Ram horns curled off his head, and his bottom half was that of a goat. A curling forked tail wrapped around his waist, flicking here and there. He opened his mouth in a silent roar.

Peta peered over the edge. "That can't be good."

Giselle turned the card over. "Someone else is searching for the Tracker. They," she frowned and her eyes went distant, "they don't have anything to do with you on this journey, but on another journey they will interfere with something important to you. Right now they want to kill her. That doesn't make sense." She closed her eyes, a frown tight on her lips.

"Someone wants to kill . . . her? The Tracker is a woman?"

Giselle blinked up at me. "Yes, that's what I see when I look at this card. The monster is after a woman with long dark hair."

Well, goose shit, that was something of a surprise. "In London?"

"That is my best suggestion. I'm sorry I can't be more sure."

I stood. "Time to go, then."

The kid scrambled to her feet, then reached a hand out to me. "There is something else."

We stopped and I looked at her. She swallowed hard. "I don't understand it, but when I look at you . . . there is so much swirling around your aura. I have to speak it."

"Then do it," I said, not unkindly.

"I'm sorry." She paused, swallowed again, and then went on. "The world will balance in your hands not once, but twice before your life's journey is through."

Peta gripped my vest hard. "All nine of my lives are going to be used up on you, Lark. Why am I not surprised?"

Giselle glanced up at her. "You will save her, time and again. And in the end, she will save you."

Peta shook her head rather violently. "No, it doesn't work that way."

Giselle gave her a tiny smile. "You don't have a say in it, former bad luck cat."

I had to give it to Giselle, she was good at what she did. There was no way she could have known Peta's former moniker.

My cat's claws dug in until the leather creaked

under her grasp. I reached up and ran a hand down her back but directed my words to the Reader. "Thank you."

She shook her head. "No, thank you. I don't think I could have broken free on my own. I hope what was dispelled does no harm to anyone else."

I didn't want to burst her bubble. What I knew of dark spirits was not a lot, but a simple rule of thumb was they were never truly destroyed until they realized the error of their own ways. So in other words, the only thing we'd done was spread it out.

Giselle lifted her hand in a forlorn wave. "I wish you could stay a while. With Talan gone, I don't have anyone to talk to."

Loneliness rolled off her in a wave so strong I couldn't have missed it even if I didn't have Spirit pumping through my blood. I looked at Peta, knowing how much comfort she brought me in the dark hours of my life even in the short time she'd been with me.

I wasn't sure I could find Giselle her own Peta. But maybe something close. "Wait here a moment." I touched Giselle on the shoulder and headed to the door that led to the backyard. Cactus lifted an eyebrow and I motioned for him to wait too. Peta butted my head with her nose. "What are you thinking?"

"She's lonely. What can we do to soften our leaving?"

"I'm not staying with her," Peta said.

"No. But . . . you know the human world better than I do. Is there something we can do? A form of comfort we can leave with her?" The last thing I wanted was for Giselle to struggle after we were gone. She had a hard enough path ahead of her as it was.

Peta leapt from my shoulder and landed with a thud on the grass. "Maybe. Wait here."

She took off, a streak of gray and white, bounding across the lawn and then up and over the wooden fence. She didn't make me wait long. A few minutes later Peta leapt over the wooden fence once more, though this time in her snow leopard form. In her mouth was a dead dog. Its head flopped at a bad angle and its legs swayed with every step she took.

"Peta!" I couldn't believe what she'd done.

She spat the dog out at my feet. "Pick it up, Lark."

With a grimace I did as she asked, and realized it wasn't a dead dog. Though it looked like it. The fur was silky soft, and the eyes were made of a black material that was not natural.

"The humans use them as fill-ins for real companions," Peta said.

I touched her on the head, gently. "Thank you."

We hurried back into the house. Cactus was having his palm read.

" . . . broken over and over. That is all I can see," Giselle said, putting his hand down.

I held the soft, stuffed dog out to Giselle. "For the dark nights. It isn't the same as staying, but it—"

Her eyes lit up, and a smile curved her lips. "It's perfect. Thank you."

Peta shifted and leapt to my shoulder. "Of course it is, I picked it out."

Giselle smiled even wider but it slipped as she looked to me.

I touched her cheek. "I'm sorry, we have to go now."

Her eyes welled up and a tear trickled down as she clutched the stuffed dog. "This path you are on won't end well. You should stay here with me."

I took a step back. "I'm sorry, you know we can't." Not wanting to drag the goodbye out longer than we already had, I gave Cactus a quick look.

He slid a hand through my belt loop and I reached up and twisted the armband counter clockwise. We had to go back to the Traveling room in the Rim before we could Travel to London.

The memory that washed over me as we Traveled was not Cactus's this time, but Peta's.

Her body was tiny, she knew, but already she'd been chosen for an elemental. Her first charge! How exciting. Wouldn't her mother be proud . . . no, her mother was a simple snow leopard. Yet she, Nepeta, had been chosen to become more. To become a familiar who could talk and teach and help an elemental.

How wonderful! Her purrs grew with each step the mother goddess took toward wherever they were going. It didn't matter, she knew it would be good. That she would belong. She trotted beside the adult snow leopard who resembled her own mother, the deep snow making it difficult.

"Nepeta, your life is going to be different from other familiars," the mother goddess said. Her voice was kind even though the words were a little concerning.

"But I will have my charge, and he will love me."

"He will love you, that is true. But he will be the only one to truly love you for a long time."

Nepeta frowned, her lips turning downward. How could that be? Would she not only have one charge? Rare was the case where a familiar outlived their charge, or was handed to another elemental.

"Whatever you wish for me, Mother, I will do," she said as they trotted through the belly-deep snow.

"I know. That is why I must ask this of you." There was a thread of sadness in her words but there was no time for more questions. They stopped at the bottom of the mountain where a young man waited for them. His hair was a deep brown, but his eyes were blue, so blue they made her think of the sky high in the mountains after a storm. So blue they pierced. Yet on closer inspection the blue was rimmed with a pale gold edge.

The mother goddess nudged her forward. "Go to him, he is the first of your charges, and only one other will know your heart better."

She trotted forward, eager to meet him. He crouched down and held his arms out to her.

"Peta. My very own snow kitten."

With a leap of both body and heart, she jumped at him. They tussled in the light dusting of snow until they both were short of breath. He grinned at her as they sat side by side, and the sun dipped down behind the mountains.

Contentment rolled through her. Here was safety, here was her heart and the place she'd longed for since the moment she'd been brought into the world. Not that long perhaps, but her whole life still.

"Talan, what will we do first?" she asked as the night fell around them.

He leaned back in the snow and stared up at the sky. "There is so much to do, Peta. So much. In the morning we will talk about it."

I opened my eyes and stared at the interior of the Traveling room. I wanted to think about what I'd seen but I didn't have the luxury. Unless Vetch was a fool, there would be a guard—or guards—on the door.

Cactus's hand still gripped my belt. I put a finger to my lips. The interior of the globe glowed softly so there was no need of light. I lifted a hand and positioned the globe over London. Peta sat on top of my right foot, a light shiver running through her body.

Almost there. I lifted my finger to touch the spot over London.

"Why is that door shut?" Vetch boomed from the hall.

Cactus jumped, which yanked me off balance and away from the map. We thumped to the floor in a tangle of limbs far too loud to be missed even through the thick doors.

We were so screwed.

CHAPTER 8

"Get that door open now!" Vetch yelled.

I lurched, dragging Cactus with me. Peta dug her claws into my leather boots and I fought to get to my feet. The door swung open and three guards stared at us, shock on their faces. One was my ex-lover Coal.

He gave me a strange look, his eyes a mixture of longing and frustration. He shook his head. "Take her. She can't make the jump if more than one person is touching her."

I couldn't stop the scream that ripped out of me as the first guard put his hands on my shoulders. "I don't want to hurt you."

The guard laughed. I snapped my elbow into his throat, cutting off the laughter, dropping him to my feet. He writhed but I ignored him and his gurgled attempts to breathe. From behind the men, a hand snaked out and grabbed the second guard, yanking him backward; Ash was doing what he could to help.

Vetch glared at me and Coal approached from the other side. I lifted my hand and touched the armband, twisting it forward. Ash had bought us enough time, but we wouldn't be able to come back to the Rim after this.

At least, not without Father.

I yanked the armband clockwise, which would take us to London. The world started to dissolve and a hand clamped around my leg.

Pain danced up through my nerve endings and arched my back. My mind felt as though it were being pulled in two directions. I fought it, but the enormity overwhelmed me.

"Lark, use Spirit to pry him off! You must!" Peta's voice cut through the pain, and I latched onto her words. Spirit flowed through me. In the distance Ash's voice rose up and I knew he was fighting for me, for all of us. I slammed Spirit into Coal. There was no attempt at delicacy, no way to be gentle; I grieved I had to do it at all. But it was not only my life I felt drifting on the lines of fate, but Cactus's and Peta's. They were attached to me, and if I died, they would too.

I couldn't lose either of them. With a final shove of Spirit, I pushed Coal away.

Coal's heart burst with the power, and his hand dropped from my leg. The armband sucked us through the globe, like an elastic band held too long and finally released as we were catapulted. Yet a memory hovered, thoughts fleeting even as their owner died.

I loved her. I hate her. I loved her again. She took my hand. Yet I still loved her. I hate her. Damn her. I want to save her. She doesn't want me.

She broke me and now she is my end.

The words were echoes of all the things Coal had said to me. They swirled over and over in my mind as we were taken across the world. I couldn't escape them, or the feeling of betrayal that came with them.

Coal had loved me still.

With an audible pop, we split the air and landed on a soft, mossy turf.

A hard, throat-tearing gasp wrenched through me. My legs wobbled as I tried to get my footing on the grass, yet it was as if I were learning to walk again. Coal's emotions stung, biting at me even as I knew he was gone.

I'd killed him.

Perhaps I was the monster so many thought I was.

I stumbled to a stop, my hand coming to rest on a gravestone, forcing myself to put Coal away for a moment. The etched name and date in the stone blurred and I used them to help center myself once more, focusing on the details.

Brittany Ann, beloved daughter taken too soon. 1912

I looked around. Night darkened the sky here. A slow circle showed me we were in a human graveyard. In the distance was a church with a high steeple. Where were Cactus and Peta? "Peta?"

"Dirt Girl, that was not a ride I want to repeat,"

she said as she stumbled out from behind another tombstone. I crouched and picked her up, burying my face against her neck.

"I killed him." My words were a bare whisper. "I didn't want to hurt him, Peta."

"I know." She licked my cheek, and it was only then I realized I was crying. Coal was not the man I'd thought him to be, but he had been the one I'd thought I'd marry for a long time. For me to be the one to end him . . . my heart lurched and with it my stomach. Biting down on the roll of nausea, I took a step. "Cactus?"

A groan led me around to the back of a stone winged angel. Cactus lay face down with his hand over the back of his head. "Lark. Remind me not to Travel with you anymore. I have a headache that could split stones."

Anger snapped through me at his callousness. How could he think only of himself when we were lucky to be alive? When we were lucky it was only Coal who'd had to give up his life? "May I remind you I could have left you there, which would mean Vetch would have killed you? I killed Coal to save us, and you're lying there complaining you have a headache? Grow up, Cactus."

I spun on my heel and strode away. My emotions ran with me, and at the forefront of them, grief.

No, I would not cry any longer for Coal. A strange twist began in my gut, like an uncoiling serpent.

Coal didn't deserve my tears. Not only had he tried to manipulate me during our relationship, he'd been a bastard afterward and tried to make me think I was weak. I strode through the cemetery. Peta kept up easily. "You can't blame Cactus. He didn't know what you had to do."

"Doesn't matter. I have to find the Tracker. We need to look for something chaotic near the Tower of London."

Peta bobbed her head. "That would be the easiest thing to do. Though you might want to calm yourself."

I swallowed hard, struggling to do what she suggested.

We'd been walking for ten minutes before Cactus caught up. "Want to tell me what the hell that was all about? I thought we couldn't Travel with more than one person?"

I opened my mouth but Peta spoke for me, bless her. "Coal grabbed Lark as we started to make the jump. She was forced to use Spirit on him to make him let her go and it killed him. She felt him die."

Cactus grabbed me and spun me around so fast I didn't even try to stop him. He wrapped me up in his arms and held me tightly. "Mother goddess, Lark. I didn't know. I wasn't trying to be flip back there."

His apology was all I needed to let the anger go. I hung onto him. "I know. I . . . we have to go, Cactus. We are running out of time. I feel it."

Though I said the words to hurry him, the moment they slipped from my mouth I knew they were true. We only had so much time, a countdown of minutes and hours we couldn't see before something terrible would happen. What and where, I had no idea, which only made the sensation of impeding doom that much worse.

I pulled back from him and started down the street once more.

Across from us, a building seemed to beckon and I followed my instincts. The word "Police" was etched into a plaque over the door. "Like guards, if I remember right." I knew enough about humans and their world to get by, enough to be dangerous.

I crossed the street and ran up the steps of the police building. As I lifted my hand to knock on the door, it was jerked open and a redheaded man stepped out. He looked to be about my age though he was a few inches shorter than me.

"Get the fuck out of my way, woman," he snapped as he pushed past me.

"He's a Tracker, grab him!" Peta yelled.

I didn't hesitate. I grabbed his arm and spun him to face me. His fist came up and caught me under the jaw, dropping me to my knees. I didn't let go. "Stop, I need your help."

"I don't fucking well help anyone. Piece of shit police are dumb fuckers who should just—"

"Stop!" I held up my free hand. "Please, I'm not police."

"Of course you're not, blondie." His voice softened. "Damn, sorry about the shot to the jaw. That's going to bruise." He put his hands on my arms and helped me to stand, then grinned at me. "You are a tall drink of beautiful. Fuck me."

"No, I think not." I brushed his hands off. "I need you to Track someone for me."

He grunted. "You got a picture?"

It took me a moment to remember what a picture was. I shook my head. "No, a name."

His tri-colored blue eyes swirled as he grimaced. "You need Elle. She's the only one who can Track without a picture. Me and Brin are useless as tits on a bull when it comes to that."

My shoulders sagged and he swatted me on the ass. "When you see her, tell her Jack says hi. And she owes me a batch of cookies."

With nothing more, he walked down the street.

A thought slammed into me. "Wait, do you know where she is? Can you Track her? Please."

He paused and turned his head back. "What you going to give me for it?" His eyes roved my body. Cactus stepped between us.

"She already can't handle one redhead."

Jack's lips curled up. "She was here in London, but she's on the move. She's headed south. That help?"

I nodded. "I'll take it. Thank you."

"Don't fucking thank me. Getting tangled with us assholes has killed more than one dumb fuck."

He tugged his collar, ducked his head and strode away from us.

Peta laughed softly. "Trackers, foul-mouthed bunch to the last drop. Come on, we need to keep looking. Even though she may be gone, we have to see if we can get a solid hit."

I agreed. We turned away from the direction Jack went.

"Here, what about these?" Cactus asked. He pointed at a wall along the edge of the sidewalk plastered with signs and maps. I ran a hand over them, stopping when I saw one that spoke of the Tower of London. Yanking it off the wall, I opened it to a folding map. Cactus peered over my shoulder.

"We aren't far. A few streets up and then four to the west and we'll be there."

I tucked the map into the back of my belt and broke into a jog. We were close enough I didn't want to hold back. I reached for the power of the earth to propel me forward and got a distant buzz that brought me to a standstill.

Cactus stopped beside me. "What?"

"Try to reach the earth," I said as I took a slow circle. Lines of power flickered up his arms, but he was no more successful than me if the widening of his eyes was any indication.

The ground was buried under a thick coating of cement. Lips tight, I held my hand out, palm down, and called the earth upward. Such a strange thing; it was akin to calling on the bottom of the ocean from the surface of the water. I could feel the earth, but it was far away from me.

"I can't reach it." Cactus shook his head and there was no small amount of fear in his eyes.

Beside us, a car roared by, its lights blinding me before throwing me into night blindness. I covered my face with one hand. "I can, but it's a strain. How do they live like this?"

"They don't know anything else, Lark. You

probably thought the same thing when you were in the Pit." Cactus took my hand and we started toward the Tower again.

"Maybe, but the Pit at least was natural. This is anything but."

Peta was between us, keeping up easily. "Not true. The cement is made up of tiny particles that are of the earth, as are the buildings and even the car that went by. Humans have gotten good at manipulating the elements around them and bending them to their will."

We took our corner and kept moving as cars zipped past us and the fumes choked my lungs. Cactus seemed less bothered by what was going on than I was. He grabbed my arm as he pointed to the skyline above the buildings that crowded around us.

A plume of smoke swirled up, a hint of orange glow coming from underneath it. Damn, that was in the direction of the tower.

"Move, she won't stick around with that going on." I was running before the words were out of my mouth. We burst around a final building and skidded to a stop.

The tower was actually a large square with four main towers. The front two were on fire and humans poured out of the buildings. Cactus grabbed me. "This is our chance to get in and out without being noticed."

"Are you crazy?" I made a face at him as he tugged me along.

"Only for you, Lark." He smiled at me and my heart gave a traitorous thump. "Come on, I can protect you from the fire. We can grab your Tracker and be done with this."

I glanced at Peta. She gave me a subtle nod, which was all I needed. I raced after Cactus. We pushed our way through the growing crowd. There were men holding a long snake-like thing that shot water out of the end of it.

"You can't go in there!" one of the humans shouted. We ran harder, dodging their efforts at stopping us. Cactus let out a laugh, and I had to admit, his recklessness made me giddy. Like we were kids again sneaking tarts from the kitchen and running from the cook. We were through the main gates and into the courtyard before we had to stop.

"Where now?" Cactus asked.

Behind us, the men ran toward us. Worm shit and green sticks. "Can you slow them down, please? I need to figure this out!"

He flicked a hand, red lines lit up his arms, and flames raced out along the ground bringing the humans to a screaming halt. They shouted at us, but we ignored them.

Peta shifted into her snow leopard form. Her green eyes narrowed as she stared around us. "I can protect you from the heat better this way."

"Shouldn't need protecting, Peta. We're here to talk to the Tracker, not fight her."

She snorted. "Did you not get a fist slammed into your jaw only a few minutes ago? And that was by a mildly irritated Tracker."

My lips twitched. It couldn't be all that bad.

Trackers might be a bit rough around the edges, but I doubted they were going to go out of their way to cause trouble. My jaw might disagree with me on that, though.

We wove our way through the buildings, and it didn't take long to realize all the doors were locked. Except one.

At the top of the northwest tower, which was only beginning to burn, a single door was open as if in invitation. No, that was being too kind; what we saw was no invitation, but an invasion.

I ran a hand over the jagged edges of the door frame where they'd been ripped off. The metal hinges were sheared in half and the door was nowhere to be seen. Unless the tiny splinters littering the floor were what was left of it.

I stepped inside as Peta let out a low snarl.

"What?"

"I smell something rather alarming. Troll shit."

The fetid stench curled up my nose as she spoke. As if the human sewers had spewed up after festering in heat for a year. "Mother goddess, that is horrid." I put a hand to my nose as my eyes watered. Forcing myself to step further into the room, I dropped my hand and looked around. The room was laid out simply, a table with a few books on it, two chairs, and a window on the far side. Glass covered the window frame as if blown inward. Two strides and I stood at the window. Blood splatter covered the frame and a fingerprint on a piece of glass still left in the window drew my eye. I put my own hand up to mimic it.

Several strands of long dark hair caught on the top of the window frame. "She jumped out."

"She would have died," Cactus said.

I peered out of the window to the cobblestone below. "No body."

"Doesn't mean she didn't die. Maybe the trolls got her."

Somehow I doubted she would be that easy to take out. Call it a hunch. "No, she made it out. Now we have to track the Tracker. Cactus, check the books for something. A clue, anything that will give us an idea of where we're going."

I turned as he picked up a book by the edge, something dark brown dripping off it. His nose wrinkled up. "I found the troll shit."

"Disgusting creatures," Peta said as she crept around the edge of the room, her nose twitching. "Their scent makes it hard to pick up hers, but I think I have it."

"So you can smell her if we get close enough?"

"Yes."

A low, deep laugh turned me around, my hand instinctively going for my spear. In the doorway stood a large, orange-skinned troll. He filled the door frame, his head pushing against the top as his six-fingered hands gripped the edges. At least I knew how the door had been ripped off now. His fingers clutched what was left of the frame, making the wood creak.

Three eyes peered at us, one from each cheek and one in the center of his head. His mouth had wide, flat teeth for crushing and his jaw looked as though it had been modeled after a boxer dog, the way the lower section shot forward. "You looking for the Tracker? Me too. Maybe we can team up."

He thrust his hips my way as he ran a hand over himself as if that would somehow endear him to me.

"Yeah, I think not." I took my spear from my side and twisted the two halves together. From Peta rolled a flash of excitement. She wanted to fight with the Troll.

I raised an eyebrow at her and she shrugged.

"Not my first time dealing with them. Watch him, he's a Firestarter."

The Troll looked from me to Peta and back again. Of course, he couldn't hear her.

"Too bad. Pretty girl like you should have a real cock in her bed, not a redheaded weakling." He grinned at Cactus, then flicked his hand that had been wrapped around his shaft at him.

A slimy substance I didn't want to guess at slapped Cactus in the face.

His green eyes flashed and he let out a breath. So much for getting in and out of the tower with ease.

CHAPTER 9

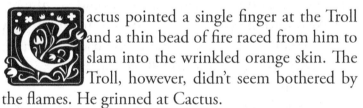

actus pointed a single finger at the Troll and a thin bead of fire raced from him to slam into the wrinkled orange skin. The Troll, however, didn't seem bothered by the flames. He grinned at Cactus.

"Witch, I'm going to enjoy eating your skinny ass."

I grabbed Cactus and yanked him behind me. "You can't help with him."

The hurt on his face should have bothered me, but all it did was irritate me. I didn't need anyone saving me.

My back was to the Troll and I held still, knowing he wouldn't be able to resist. Predators always thought they were clever bastards.

Peta watched from under the window ledge and I

kept my eyes locked on her for a sign. She blinked and I spun with my spear arced outward in a sweep. The blade buried into the Troll's side. He let out a roar and swiped at me with his oversized mitts. "Sneaky bitch!"

Peta shot in between us and swiped at his legs, taking him out at the knees. He dropped to the floor, clutching his side. Peta danced back from him, her tail lashing.

I yanked my blade out of his hide and held it to his neck. "Easy or hard, Troll?"

"What are you? Humans don't move fast like that, and you don't smell like anything but trees and dirt."

I pressed the blade harder until it cut through the first layer of flesh, peeling it as though I were fileting a fish. Fire raced up his arms and he flicked them at me. I held my ground, knowing Cactus would . . . the fire slammed into me and threw me backward, all the way to the window. The glass dug into my back and hands as I scrambled to keep from falling out.

"Cactus!"

He stood to the side, his arms folded. "I can't help with him."

Peta grabbed the Troll as he got to his feet, jerking him back to the floor. Fury like I'd never known ripped through me. "Good way to show you're a better man than Ash, Prick."

I tumbled off the ledge and into the room, grabbed the table and flipped it onto its side. Cactus let out a sigh, "I'm sorry, I just—"

"Now is not the time," Peta said. The Troll lurched to his feet, bleeding but otherwise not bothered by the injuries we'd inflicted. He backed up and I shot forward. We needed to get moving, and obviously the Troll wasn't going to have any answers.

I drove my spear into his neck and jerked it to the left, cutting his head most of the way off. Cactus gagged, and from Peta through our bond came a definite sense of satisfaction that lasted a split second.

The Troll was a Firestarter, which meant his death was not going to be as easy as taking his head.

His body combusted as it fell, bright orange flames the exact shade as his skin curling up in the doorway, completely blocking it. The flames were so hot, I had to back up as they reached for the ceiling.

Worm shit. I refused to ask Cactus for help. Which only left the window option. Peta nosed the book on the floor that had the least amount of troll shit on it. "I think this actually might help us."

I scooped the book up and tucked it into the back of my pants under my belt.

"Peta, you ready?" I tapped my shoulder. She shifted and leapt into my arms. I put her onto my shoulder and went to the window.

"I can stop the flames, Lark," Cactus said, his voice contrite.

"No, please don't bother yourself. I'd rather climb than put you out again." I kept my voice as neutral as I could make it.

"Don't be like that."

I spun and jabbed a finger into his chest. "Be like what? Expect you to be a team player? To know your strengths and mine? To think you would be there to help me when I *did* need your help? Pardon me for thinking you were adult enough to actually be a help and not a hindrance."

I turned away from him and pulled myself into the window. Anger fueled me, which made it easy to manipulate the stone the tower was built of—at least that was what I was banking on. I knocked the last of the glass out of the window and then eased out so I hung by my hands.

I placed one hand on the stone wall a foot down from the window ledge. The rock eased around my fingers like soft clay before firming up.

"Tell me again why I shouldn't be able to do this?" I asked Peta as I made my way down the wall, handhold by handhold as I created them. The last thing I wanted was a lecture from her about being nicer to Cactus.

"From what I understand, what you are doing is manipulating the material down to its most basic matter. As a Terraling, you can move sand the way sand moves, you can encourage plants to grow, you can communicate with animals. But taking a hard stone and softening it to the point of reforming it is something not done since the beginning of Terralings. It is an ability thought to be lost."

I dropped to the cobblestone at the same time Cactus stepped out of the main doors. He wouldn't look at me, and I was glad. I strode toward the side wall of the courtyard and flicked my hands at it. The stone blew apart and I walked through, ignoring the humans staring at me as I strode out.

"He's making it easier on you to choose Ash," Peta said.

"That he is." I stared straight ahead.

"I hate to be the voice of reason, because I do not think Cactus is the right one for you . . . but does it seem like him to pout? To put you in danger?" Her words were soft, and they gave me pause.

"Why would he do it, then? Why would he put me in danger?"

"I can only think of one reason."

I glanced back to see him trailing behind us, his hands stuffed in his pockets and his head lowered. "What reason?"

"He knows he's already lost you to Ash, and so he is going to make it easy on you."

I came to a complete and total stop. My heart thumped wildly against my chest. No, no, no. I did not want to believe she was right, but . . . it was something Cactus would do. He'd taken pain for me before, when we were children and had gotten in trouble together. The strap had fallen on him, not me.

I closed my eyes and tried to slow the beating of my heart. Cactus stopped a few feet behind me. I slowly turned to him.

"Are you trying to make me angry with you? Trying to drive me away?"

His eyes never left mine. "I want you to be happy, Lark. I love you enough to lose you if it means you will be happy."

Damn him. My lower jaw trembled. "I cannot focus on this while we are trying to save my father. We can discuss this later, but I need to know if I can depend on you or not."

He stepped forward and took one of my hands, raising it so he could kiss the underside of my wrist. "I am always here for you. I'm sorry, I . . . I could see the guilt in you, and I didn't want to make it worse."

I let him pull me into his arms. Slowly I dropped my head to his shoulder. "I can't choose, Cactus. Don't make me."

"One day you'll have to." He kissed the side of my head.

"Enough. We have to go," Peta said, her voice sharp.

I stepped away, my hands lingering in his. "You almost got me killed."

"Nah, you handled it fine. I knew you would." He patted at a few charred spots on my vest as he winked at me. I could admit I was relieved even while I was exasperated.

He reached around me and tapped the hard-backed book I'd taken. "Let's see what we've got, then."

Taking the book out, I held it in front of me. The title was *Africa in Pictures*. I flipped it open and grimaced as the scent of troll shit wafted up. "Disgusting creatures. I can't understand who thought they were a good idea."

"Some witch on a power trip," Peta muttered.

Figured.

The pictures were bright and vibrant, stark and desolate all at once. I'd never been to Africa, though there were parts of it I knew would call to me. The deep jungles, the grasslands filled with animals, the mountains where the earth stretched to reach the sky.

I turned the page and a bloody fingerprint stopped me. The same as the one on the glass, it had been smeared a little over the blue water. Sand dunes stretched out into the ocean, triangular and shaped very much like dragon's heads. "There. That's where she is."

"Are you sure?" Cactus leaned over my shoulder, his body brushing against mine enough to make me forget for a moment what I was going to say.

Peta cleared her throat. "Head in the game, Lark."

Mentally I shook myself. "Yes, I'm sure. This is her fingerprint."

"Could be a trap."

"Not for us. If anything, she was trying to draw someone else."

From my shoulder, Peta nodded. "I agree. Trackers are smart, tricky beggars. Giselle said someone else was looking for her; maybe she's leading them on."

With a quick tear, I ripped the page out of the book and folded it up. "The sand dunes are huge. We need to get above them to find her fast."

"How are we going to do that?" Cactus asked. "It's breeding season for dragons, which will make them next to useless. No Sylph will give us the time of day. And I wouldn't trust a Harpy further than I could throw her."

I situated myself, finding east easily. The sense of where the sun would rise was bred into me as surely as the power of the earth and the power of Spirit. "Peta, what do you think?"

"I think you need your second familiar. A winged creature big enough to carry you would be helpful. That being if I could choose your second." She tipped her head to one side.

"A dragon?" Cactus's tone was hopeful even though he'd just disparaged the big lizards.

"No. They only bond with demon slayers. Something else. Hmmm." She went quiet and I kept moving. Regardless of what she said, we needed to get across the channel to the continent. Once there, we could find a way to get airborne. There were several supernatural creatures we could reach out to. Harpies, though tough, could be reasoned with for a price. There were several clutches of griffins who resided there as well.

But I had a feeling that whatever Peta came up with, it would not be—

"The Bastard. He's our best shot, I think."

Cactus let out a laugh. "You're kidding, right? Isn't he in Greece?"

Peta bobbed her head. "Yes, I've met him before, though it was a long time ago. I think he will remember me and I could convince him to help us. We have to go almost that far anyway. Unless you want to convince a human to take you up in one of their whirly bird things."

Nausea rolled through me at the simple thought of trusting my life to a human contraption. "No, we'll go to The Bastard. If you're sure."

"The only choice we have, I think," Peta said, "and until you get your second familiar, maybe we can convince him to help us. He is a bit of a glutton, so a food reward would work. Or the offer of some attractive ladies."

I grimaced. I'd heard The Bastard was difficult . . . one of those few creatures who was truly alone in the world since he was a creation, not a natural occurrence. Even the Trolls got to breed and have babies. The Bastard, not so much.

"Then it's set, we're off to see him. And hope we can convince him to help."

I had a feeling it wouldn't be all that easy, but it was a long road between us and Greece. Perhaps in the interim we'd find a simpler way.

Somehow I truly doubted it, but one could hope.

CHAPTER 10

"You think the ferry is safe?" Cactus crouched by the edge of the boat while we waited for the sun to rise and for the human who owned the boat.

"You want to swim across the channel?" I lifted an eyebrow at him and he shook his head.

"Nah. It'll ruin my hair."

Peta snorted and shivered lightly. "Lark, I have a funny feeling—"

There was no warning other than Peta's words. A wave shot up above our heads with a speed that could only mean one thing. An Undine had decided we were a threat.

I bolted backward, Cactus and Peta with me, as the wave crashed down where we'd been standing. The tail end of it caught my legs and sent me sprawling onto the rough cement that touched the docks.

The jagged footing tore at my pants and ripped at my skin. Hissing, I rolled to my back to stare at where we'd been only moments before. A high-pitched giggle rebounded toward us and for a split second I thought Finley, queen of the Undines, was playing a prank on us.

A figure rose up out of the water and stepped onto the docks. Not a girl, not even a woman, but a rail-thin man stared at us. His eyes flicked from me to Cactus, to Peta, and then back to me. A full-body shiver rocked through him and he snapped his head back as it reached the top of him. He had dark eyes and darker hair and looked far too much like Requiem for my liking. Requiem had raped Bella, tried to kill Ash and me and had nearly taken the throne of the Undines. To say he was not one of my favorite people would be an understatement. If he'd still been alive, that was.

The Undine shivered again, softer this time. "Do you know who I am?"

"Peta, he look like anyone to you?"

"Mouse turds, he looks like Requiem." She clicked her teeth together. "I thought we killed him?"

The Requiem look-alike dropped to a crouch and scuttled forward, like a crustacean. "Requiem, Requiem, he was my brother. A bastard to the core, he had me banished and here I am, mad as a hermit crab with no shell. No place to call my own, cut off from the place that feeds my soul."

He scurried toward us and I took several steps

back. A banished elemental . . . already mad with the loss of his home. I grabbed Cactus's hand. "I don't want to hurt him. If Requiem banished him, he was probably one of the good guys."

"We may not have a choice." Cactus turned me to the side where a second elemental crept our way. Another Undine, by the fins that sprouted along the edge of his arms and legs.

"Peta, tell me we can talk them down."

She whimpered. "No. The banished are to be killed on sight. Not because they should die, but because they are dangerous—"

The Undine on our left roared and leapt toward us, his arms and legs spread wide as he shifted into a giant octopus, tentacles reaching for us. I dropped to one knee and yanked my spear clear of my belt. The octopus shifter landed on top of Cactus and me. Before I could get my spear free, the tentacles wrapped around us with a speed I'd previously reserved in my mind for striking snakes. We were jammed together as the Undine tightened his hold on us. My head pressed up against his bulbous eye and his thoughts rushed through me.

Kill them show loyalty, don't question, kill them take me home please take me home don't leave me out here I'm dying my spirit fades kill them take me home find me a place kill them.

His pain and sorrow flooded my mind, and if I'd been standing, the emotions would have brought me to my knees. Cactus groaned and then a burst of flame lit him up, covering his body long enough to make the tentacles release him. Except that they re-wrapped around me.

We slipped backward toward the water. Panic reared its ugly head.

"Worm shit, Cactus, help me!"

"I'm trying." The sound of flesh sizzling under a ball of flame met my ears a split second before the Undine holding me dropped over the wooden dock edge and into the icy channel.

With my arms trapped to my sides, all I could do with my spear was swipe it uselessly through the water and hope I hit something. We rolled and I was looking up at the surface of the water. The tentacles tightened and then loosened a fraction of an inch. Enough to turn and get my spear up.

Time seemed to pause as our eyes met. He blinked once, shook his head and reared back. The parrot-like beak of his mouth aimed for my face. He let me go another few inches, and adjusted my position with his tentacles.

Lips clamped shut tightly, I thrust my spear tip up into the center of his head as I tried not to think about why he was banished. Because he'd opposed Requiem? Because he'd tried to stop a raging tyrant from taking over his home?

Forgive me.

I don't know if it was his thought or mine. I drove the spear further in, pushing the blade hard and twisting it. Blood flowed into the water and his tentacles slowly released me. The creature convulsed and its questing tentacles drooped. His body slid down into the inky black water, his body shifting one last time as he breathed out his last gulp of water.

Keeping my hands tightly on the haft of my spear, I swam to the surface. I broke through to the sounds of fighting, and Peta snarling. Grabbing the edge of the dock, I pulled myself up but kept my body low to the wooden surface. In front of me, Cactus and Peta barely dodged the first Undine, keeping free of him but only just.

I stood and arched my hand back, took two running strides and loosed my spear. There was a slight wobble in it—it wasn't meant for throwing like that—but it still slammed into the left center of his back. He threw his arms wide with a roar and fell to the ground. Scrabbling at his back, he tried to reach the spear, but failed and dropped forward onto his face.

"I am done," he said, but his back still rose and fell. I approached him cautiously before crouching by his head. His eyes lifted to mine but not much else. Dark, so dark they were, like the night sky.

"You fought Requiem?"

"I did. He was a bastard."

Snarling, he took a swing at me. I pressed his head to the ground and knelt on his hand closest to me. "Peta, can we call on Finley?"

He shivered under my hand. "The child cannot help me. No one can. End it now. You are an Ender. I demand you END ME!" he screeched and lurched toward me, but he had no strength in his body.

With my free hand I pulled the knife tucked into the top of my boot.

"Are you sure, Lark?" Cactus asked. I knew what

the real question was. Could I live with killing the Undine in essentially cold blood? But what Cactus didn't understand was that it wasn't going to be in cold blood. Mercy was an act of love, an act of understanding. I could do for this Undine what he needed.

"Last words, if the madness is not so far eaten into you?" I asked.

Below me, the Undine shuddered. "Requiem is dead?"

"Yes."

"Then I am at peace and need no last words. I go to the mother goddess's embrace."

I didn't wait for him to say anything else. As hard as I could, I drove the blade into the back of his neck, angling it upward for a clean kill. His body jerked once, all his muscles contracting at the same time before he relaxed into his death.

Pulling both blades, I wiped them one at a time on his back. The salt water would rust the blades if I was not careful.

I put the blade back into my boot and the spear I reattached to my belt, my movements automatic. Without a word, I took the dark Undine's arms and dragged him to the water's edge. I laid him on his back and folded his arms over his chest. Peta moved to my side and pressed herself against me. "There was no other choice."

"I know. But banishment from the Deep for fighting Requiem . . . I thought Finley would have made these things right." I pressed my hands over the unnamed Undine. The queen of the Undines should have been bringing home those Requiem had banished. Why wasn't she? A question I did not have time for.

I rolled the Undine into the water. "Go to her embrace then, and find your peace."

The water splashed up, engulfing him with a single wave that settled within seconds as if he had never been. Being banished, perhaps *that* was the truth. Those banished were considered anathema, as if they had never existed.

Peta must have picked up on my thoughts. "Their names are wiped from any record. Finley likely doesn't even realize they are missing."

A hand brushed along the side of my face and I leaned into Cactus. He was softer than Ash in many ways . . . but right in that moment he knew what I needed. A touch, and the knowledge that he was there with me, with no pressure beyond what we could see in front of us.

I stood and let out a long breath. "Let's take the boat."

Cactus gave me a sideways grin. "Theft?"

"I think it's the least of my sins tonight." I meant it as a joke, but it fell flat and killed whatever levity he'd been attempting. "Sorry, my timing sucks."

"You're telling me," he grumbled, but again the mood lightened. In a matter of minutes we had a boat untied, a small one with a sail attached to it. Peta paced the dock. "It's small, are you sure this is a good idea?"

"No, but you want to get to Greece. How else would you like to do it?"

"I would rather drag my belly the whole way than get into that boat. I don't like water, Lark." She blinked her large green eyes up at me. Yet she'd dived into the water to save me before she'd ever been my familiar. Peta had the heart of a dragon beating inside her chest.

"Not overly fond of it myself, but we all do things we don't like. Come on, you can sleep the whole way." I pointed at a small orange padded material with a hole in the middle. A perfect cat bed if I ever saw one.

Sighing, she shifted into her housecat form, then jumped into the boat and settled down. "This is not very comfortable."

"Stop complaining, bad luck cat," Cactus said.

She hissed at him but said nothing more. I stepped into the boat last and pushed off the dock with my boot.

"How in the seven hells are we going to get to Greece exactly?" Cactus asked. "Not that I'm doubting you, princess. Just curious."

I ran my hand over the leather pouch at my side. Ash I would have trusted in an instant, and that was what made me pull the smoky diamond out of the pouch. With a quick flick, I put it on a leather strap, slipped it over my head and tucked it under my shirt. "Don't tell on me, Cactus."

His eyebrows shot up. "I never told anyone you put pig shit in Cassava's dinner that one night. And I had my ass tanned for not saying who did it. They all knew, Lark. But I held my tongue."

Peta let out a laugh, rolling onto her back. "She did not."

He laughed with her. "Yeah, she did. Of course, she let me take the beating."

I smiled, and rolled my eyes. "We were ten. I knew what the lash felt like all too well. If I remember right, I'd taken a licking for you the day before."

"You think I didn't know what the leather strap felt like?" He fell back into his seat. "I'm quite sure I have the scars to prove I was well acquainted. I could show you, if you don't believe me." His green eyes locked onto mine and he gave me a slow wink. No, I was not going there.

"I'll pass."

"The offer stands, princess."

I widened my stance and slowed my breathing. Using the power of another element was not something I took lightly. But our time was slipping away and we had to get to Greece. "Tell me why I don't take us straight to the Namib Sand Sea?"

"Because it's huge, Lark," Peta said. "We could search for weeks and not find her, and then she could be gone. We need a faster way to sweep the area. Besides, I have a feeling about The Bastard."

I looked down at her. "What do you mean?"

She rolled into a ball, her tail wrapped around her nose. "Trust me. We need him."

There was no way she was going to say anything if she wasn't ready to. Pressing the smoky grey diamond hard, I focused on calling up a wind to fill our sails and push us toward Greece.

The power of air was strange on my skin, the feel of it so light, as if it could sweep me into the sky. I held my arms out in front of me and watched the foreign lines of power as they crept up my arms. White, misty tendrils wrapped me tight and beckoned me to use them.

Acting on instinct, I pursed my lips and blew out a breath as softly as I could.

The water ruffled and a blast of air slammed into us, scooting us forward. Cactus and Peta let out twin yelps.

I wobbled but balanced myself quickly. The sails of the boat were full and I pointed at the rudder. "Steer us, Cactus."

"Aye, aye, captain!"

I didn't look back at him but kept my eyes forward as I breathed through the power. Each exhale sent the boat scooting forward. So as long as I could breathe, we could make good time.

I only wished I didn't feel so threatened by the simple thought of trying to make sure nothing stopped me from breathing.

CHAPTER 11

Boating wasn't as bad as Peta made it out
to be. I even caught her once or twice
with her eyes closed as she breathed in
the clear salty air. We stopped where we
had to for food and water. Rested only when necessary. No trolls showed up, no more banished elementals lost their minds and lives. If it weren't for the fact
that we were searching for my father, it would have
been enjoyable.

The first day, Cactus told dirty jokes.

The second day, Peta told stories of her past and
the stupid things her charges did until we howled
with laughter and cried bullshit on the ridiculousness
of her tales.

The third and what would be final day on the water, they both looked at me in perfect unison.

I arched an eyebrow. "What?"

Cactus grabbed the heel of the bread we'd snagged at our last stop and tore it into pieces, handing one to me. "We've been doing all the talking. Now it's your turn."

"Nothing to say. You two have had interesting lives. I haven't."

Tipping her head to one side, Peta blinked up at me. "That may have been true in the past, Lark. But I think the last while has been anything but quiet."

"But you know about that. Telling you about being in the Pit . . . you were both there." What were they getting at, anyway? What did they want me to say?

Being who she was, Peta braved the waters of my past first. "Tell us about Cassava. Why do you think she's the one behind your father's disappearance?"

I sighed heavily and the wind whipped up around us. I eased off on the diamond so my breathing would not be connected to it while we had this discussion. The last thing I wanted was to have the power of air running though me as I raged about Cassava. About how she'd destroyed my family.

I tore the piece of bread into bits, one for each thing Cassava had done.

The bottom of the boat gave a thump and the water around us rippled. I froze. "Peta. Tell me you didn't see that."

"Sorry." She shifted into her snow leopard form. Worm shit.

The boat swayed to the left, out of the current

as though something were pushing it. Cactus stood and I waved him back down. "Standing is a bad idea. Don't rock the boat."

He clutched the edges of the boat. "Then what do we do?"

I dared to lean over and stare into the water. Scales undulated around the hull, twisting and turning. A flicker of deep green against the blue, and here and there flashes of yellow.

"Peta. Snake-like, big coils. Green and yellow."

"Sea serpent," she said. Her words were like a trigger. The water around us erupted and a serpent burst out. Its head was easily fifteen feet in the air, with an elongated jaw like a crocodile and teeth the size of my hands. The thing's body was easily as big around as the boat and there seemed to be no end to it.

It snapped its jaw once and dove back down under the water. The boat rocked and swayed; the water stilled as if there had never been anything there. I hunched my shoulders.

"That was easy," Cactus said, and my muscles tensed further. Peta's eyes met mine. She dug her claws into the bottom of the wooden boat.

"Hang on," I said.

"What? Why?" Cactus spit out.

Heartbeat.

Breath.

Heartbeat.

The boat lifted up with no warning, straight into the air before tipping to one side. Cactus went flying with a yell, but Peta and I dangled from the boat as it flew through the air. Flashes of scales, a coil crashing down in the water. I lost my grip on the wood and fell separate of the boat. I didn't land in the water, though. I landed on the sea serpent.

Straddling the coils, my legs stuck out to the side, like a child riding a wide-backed horse. I slipped to the side and into the water, pushing off the creature with my feet. Its head spun around and it grinned at me.

"Tasty morsels, oh so fine. Elementals out of their element." Water sprayed as the serpent spoke, its voice high, and distinctly feminine.

She drove her head straight at me, jaws wide. One gulp is all it would take to suck me into her maw; I'd barely be a single bite. I flung myself sideways at the last second but she caught my left leg, right at the ankle, and bit down.

I was going to lose my foot.

And go mad like Coal.

I sat up and dug my hands into the ridges around her eye. I didn't think, I reached out and let Spirit guide me.

Her mind was a tangled mess. In it I saw the hand of another Spirit user. Someone darker than me.

"I am not him," I whispered. A shudder went through her.

She spat my leg out and lowered me into the boat. I didn't let her go, knowing the connection of touch was the only thing keeping her mind easy. "I am not myself any longer. The cloaked one did this to me. I was a familiar once, to the Undines' king."

"Finley's father," I said. Her big eyes blinked in confirmation.

"Yes. I would have stayed. But the cloaked one took my mind. This respite . . . I am not sure it is welcome, for I know the danger I represent."

Cactus tugged on me. "Stop playing with the snake, Lark. Let's go."

I ignored him. "Serpent, I can't heal your mind."

"I know."

She didn't move, but her tongue flicked out and touched the tip of my spear. "You could save me from this."

Peta stepped closer. "You could be healed. There is another who wields Spirit. More experienced than Lark or the other one."

Her eyes flicked to my cat. "Are you sure?"

"Yes." Peta bobbed her head.

The serpent let out a sigh. "I still do not know if you can get past me. Why are you here?"

"Looking for The Bastard," I said.

She snorted and salt water sprayed over us in a fine mist. "There is no love lost in him for supernaturals or elementals. I will wish you luck with him, and me."

I softened my touch on her face. "How do we pass by you?"

Her eyes fluttered closed as she slowly lowered us and the boat to the water. "Put it in my mind that there is better prey elsewhere. It is the only chance you have."

I closed my eyes and thought about fish to the south of us, schools of fish fat and lazy, replete with a feed of their own. "Here we go," I said, and slid my hands away.

Without a word, the serpent jerked away, her eyes going to the south of us. One snap of her jaws and she dove under the waves.

I put a hand to the smoky diamond and blew hard, scooting the skiff along the water. An hour at a wicked pace took us far enough away that I finally felt I could ease off, and sat down to catch my breath.

Peta put her big head on my lap. "That was unexpected."

A laugh escaped me. "You said I would bring trouble to us."

"Yes, but even I didn't think you would bring a sea serpent. There aren't many left."

I nodded and leaned back on the wooden bench. Using the diamond tired me out. Or maybe it was the fact that we'd narrowly escaped death.

Peta butted me with her head. "Finish what you would say about Cassava."

Damn. I was hoping we'd skip by that.

"She killed my mother and little brother, Bramley. Manipulated my father. Blocked me from my power. Tried to wipe out our family with the lung burrowers. What more reason do you need? She is the cause of our latest problems. I know it."

Cactus leaned forward as he steered the boat. "It's not about reason, it's about facts. Evidence. How do we prove she was the one to do this? That is what you want, isn't it? To prove she is behind everything wrong in your world."

I knew he wasn't being mean or trying to upset me, yet a part of me wanted him to believe me. To say I was right, Cassava was a bitch, and that was all there was to this story.

"Unless she confesses in front of the right people, there is no way to prove it. It's her word against mine. And we all know she is too smart for that."

"Why would she take your father?" Peta asked, stretching her back in a perfect arch. She yawned. "Surely your father is stronger than her in his connection to the earth."

I nodded. "Yes, he is. But his mind . . . it's so broken, I don't know how easy he would be to manipulate even without Spirit. If Blackbird is working with her as we think he is, then . . ." I didn't have to say the rest. All three of us knew Blackbird could control Spirit.

The desire to believe he, my father, was still the man I remembered from my childhood was strong, yet I knew it for what it was. A last desperate hope that he could be saved not only in the physical sense, but from mental deterioration too.

Cactus shook his head. "Why would Blackbird work with her? He carries all five elements; he doesn't need her."

Frowning, I stared over the water. "Why was he working with Keeda, then? That makes about as much sense. He doesn't need anyone . . . yet he was about to set Keeda on the throne in the Pit. That has Cassava written all over it."

The more I thought about it, the more sure I was

that I was right. Cassava was pulling the strings on Blackbird . . . it made a twisted sort of sense. With him working for her, she would be able to attack anyone, control anyone with Spirit, and unlike her usage of the pink diamond, the only way to stop her from using him would be to kill him. Something I knew from experience was more than difficult. Not to mention he was a coward, the slippery little bastard.

"Lark, you have to look at his motivation," Cactus said, pressing his case. "There is no reason for him to help her."

"Unless they're lovers, as we suspect," Peta said. "That would be enough for him to work with her, to do as she wishes."

A shudder ran through me. "If she got pregnant with his child, she'd have what she wanted. A second child who carries all five elements. Exactly as she and Requiem were planning."

A snort escaped Cactus and I really looked at him. He wasn't buying into the theory, I could see it in his eyes. "What?"

"Why . . . Lark, you need to start asking why. Why would she want your father?"

"How the hell should I know?" I snapped at him.

He stood and stared down at me, his words harsh. "You should know. You're accusing her of treason, attempted regicide, and genocide."

I shot to my feet. "Why aren't you on my side?"

"I am!" he roared. "But you have to think. You can't assume anymore. We aren't children, and this isn't a game of hide and seek. Lives are at stake. Yours. Mine. Peta's. Your father's."

Incredulity whispered along the bond between Peta and me. I had to agree with her; I couldn't believe Cactus would stand there and yell at me, telling me I needed a reason to believe Cassava was the bitch we all knew she was.

"I know that. Do you think I'm stupid?"

His whole body shivered. I knew because I knew him so well that he wanted to pace. But the size of the boat prevented much more than standing and sitting. "I think you have a one-track mind. You need to ask questions, Lark. You need to see the wider picture, because I don't think this is about Cassava. It feels . . . like there is more at stake. This is about more players than a single woman who's lost her mind."

Peta jumped onto the wooden seat between us. "Wait, do you mean a premonition?"

He scrubbed his hands through his hair. "This doesn't make sense. Cassava escaped with her life. Your father was going to hunt for her. Blackbird wanted Giselle. We're going after a Tracker. What are the threads that tie it all together? If you can pluck those out, then we will know what we're up against."

Suddenly I understood what he was saying. The pieces of our lives were threads and they bound us to certain paths and people. And he was right, I could no longer assume Cassava was always at the center of the evil in my world.

I closed my eyes and let the rocking of the boat

flow through me as I let the things he said sway through my mind.

Cassava. Blackbird. My father. Giselle. The Tracker.

They brushed against one another, slowly revolving until I saw the pattern and the pieces. There was only one that truly didn't fit, and that was the Tracker. But the rest . . . the rest revealed themselves to me.

What I saw made my muscles clench and my stomach roll with dismay.

"If my father is dead, Vetch would rule, and Cassava would be able to come back to the Rim with Blackbird at her side as her new lover. Giselle would have been able to tell them how to do it, how they could accomplish the task." The words slid out of me and my eyes widened. "Mother goddess. That's it, isn't it?"

A wry grin twisted over his lips. "I think I should piss you off more often."

I reached to him and brushed my hand against his. "Cactus, you didn't piss me off. Not really."

His fingers wrapped around mine. "No? Then shouldn't I get something for helping you? A gift?"

Peta snorted and turned her back. "Not while I'm in the boat, Prick."

I gave him a wink. "Maybe later." What was I saying? I turned away as heat curled up my neck to my face. I was not giving Cactus another reason to hang onto me. Pressing my hand to the smoky diamond around my neck, I breathed out. The wind picked up again, pushing us toward our destination.

Behind me, Peta and Cactus spoke as though I weren't there.

"Stop pressing her to give up her heart. You heard what Giselle said, she is not meant for the yoke of marriage."

Cactus laughed. "You don't know much about Terraling partnerships, do you? Often we don't marry. And as in the case of Lark's father, if there is a marriage, it is more often than not rather . . . open. We follow our hearts wherever they lead and believe that is the nature of our people."

"You would share her with Ash?"

I closed my eyes and focused on my breathing. We all knew I heard what they were saying, but I chose to pretend I couldn't hear a word.

"No, I wouldn't. I'm just saying things are not cut and dried when it comes to love and sex with Terralings. Salamanders, on the other hand, are jealous types. I suppose I have a bit of them too."

A roll of satisfaction from Peta tipped me off. I cranked my head around. "Don't you dare."

Her mouth tightened in a thin line and her ears drooped. "I would never."

Instantly I regretted not trusting her. "I'm sorry."

"What," Cactus said, his tone deceptively innocent, "you don't want her to tell me you've slept with Ash?"

My mouth dropped open. I would have spluttered except the boat grounded itself, throwing me backward. I hit the edge of the boat and flipped out. Thoughts of jagged teeth and long tentacles in the water kept me clinging to the edge. Until my feet touched the sandy shore and I realized we were in the shallows. I stood and looked around where we'd beached. The sand, the trees, and bushes. The statue of Zeus staring down at us. This was the place the humans had named Greece.

But we knew it as the birthplace of monsters, a place of mystery and danger even elementals of great power avoided. There was too much wildness in the earth and elements here; too much of the supernatural to be anything but chaotic.

"You sure about this, Peta?" I asked as I pulled the boat forward.

She stood on the prow of the boat, her eyes staring straight ahead. "I may not be a Reader, but I know when a certain path is right. This is the path we have to take if you want to succeed, Lark."

Cactus leapt out of the boat and helped me pull it the rest of the way up the beach so it was fully out of the water. "You aren't going to say anything?"

I had a choice. I could give him hell for trying to control me, or I could be honest with both him and myself. I went for the second choice.

I grabbed his face in both hands and pulled him to me. The kiss ignited an instant fire in my body, a flame of love and bonds rooted in my earliest memories. He crushed me against his body until we had to break apart to breathe.

I stumbled back, panting for air. He stood a few feet from me, his hair wild from my hands skimming through it, his eyes dark with a heady desire that still rushed along my skin. "The truth is I love you both. That is all I know."

Peta groaned. "Why, why did you have to tell him?"

"Because I can't lie, not to either of them," I said. "I may be a lot of things, but a liar is not on the list."

"Fine, but you deal with this little love triangle when we have your father home, and things are settled enough for you to see clearly." She turned, and stalked up the beach, her long tail twitching like mad.

"I can wait, Lark. For as long as it takes for you to realize I am the one you need." Cactus grinned at me, and I couldn't help but smile back.

"So sure of yourself?"

"Lust is not the same thing as love. I don't care that you bedded him. It doesn't mean you love him." He walked ahead of me and I couldn't help but stare. He and Ash were not so different in height. But the muscle on Ash was thicker from years of fighting and training with weapons. Cactus was leaner, like some of our Runners who took messages.

Neither was weak, but they offset one another. As though one called to my dark side and the other to the side of me that believed fairy tales always ended with a happily ever after.

I frowned as I followed Cactus and Peta, and my thoughts bounced between my situation with the two men, and the situation with my father. I'd almost rather deal with Cassava and my father than decide between Ash and Cactus. My heart had been broken too many times with loss and betrayal to lose another person I loved.

And that was the crux of it: I loved them both in ways I never thought possible. In ways I'd never experienced, not with Coal. My heart stuttered ever so slightly and I gave a silent prayer for his soul. That he would find peace on the other side of the Veil in the arms of the mother goddess. That he would forgive me for not loving him the way he wanted me to. The way I loved Ash and Cactus.

"Keep your eyes open, and tread softly. He didn't get the name The Bastard for nothing," Peta said. "We're close to the glade he uses as his launch pad."

Around us the trees and brush had grown thick, and the sounds of the ocean had faded to nothing. In all my musings, I hadn't realized how far we'd come. I looked behind us, and could see nothing but green. No ocean. In fact, we were surrounded by foliage so thick I couldn't even see the sky. "You get us lost, cat?"

She shook her head. "Of course not. But there are no paths to The Bastard. Would you make one?"

I nodded and did as she asked, tapping into the earth. The power ran up my arms, warm and inviting. A touch of the mother goddess, like a caress of my own mother nearly remembered. The plants ahead of us bent outward, opening a path. I put a hand on Peta's head. The power of the earth ran through me and into her like a fast-flowing river and she trembled. "I can feel your power under my fur. How is that?"

"I don't know." I stepped forward and she moved with me in perfect tandem. A thought occurred to me and I ran with it. I released the earth and the plants closed around us again. "Try, Peta. Ask them to bend for you."

"Ridiculous. Familiars do not have the power of their charges," she said, but her words held no real heat.

"Try anyway. Cactus won't tattle if you can't. Or if you can."

"Your secrets are safe with me, kitten."

She glared at him over her shoulder. "I'd rather you call me bad luck cat than that."

Kitten. That was what Talan had called her. I made myself focus on the present. "Try, Peta. Try, because maybe there will come a day when you need this connection." I paused, thinking of how the power felt when I'd touched her. "Run it through me. I think it will work."

She let out a sigh, but under my hand I felt her eagerness. There was a tentative pull through me, but I didn't reach for the earth's power. Around us, the path opened again, the branches pulling back. Cactus stepped up close behind me. "Is that her or you?"

"It's Peta. Apparently you were meant to be with a Terraling all along." I smiled, not only because I was pleased but because of the way Peta felt.

She was ecstatic. "I'm really doing this?"

I nodded and urged her forward with my hand, then took it from her back. "Lead on."

Her green eyes met mine and in the look so much was encompassed. Love, friendship, loyalty and sheer joy. Smiling, I waved at her and she stepped forward, the plants moving out of her way.

"You know this shouldn't be able to happen," Cactus said.

I shrugged. "Seems to be a recurring thing with me."

Ahead of us, Peta dropped to her belly. The sound of voices floated in the night air to us. I lowered into a crouch as I took my spear from my belt and twisted it together. Cactus did the same and we moved forward with quiet steps, moving only the bushes we had to.

Through the screen of the foliage, the flicker of fire danced. A bonfire, by the height of the flames that reached the top of the trees. So we'd found the clearing, but what was The Bastard up to? He had no need of a fire to keep warm.

I crept closer until we were at the edge of our cover, Peta on the right of me and Cactus on the left.

In front of us, circling the bonfire were a number of people. I looked closer, picking up on their auras. Not people, supernaturals. "Count them," Peta said.

A quick tally told me all I needed. Thirteen—a coven of witches. That wasn't the disturbing part, though. Thirteen witches, and one more tied to a stake driven into the ground. The captive was male with deep brown hair and a pretty face, nearly feminine in its beauty. He stared around, pulling at the binding. "Let me down, this was not the agreement." His voice made me jump, the depth of it a juxtaposition with his features.

The other witches ignored him, as if he'd not spoken at all.

Cactus shifted his weight and I glanced at him. His eyes were deadly serious. "If we take them by surprise, I think we could handle them all. He needs our help. We can't leave him."

From the glade, a slap resounded in the air. We turned at the same time. A woman stood in front of the man tied to the stake. "Winters, you do not deserve to be freed. The demon asked for you, and that is a small price to pay for his knowledge."

He shook his head. "You can't control him. Once he comes through, you will be at his mercy. Trust me."

She spat at him. "Trust you? Maybe you are the strongest the world has seen, but your mind and spine are soft. Which makes you unworthy of leading us."

Backing up, she snapped her fingers. The coven swirled around the bonfire and a faint whinny snapped my head around. One of the witches ran toward the stake, a bowl in her hands. The liquid within it sloshed dark in the firelight.

"Peta," I said. "Is that what I think it is?"

"That's The Bastard's blood. I'm sure of it." Her eyes met mine. "They're calling a demon forth. If they need his blood to call this particular demon . . . it's a bad one."

Worm shit and green sticks. We had no choice. Even if The Bastard wasn't in trouble, we couldn't let these idiots bring a demon into the world.

I stood and strode out into the clearing. I flicked my hands at the ground, sending it up in a spray of dirt that tamped down the bonfire. Cactus was right with me, his hands raised.

We were too damn sure of ourselves, though. These were not elementals who played by the rules.

A bolt of pure power slammed into me from the left, sending me through the air. I hit a tree and slid down the trunk. The fight surrounded us, witches flinging spells and Cactus fighting for all he was worth. Peta stayed in front of me, dodging blows and delivering her own.

But all I saw was the heaving side of The Bastard in front of me. His white coat splattered with blood and his wings shivering as though tiny currents rippled through his body. A faint wheeze squeezed out of him.

"Useless elementals, hiding when you should fight," he bit out, his dark eyes rolling to me as his hooves dug into the ground. Something about him pulled me closer, I knew I should have been fighting to keep the witches at bay, to stop the demon . . . but . . . I couldn't keep my hands from The Bastard.

I pressed one hand against his muscular neck, and ran the other over his side as far as I could reach. Spirit roared inside me; fear made me hold back. A shudder slipped through him and I felt him slip further into the Veil as if I could see it happening.

Was it worth trying to save him? I had to believe it was; not because of his value to me, but because it was the right thing to do.

If I was wrong, I was willingly giving up a piece of my own soul by saving him.

"Mother goddess, help me," I said, and opened myself to the power of Spirit.

CHAPTER 12

As carefully as I could, I threaded Spirit through his body. His wounds ran through his belly; they'd split his stomach and spilled his guts onto the ground. I didn't think about how it would heal, only that it needed to. The Bastard let out a low groan.

Inch by inch, I closed his wounds. Sweat poured down my face and arms as I stitched him together. Equine stomachs were monstrously huge with coil after coil of intestine, and I had to wrap it together. His legs and hooves twitched as I worked, and his wings shuddered here and there. But otherwise, he was quiet.

Around us, fire and magic lit the night air and time passed. Peta pressed against my side, and Cactus knelt down in front of us as he lifted a wall of flame. I didn't understand what was going on and couldn't pull back from Spirit. The power flowed through me and into The Bastard until the final portion of his hide was closed and his belly inside.

Slumping, I leaned forward to press my cheek against his ribcage. I had nothing left in me.

The Bastard lifted his head and looked at me, peering through his mane. His tail flicked once.

"You are not an elemental?"

"I am," I said, though my words were slurred. I knew in a few moments fatigue would win over my need to stay awake.

"Lark, I can't stop them on my own," Cactus said at the same time the shrieks from the other side of the glade began. Soul-piercing screams tore the night air as they pitched higher and higher, closer together, until it was a continuous wail with no space for a breath.

I pushed myself to my feet, wobbled, and locked my knees. "Let's do this."

The scream cut off so my last shouted word was loud and clear. The Bastard rolled his legs under his body and then lurched to his feet. I reached for the power of the earth and wrapped it around me, using it to give me strength. Striding forward around the now-smoldering bonfire, I realized the night was nearly over. The time spent healing The Bastard had allowed the coven to complete their heinous ritual.

Winters, the one who'd been tied to the stake, stepped toward us, a grin on his lips. His eyes were no longer the bright green they'd been, but a flickering red glow that told me all I needed to know. The demon possessed him.

"Well, well. A pair of elementals?" His voice was gritty, and no longer the high tenor of Winters's, but a deeper baritone. He put his hands on his hips and smiled at me. "What are you doing out of your designated prisons?"

Several of the coven members slunk forward behind him. Cactus had cut their numbers, but he was right. To take them on would be hard. A nose pushed hard between my shoulder blades, shoving me forward a step. "Go on, kick him in the ass," The Bastard said.

Winters held up both hands. "Shall I quote Elemental Law for you? You are not to interfere unless you've been asked for help, and then you may only do the bare minimum."

My whole body stiffened. I didn't like that he knew Elemental Law. Didn't like that he could quote it to me.

Hell, I simply didn't like him.

"What is your name, demon?"

"Who, little old me? What could you possibly want to know about me?" He put a hand to his chest and grinned. Behind him the remaining coven members laughed.

I swung my spear tip so fast it blurred, and laid it against the hollow of his throat. "I am not like other elementals, demon. Do not mistake me for them. Rules are made to be broken as far as I am concerned."

His eyes widened as I pushed the blade harder. "I see. That is interesting." He paused and his red eyes widened further, though I was surprised that was possible. "You met Astrid, didn't you?"

"Yes, and now she is no more. So may I suggest you are careful with what you say, demon," I said, keeping my voice even.

With great care he shoved the blade away, a funny little smile on his lips. "Oh, I doubt you've seen the last of Astrid. She shows up when you least expect. As to your question, though . . . I have been summoned into this body to train these coven members."

"What did they offer you in exchange?" Peta stepped up beside me, her coat orange in the firelight. His eyes dipped to her and he opened his mouth, but I stopped him.

"If you lie, I will know, and I will end you where you stand."

The coven members sucked in a unanimous breath. The demon that'd once been Winters pursed his lips. "I want a promise, then. No matter what I say, you will let me go. You will not pursue me regardless of what comes out of these lips."

The desire to kill him, to end his life and stop whatever mayhem he had planned, rippled through me. I lifted the spear, centering it over his heart.

He flicked his eyes to the spear and then to my face. "Do not be hasty, Elemental."

"I'm not." I tensed, ready to run him through.

"Winters is dying. He is dying, and I will be able to keep him alive long enough to pass on the training and knowledge both he and I have." The demon spoke fast, and the fear in his voice and eyes was enough to give me pause. Without thinking of the consequence, or perhaps not caring, I spun Spirit through him.

The man Winters was indeed sick, and the disease curled through him in every cell, every part of his body. So that much was true. "What do you get in exchange? Demons are not known for their largesse. I doubt you are here out of goodwill."

"A little freedom from the seventh veil. I have a time limit here, Elemental. Winters will die and when he does, I will be sent back." But that was not completely true, and the lie was thick in the air between us.

Indecision flickered through me. I could kill him, and Winters would die with him. But the man was already dying.

Cactus, Peta, and The Bastard said nothing. This was my choice. "Tell me what you are truly getting for your help, your real name, and I will let you go."

His eyebrows shot up. "Give your word."

My lips curled as I spoke. "You have my word that *this* time, I will let you go if you tell me the truth. Lie, and I will end you. If I meet you again, I will end you."

The demon nodded. "Done. My name is Orion. And I have been promised a witchling child of my choice from the coven."

One of the coven members gasped. "No!"

Apparently not everyone had been aware of the deal. I lowered my spear, feeling the truth of the demon's words. I didn't like it, but I had given my word.

"I hope we meet again, demon. I look forward to sending you back to the seventh veil."

He barked a laugh as he stepped away from me. "You fancy yourself a Slayer now?"

Peta leapt toward him, landing in a crouch at his feet, swiping at him with one big paw and knocking him on his ass. "Blood of the Slayers springs from a single well, demon. Do you not wonder where that well is grounded?"

He scrambled backward, scooting across the grass, the firelight illuminating the fear on his face.

"Then I hope we never meet again, Elemental. Slayer. Whatever you are." He spun and strode away, the coven encircling him.

As they disappeared into the night, a trickle of anxiety spread upward through me. "I should have killed him."

The Bastard snorted. "And break your word? You'd sooner give up your connection to your element."

I didn't answer, just stared into the bush where the coven and the demon had disappeared. I didn't realize I'd taken steps in their direction until Cactus stopped me. "Lark, that is not our battle. We have to get to your father, and for that we need the Tracker."

He was right, but that did not mean I had to like it. "I should have killed him. Worm shit." I jammed my spear into the ground several times, digging up the turf.

Peta cleared her throat. "Before The Bastard leaves, you'd best ask him for help."

I spun to see that the Pegasus was indeed flexing his wings. "Wait, I need your help. Please."

He tipped his head to one side and blew a breath through his lips, making them wobble. "What kind of help?"

"We are looking for a Tracker. She's gone to the Namib Sand Sea. It's too big to search on foot in a timely manner. Will you take us?"

He shook his head and ruffled his feathers. "Normally I'd tell you to buck off. But since you put my guts back together, I think I can give you this one flight." He bent a knee and I leapt onto his back before he could change his mind. Peta shifted into her housecat form and did the same.

A breath of relief escaped me, chased by a surge of anxiety. We were one step closer to finding my father. I gripped The Bastard's side with my legs. Cactus swung up behind me and tucked in close so as to stay out of the path of The Bastard's wings.

Beneath us, The Bastard's muscles bunched and he leapt forward, going from a standstill to a gallop in one stride. His wings beat furiously as we reached the edge of the clearing, and he lifted. His legs treaded the air as if he were still running as his wings did the work of holding us aloft.

"Do you have a name besides The Bastard?" I asked as we swept toward the coastline.

He gave a low grunt. "We aren't friends, Elemental. I did that once, it did not end well. You don't need my name for this exchange of favors."

I tightened my grip on his mane as we swooped

through a bank of clouds. "You mean you had a friend? Or you were friends with an elemental?"

He tipped his head so his large dark eye could look at me. "Both."

Peta squirmed into my lap. "Bastard, I have worked with you before."

"You are not an elemental, Peta. You are a familiar and a child of the goddess. That I can respect. The elementals are a spineless lot who cower in their homes like ostriches with their heads buried in the sand and their asses in the air."

His words were not untrue, which made them sting all the more.

"Lark is not like the others," Peta said. "It is why . . . why she is worth fighting for." Her green eyes locked with mine. "She is different."

The Bastard snorted. "All that means is she will be killed. Or banished, which is the same thing."

"How do you know so much about elementals?" Cactus beat me to the question on the tip of my tongue.

Peta shook her head, but The Bastard answered. "Elementals were what the humans thought were the Grecian gods. They set themselves up to rule. They were petty and cruel and thought nothing of manipulating people."

My jaw dropped, I'll admit it. "That can't be."

"I was there, Elemental. I saw it with my own eyes and lived through it." His wings stilled as we coasted high above the treetops and then over the ocean. "Your kind . . . they have done far more harm than good to this world because of their pride."

His words shouldn't have stunned me, yet they did. I wanted to believe my people weren't the problem. That it was the humans who'd caused all the destruction of the earth and the elements . . . but maybe if we'd shown them the way. If we'd been a part of their world instead of separating them, things would be different. Cactus slipped an arm around my waist. "He's wrong."

I shook my head. "I don't think he is, Cactus. Where would we be if we had helped the humans? If we'd shown them how to care for the elements and our world?"

He sucked in a sharp breath. "That would mean exposing ourselves to them."

I said nothing more, feeling the weight of The Bastard's words on my soul. He was right.

The elementals had been selfish. They had caused harm to the world, and now they acted as though it was not their place to fix anything.

Hours passed, the day came, the sun rose and waned, and as the west lit up with the final rays of the day, we reached the Namib Sea.

The sand dunes reared out of the desert into the sea, the triangular dunes mimicking that of a dragon's head in an eerie replica.

Below me, The Bastard shivered. "I smell a dragon. This does not bode well. Breeding season is on us and it makes them moodier than usual."

Cactus twisted around. "I don't see any dragons. And even I couldn't miss that."

A laugh burst out of The Bastard. "How many dragons have you dealt with, boy?"

My shoulders twitched as though we had eyes on us. I slowly turned my head, searching the skies around us. If I were a dragon, and so large as to be seen from miles away, I would not swoop in from the side or behind my prey. I tipped my head back and stared into the sky above us.

The body of a dragon swept downward, silent on its leathery wings, its mouth open in a soundless roar. "Above us!"

The Bastard dropped, tucking his wings tightly as he spiraled to one side. The dragon whooshed past, sending out a wave of air in its wake.

"I cannot avoid her in the air. We have to land," The Bastard hollered.

He didn't waste any more time or words, but barreled straight toward the closest dune. We hit the ground hard enough that the three of us were bucked off and into the loose sand. I scrambled to my feet, as did Peta and Cactus. From above, the dragon roared and spat a straight blast of fire at us. Cactus lifted his hands and deflected it before it could do any damage.

The sound of feet running on the sand spun me around. The Bastard pranced, then reared up as a whip curled around his neck right behind his jaw. I rushed forward, swung my spear in a wide arc and cut through the leather. There was an "oomph" on the other end of the line and the sound of someone hitting the sand.

A flash of white fur and Peta put herself between whoever wielded the whip and me, blocking my view of them.

The Bastard shook his head, his long mane flipping in the air. "Damn Trackers, always so touchy about every little thing. I didn't mean to step on you."

"Fuck you, horse!" someone yelled back from what seemed like a far greater distance than she should have been. Wait . . . Tracker . . . then we'd found her.

Peta stayed where she was, crouched with her belly pressed into the sand, ready to leap on whoever was attacking. I stepped beside her and saw why I'd not been able to see the Tracker sooner. She had tumbled down the edge of the sand dune into a shallow valley perhaps thirty feet in depth. I spun my spear and buried the haft into the sand.

The Tracker stood and stared up at us, covered in sand, her eyes flashing with anger visible even at a distance. Her hair was cut short, barely brushing the edges of her shoulders; it was the color of obsidian. Her eyes narrowed. "You want to fight? Then get your ass down here and we'll fight, witch."

I did not correct her as to my designation. "Tracker, I want only to talk to you. I'd like to employ your services."

"That's more than talking then, isn't it?"

Above us the dragon roared. I flattened myself to the sand out of instinct. Claw tips raked either side of me, missing me by mere inches. Peta screamed, and I rolled in time to see her scooped into the air. From my knees I snapped my arm back and threw my spear with everything I had. The blade buried into the dragon's leg, right above the claw that held Peta in a death grip.

The red dragon roared and its claw opened. Peta fell, but like any self-respecting cat, landed on her feet. My spear fell beside her, blade in the sand.

I ran to her side and crouched so I could put a hand on her back. My familiar's bond with me was humming with energy so intense it felt as though she would fly away at the drop of a leaf. She shifted into her housecat form and I lifted her to my shoulder.

"Thanks, Dirt Girl."

"Any time, cat." I spoke to her, but my eyes were glued to the Tracker. She had stepped back and waved at the space around her.

"If you want to talk, then fucking well spit it out," she yelled up at me.

I scooped up my spear and started down the slope, taking my time. "Call off your dragon."

"Ophelia," she waved a hand above her head, "ease off, you big bitch."

The dragon dropped like a giant red rock, thumping into the sand and sending up a wave as if it were water and not earth. I made myself not look at the enormous creature. But even from the corner of my eye I couldn't help but pick up details. The dragon was easily twice the size of the adult Firewyrms I'd encountered in the Pit, and her wingspan was impressive. Not to mention the size of her teeth and claws. Her hide caught the sun, sending flickers of red light dancing across the sand like a prism.

A formidable creature indeed.

I reached out to the power of the earth and tugged

it to me. In case this discussion with the Tracker went in a direction I did not like.

"You know," Peta said, her body swaying with each step I took, "I can't help but think this is a crossroads for you."

"Why?" The question escaped me before I thought better of it.

"You mean besides the fact that you're willfully breaking rules?"

We were halfway down the slope. "Yeah, besides that."

Her whiskers tickled my cheek as she spoke. "Trackers bring chaos to all they do. Like you, they can't help it." She blinked several times. "It's because of their heritage. Add a Tracker to your own tendency to cause problems . . ."

A chill swept through me. I had a feeling I knew what she was going to say. "Should I guess, or are you going to tell me?"

With a shrug and her tiny cat smile, she shook her head. "You know already, I see it in your eyes. The Tracker has Spirit Elemental blood running through her veins, as do they all."

I slid to a stop at the base of the sandy valley. Once more I planted my spear haft into the sand. "My name is Larkspur, and I need you to Track my father."

The dark-haired Tracker arched an eyebrow at me. Her eyes were tri-colored: emerald green, chocolate brown, and a deep gold that swirled within and around one another. She didn't hold her hand out, only tipped her head ever so slightly forward as her eyes narrowed.

"My name is Elle, and you already know I'm a Tracker. But what the fuck are you?"

CHAPTER 13

Teeth and muscles clenched, I had to fight the response that rose to the tip of my tongue.

"Tell her you're a witch. It will explain any usage of your elemental power around her," Peta said.

Elle's eyes never wavered from my face. I mimicked her head-tipping motion. "I'm a magic user, as you thought."

"Weird fucking way to say witch." Her eyes narrowed until they were mere slits.

"Not as strange as a Tracker having a Slayer's dragon with her as protection," I countered.

She grinned, a flash of white teeth and a smile that softened her face immensely. "Ah, Ophelia isn't mine. She belongs to my husband, Bram."

Bram . . . could it be? No, I must have heard wrong. "What is his name?"

The smile disappeared and her gaze darkened once more. "Bram."

I gripped the spear until I was sure I would break it in half. "Is he here?"

Her frown deepened. "Why?"

Calm, I had to remain calm. The chances that my brother had somehow survived Cassava's attack were slim, and the rational part of my mind knew that. But my heart . . . ahhh how my heart hoped it was possible. "I knew someone by that name. It is an uncommon one. I wonder if he is the same Bram."

"A lover?" Her eyebrows went up at the same time. She tried too hard to look like it wouldn't bother her if that were the case. I shook my head and laughed quietly.

"No. Someone I knew a long time ago."

"Couldn't have been that fucking long, you aren't much older than me." She turned as she spoke. It was only then I realized I'd lost Cactus somewhere along the way.

I turned to see both Ophelia the dragon and The Bastard staring toward the water's edge, away from Elle and me. Shit on green sticks . . . I had a bad feeling about what exactly they were staring at. A shout floated down to us. I looked at Elle, our eyes met, and we scrambled up the slippery slope at the same time.

We reached the top, me a few steps ahead of the Tracker. Cactus and the man I assumed was Bram circled one another with their fists up.

"Bram, what the fuck are you doing?" Elle hollered. Bram glanced at her and it was enough of a distraction. Cactus shot out a fist that caught Bram in the side of the head and he went down in a heap. "Hah! You owe me."

What in all that was holy was this nonsense?

"Cactus," I strode toward him, "what is going on?"

"Oh, well, it's funny really."

Bram let out a groan from where he lay in the wet sand. "Not all that funny, if you ask me."

I allowed myself to really look at him now that I was closer. His hair was a dark auburn, and his eyes were hazel. Nothing like my Bramley, who'd been blond-haired and blue-eyed. Disappointment, and at the same time relief, flooded me.

Introductions were made all around.

"Cactus, what were you two doing?"

He grinned at me. "It's funny, really."

"That's what you said, but I doubt it." My tone was about as dry as the desert sand we stood on.

Not that it stopped Cactus from grinning like a fool. "I could have killed him, but I knew you wouldn't want that. He really wanted to fight. I suggested fists only. Loser buys drinks."

Elle rolled her eyes heavenward. "Bram, seriously?"

He shrugged. "He's scrawny, I figured I could take him. Little buggar is fast, though."

Little was not the word I would use for Cactus. Then again, Bram was a big man, solid muscle, and probably had two stones on Cactus and a good four inches.

"Fine, we're all getting along now," I said. "Elle, I need you to Track for me."

She folded her arms and squinted her eyes. "Your father is missing, that's what you said."

"Yes."

She held a hand out, palm up. "Fees are steep. A thousand dollars a day, bonus for bringing him home alive. No deductions if he's dead." Her eyes were hard with no sign of mercy in them. That was not going to be good, since I had no idea what she was even talking about, dollars and bonuses.

"A way of paying for things, Lark," Peta said, and from my other side Cactus nodded.

"I have no money or bonuses to give you, but—"

Elle shrugged and walked away, speaking over her shoulder. "Then you're wasting my fucking time and yours."

Damn her and her greed. Obviously she had too much human blood running in her veins, and whatever Spirit she had in her was not enough to combat it. But I needed her, which meant I had to play by her rules.

"I'll give you something better than money."

She stopped, turned, and looked at me. Between us something shifted, like a cog slipping loose. Spirit flickered through me, reaching for her. As if it recognized one of its own. I did not want to use Spirit on Elle to get her to do what I wanted. I fought the panic and Spirit at the same time; neither listened to me. This was not in the plan, and yet I couldn't seem to rein in the damn element. It wrapped around her and slid past whatever defense she might have had.

Worm shit. I held my breath, praying Spirit didn't rape her mind as it had done to my sister Keeda.

Elle's face softened and her lower lip trembled so slightly I would have missed it if I hadn't been staring at her. Yet Spirit did not force her hand. I let out the breath I'd been holding.

She took a step toward me, her fists raised. "What could possibly be better than money? Let me tell you, not all that fucking much, Larkspur." Her tri-colored eyes welled with tears. "You grow up without food, without anything but the clothes on your back, your family and the fucking world trying to take you out at every turn and you'll learn fast enough. You'll learn the only thing that will keep you safe is money."

Bram slipped an arm around her waist and whispered in her ear. She pressed herself against him.

Keeping my voice below a whisper, I barely moved my lips as I spoke to Peta. "What just happened?"

"Spirit opened her and she spilled her beliefs," Peta said. "Spirit sometimes acts on its own, at least until you figure out how to make it work for you. That's what . . . my other charge always said, anyway. Use it, Lark."

Fantastic, that was just what I needed. An element that acted out on its own. "Elle, if you help me, I will owe you a favor. I know that may not sound like much perhaps in comparison to—"

"You're right, it doesn't. It isn't. A favor is worth shit in this world," she snapped.

I barreled ahead, knowing I had one shot at this. "I

am the strongest of my people, Elle. If you are ever in real trouble, I will get you out of it. Is that not worth something to you? Money won't always buy your way out of a tangle of thorns."

She shook her head, her face closing off. "No."

There was no one else who could help me, if the other Tracker had been telling the truth about his abilities.

I needed her . . . but she needed me too. A different tack, then.

"We killed a troll looking for you. If you have trolls after you, then they are working for someone. Which means you are going to need that favor sooner rather than later. Whether you want to believe it or not, Tracker."

I lifted my spear from the ground and turned away. "Cactus, let's go."

From behind me Bram argued with her. "Take the offer. We need to move on anyway, and why not do a job on the side?"

"You can't be serious?"

"I know you don't want to believe her, but I think she's right. A favor from someone powerful is not a bad thing."

It took everything in me not to turn around, but to keep walking and act as though I couldn't hear their discussion. Cactus fell into step beside me. "We aren't really leaving, are we?"

"What choice do we have? If she refuses to help, you know what the other Tracker said. He can't find someone without a picture, and neither can the other

Tracker he mentioned. She is the only one who can find my father."

Peta swayed on my shoulder. "Be quiet, they are coming."

I slowed my steps as Elle called out, "Prove it."

Eyebrows high, I turned to face her. "Prove what?"

"Prove you're as strong as you say. I see a weapon, and a friend who can control fire, but I've seen no magic from your fingers. I think you're a fucking liar."

A low hiss escaped Peta, but she otherwise kept her thoughts to herself. A liar, was I?

I glanced to where the dragon sat, dozing in the sun on the high ridge of sand. I could sink Ophelia under the sands, bury her and then bring her back up, or I could create an oasis on the sands as I had done in the Pit.

The chance to do either was taken from me.

Ophelia snapped her head up, and her mouth dropped open as she let out a roar along with a burst of flame. War cries cut through the air along with bursts of lightning, flame, and power bolts.

"They found us, Elle." Bram spun and ran toward Ophelia, Elle on his heels.

I didn't move an inch. This was my chance to do exactly what Elle needed to see. The Bastard bolted to my side and pushed me with his big nose. "Time to go. Those witches aren't playing around."

"Cactus, you first. And don't help me. Elle needs to see what I can do. Unless, of course, I ask." I shoved him onto The Bastard's back, then handed him my spear. She wanted magic, I would show her nothing but. "Hang onto this for me." Cactus frowned as I stepped back. "Take him out of range, Bastard."

"Wait, stop!" Cactus yelled, but The Bastard was already galloping away, his wings taking them into the air within a few strides.

"You don't have to prove anything to her," Peta said.

"I do. If she doesn't believe in me, this negotiation is over." I walked toward Elle and Bram's attackers, the sand tugging at my feet with each step. I opened myself to the power of the earth and pulled it toward me. It filled me, making my skin tingle and my muscles quiver. The desire to run, to feel the wind in my hair and the sand beneath my bare feet, called to me, begging me to be a part of the earth once more.

Around us, the sand trembled and shifted. Peta swayed on my shoulder, wrapping her tail around my neck for balance. "I don't like this."

"Neither do I. But the choices are limited at best."

As I drew closer, I sucked in an angry breath. The attackers were none other than the coven from Greece. I looked for Winters, searching for his demon-infested body. But he, at least, was missing from the group. They fired balls of flame and burning arrows up into the sky, while a portion of them manipulated the winds, driving the dragon and The Bastard closer within range.

Ten of them, working in concert to bring down a Tracker. What could Elle have done to piss them off? Sure, she had an attitude, but I doubted that was enough to cause this sort of problem.

Something else then.

"Focus, Lark, or you'll get us both killed."

Peta was right.

I stopped behind the witch closest to me, leaned in and whispered in her ear, "I warned you not to cross my path again."

She spun, her blue eyes wide. I softened the ground under her feet with a thought, sucking her down into the sand. The others turned one by one by one.

"I wondered if you'd be here with the winged Bastard." A man, warlock, stepped forward. "I will deal with her. The rest of you, capture Elena. Orion wants her alive."

Well, that was interesting. The warlock stepped toward me and I softened the ground enough to slow him down. One warlock was going to prove very little problem.

He flicked all his fingers at me and a burst of light shot at my face. I closed my eyes and dropped to my knees.

"Lark, I can't see!" Peta yelped.

I blinked several times. I couldn't see either, but Peta didn't know that. "Hang onto me."

Straining to hear his footsteps over the sounds of battle and the roaring of a dragon above us was useless. I stood and took a few steps back as the warlock laughed. "You can't run away. I have you now. Don't worry, I'm not going to kill you. I think Winters would like to get to know you too."

He was moving, walking as he spoke until he was right behind me. I spun and kicked out, my foot connecting with his soft midsection by the feel of it. He let out a grunt and I dropped to my knees. "Peta, do you trust me?"

"Mother goddess, what are you going to do?"

I swallowed hard. "Something new."

She shimmied off my shoulder and into my arms. I grabbed her and tucked her inside my vest. "No matter what happens, don't let go."

A whimper escaped her, but that was it.

I buried my hands into the sand and called the earth up.

All of it, every last piece I could reach. Power roared through me and bit back the scream that built in my throat. Sand whirled around us, but in my mind all I could see was a wave of the earth pouring over the witches, burying them deep into the ground where they could no longer harm anyone.

In my mind, I saw the sands turn into an ocean that raged on the winds of a storm, a hurricane of the earth that would wipe out those who would do us harm.

Screams erupted around us, cries for help as the world bucked and writhed under me, rising to my call.

I ignored them, feeding my power into the wave I saw in my mind, crashing it over them, swallowing them up. Hands wrapped around my throat. "You fucking bitch!"

The warlock squeezed and I buried my hands deeper into the earth, softening it under us both. I could survive being buried, I was sure of it. Him, not so much. A wave of sand pulled him away from me in a jerk as we sunk past my waist.

The world trembled with the power that surged through me and I reveled in it, feeling . . . unstoppable.

I kept my mouth and eyes shut but the sand still got into them. I didn't ease off until I could hear nothing but the whisper of sand on sand. Slowly I pulled my hands out, laying them on top of the tiny grains. My face was covered in grit, glued on with sweat.

"Thank you." The ground seemed to answer with the slightest of rumbles. Not the mother goddess . . . but the earth itself.

From inside my vest Peta shifted, breaking my concentration. "Are you done?"

"Yes, I think so."

"I have sand in places no cat should have sand," she spat out, literally, as she climbed from my vest. I was more than a little afraid to open my eyes. What if I still could not see? How in the seven hells would I find my father then?

I opened my left eye first and a sigh of relief slid from me. Though my eyes were gritty with sand, and the backs of them ached from the flash burn, I could see again.

I stood and dusted off my pants and vest. Around us the world was silent, the sand flat and unmoving, though the landscape had shifted. It looked as though I'd pulled the sand out of the desert toward the ocean, creating a new peninsula.

"Holy fucking shit. Was that for real?"

I turned to see Elle approach me, Bram beside her and Cactus pulling up the rear. Elle's eyes were wide.

"Did you have a good enough view of what I'm capable of?" I crossed my arms, mimicking her earlier stance.

She glanced at Bram, then nodded. "Yeah. You've got yourself a deal. A favor then."

Peta cleared her throat. "Technically, you just did *her* a favor. You wiped out those looking for her."

I didn't answer Elle right away but then said, "You sure that's what you wanted to say?"

Her lips tightened. "Fine, you fucking well saved our asses. That what you want?"

I nodded. "Yes. Now we can look for my father."

"You got a picture?"

"No, Jack said you didn't need one." My legs trembled and I locked my knees in place. This was not the time to show weakness of any kind. Not to this woman. Whatever her past had been, it had hardened her to the point of seeing others' plights and feeling no empathy. That was not good.

"Jack? You spoke to that dick?"

My eyebrows shot up. "He spoke highly of you. Said you were the only one with the skills I need." Okay, so maybe those hadn't been his exact words, but she was still on the fence. Even after I saved her ass.

"That doesn't sound like Jack."

"He said you owed him cookies," Cactus offered.

Elle glared at him. "I'm not baking any fucking cookies. Do I look like a—"

Bram blew out a sharp breath. "Enough, Elle. Enough. Do this job, you know you want to."

She glared at him, but there was a twinkle in her eyes too. "Pushy man."

"You love it. Now let's do this. We have other tasks ahead of us."

I liked him, maybe better than I liked her. Or maybe it was because he seemed to be working in my favor.

"I need you to describe him to me, think you can manage?" Elle asked, once more crossing her arms. Defiance radiated from her.

I nodded. "Yes, I can do that."

"Well, let's get this fucking show on the road then, shall we?"

Indeed. Time to find my father and straighten out the Rim once and for all.

Yet, I had a feeling our journey was far from over.

Looking back, I had no idea *just* how accurate that hunch was.

CHAPTER 14

"Describe him then, and tell me his name. Anything you can give me will help. Not only physical shit, but what he's like." Elle's eyes swirled as she spoke.

My words tumbled, one after another. Basileus. Long hair, mostly dark brown with strands of auburn. Gray beginning to show. Muscular body, shorter than me. Green eyes that faded to black when he was angry. Most powerful of our family. A broken soul from being manipulated. Favored some children over others. Put his family in danger because of his foolishness.

"That's enough," Elle said. I looked up, not realizing I'd looked down at any point. "He did a number on you, didn't he?" Her words were the first that showed any sort of understanding, her eyes soft with a shared pain.

I chose not to respond. "Can you find him then?"

Her eyes swirled, the three colors blending faster and faster. "Yes, I've got a bead on him. Northeast from here."

My eyebrows climbed. "That's it?"

"Well, shit, I don't know the exact location, but we'll travel with you. Make sure you find him so you can deal with your daddy issues." My jaw dropped and she walked away from me. Bram's lips tightened, and he shook his head.

"I'd apologize, but then that would be all I do. You'll get used to her."

Cactus shook his head. "I'd worry more she'll push one too many sore spots on Lark."

Bram nodded. "Yeah, that too."

They mounted up on Ophelia and I paused. The Bastard had brought us here, but that had been the only deal. I walked to his side and put my hand on his shoulder. Before I could ask for another ride, he spoke.

"I will take you. I have not had an adventure for some time."

I pulled myself onto his back. "Thanks. But calling you The Bastard is getting old. If I can't know your real name, I'm giving you one."

He grunted as Cactus climbed up behind me. "Do as you wish, Elemental. Your kind always have."

I wanted to swat him for sassing me, but I settled for winding my fingers through his mane. "There is a legend in our family about a horse that carried our first king into battle. How the horse had become the first familiar after saving the king's life by taking a blow for him. His name was Shazer."

He bucked as we lifted off into the air. "Bah."

A cold nose pressed against my cheek. "It's a good name."

My mind, though, was already moving forward. Northeast . . . the direction was not lost on me. The Wretched Peaks lay in that direction, what the humans called the Himalayans.

The home of the Sylphs was nestled in those mountains.

"Cactus, we sent emissaries to the Eyrie."

"Yes."

"And they swore oaths that my father was not in their home." I tightened my grip on Shazer's mane until the coarse strands cut into my fingers.

"Just because we are headed in that direction now does not mean he is there. A whole wide world is northeast of us." He rubbed my shoulders, but instead of soothing me, it only served to cause more friction.

"Don't, Cactus. Please don't." I didn't care that he was right.

We flew for hours, neither the dragon nor Shazer losing speed. Which gave me time to think.

Something was shifting in our world, and my mind wouldn't leave alone the pieces I could see. I'd been in the Deep and seen and helped a coup for the throne happen. I'd ousted Cassava from the Rim. In the Pit we'd set Fiametta straight. My heart rate began to climb as the pattern emerged in front of me.

I was being used to set people on the thrones of power. People the mother goddess wanted. Chills swept through me that had nothing to do with the cold air around us.

Peta spun in my lap and put her front feet on my chest so we were nose to nose. "What is this fear I feel? What have you thought of?"

I reached back and pulled Cactus closer to me. "The mother goddess is using me, Peta. I have been instrumental in the Deep, Pit, and Rim in changing the structure of who rules, or how they rule. I have no doubt we are being funneled to the Eyrie for the same reason."

Cactus sucked in a sharp breath. "Holy—"

"Do not use her name," I snapped, anger filling me. Anger and disappointment. "She has been using me from the beginning."

Peta's green eyes softened. "You are her chosen one, Lark. There must be a reason."

"Why would she let me go in blind? How much easier would it have been if I'd known what she would ask of me?"

Shazer flipped his head. "Perhaps because she knew you would fight her if she laid the harness on too tightly."

His words struck a chord. "Damn, you're right."

"Of course I am." He blew out a breath that sent a spattering of spit back at us.

I wiped my face and Peta fluffed up her back. "Stupid horse."

He rolled to the left, making her scramble to cling to me. "Shazer, enough!"

A horsey laugh rippled out of him. "For now."

If I'd known what the mother goddess was going to ask of me, I would have fought her. I'd have thought I couldn't do it, especially facing down Cassava. Or going into the Deep. Or the Pit, for that matter. Damn, I didn't want to be okay with this.

Especially now that I knew what was coming in the Eyrie. Another coup? Some sort of trial by fire like the Pit?

I tucked my chin to my chest, wrapped my arms around Peta and closed my eyes. There was nothing I could do until we got there, and maybe, maybe I was wrong.

Our direction never shifted as we flew. Sometime in the early hours of the night we began our descent and I opened my eyes.

The Wretched Peaks surrounded us. My heart climbed into my throat as we dropped. Damn, being right had never felt so horrible.

Ophelia landed first. Shazer dropped to her left with a bounce that turned into a buck. Cactus went flying over our heads and hit the ground hard, landing flat on his back. The dragon tipped her head back and let out a long laugh.

Shazer pranced where he was. "Names have power. What does mine mean?"

I blushed. "Twisting, or intertwining."

"Perhaps you should have gone with something more docile." Cactus snorted.

I swatted Shazer's neck before I slid from his back. "You don't have to wait with us here. Go home to your forest." I took a few steps before the energy between Peta and me spiked, verging on panic. I reached up and laid a hand on her back as I twisted to look her in the eye. "What's wrong?"

"That is not my energy you are feeling, Lark," Peta said. Her left ear flicked once and I followed the direction she indicated.

Shazer stood with his hooves planted in the ground as if he were frozen in the thin dusting of snow, while his whole body twitched and quivered.

"Oh, no," I whispered. "Let him go. He has done his part."

Child, you need him. And perhaps more than that, he needs you. Would you turn away a gift from me?

The mother goddess spoke to my mind, and so I could not hide my thoughts from her. Of course I wouldn't turn him away. "Shazer. You are bound to me. Do you feel it?"

His dark eyes swiveled to mine and he let out a snort, but said nothing. The anger in his eyes spoke volumes that needed no words. He did not wish to be tied to me.

I steeled myself. I'd won over Peta; I had to believe I could win over him too. I touched his side. "I will not lay the harness on you, my friend. Whatever help I need will be temporary, I'm sure."

The emotions in him softened a few degrees. "I will hold you to that."

"Elle," I turned as she approached me, "any final directions?"

She pointed up at the peak that seemed to hover over our heads. "He's up there, but how the fuck he's alive is beyond me. We circled but could see nothing."

"It's okay. I can take it from here." I held my hand out to Cactus. He offered me his hand and I frowned. "My spear, Cactus."

"Right." He tossed it to me and I twisted the two pieces together. "Thank you, both of you."

"The job isn't done until I return him to you." Elle stepped in front of me, most effectively blocking me from moving forward.

I put a hand on her shoulder and pushed her ever so slightly. "I said I can handle it from here. I will even give you that bonus. I will give you a favor, Tracker. One to be called in at any time."

Her eyes widened. "Why would you do that?"

Spirit flowed through me and out my mouth. "You will need me before your life is called to the other side of the Veil. You will give me what you hold closest to your heart."

The words were out of my mouth, but they were not my own. Chills rippled through me and Elle's body shook under my hand.

"I fucking well doubt it." She jerked away from me, but the fear in her eyes was loud and clear.

"Do not follow us, no matter what happens."

I dropped my hand and walked away. Toward the mountain's base.

"We can't stay, Lark," Elle said.

I glanced over my shoulder. "Then don't."

"We can't pull your ass out of this."

"I don't expect you to."

She threw her hands in the air. "Bram, time to go. We have things to do."

I watched as they mounted Ophelia. Her big eyes zeroed in on me and for a second I thought she might say something. Her head snapped away as she launched, her wings sending them straight into the air. I lifted a hand, and Elle raised one in return.

A funny twist began in my gut. Whatever part Elle had left in this, she and I weren't done yet.

They ghosted through the clouds for a few minutes, glimmers of red scales, and then they were gone.

Shazer snorted. "What about me?"

I looked him over. "Will you wait for me? I cannot know what we are walking into, but a backup escape plan is always a good thing to have in my world."

His dark eyes narrowed. "Call for me. I will hear you."

I touched him on the nose, the velvet of his muzzle softer than dandelion fluff. I turned and walked away, only then noticing where we'd landed. A small valley at the juncture of three mountains, the peaks towering over us so much, the sun struggled to peer through even though it was midday. Snow crunched under my boots; I had an urge to slip them off and feel it on my bare feet. In the redwoods, we didn't get snow, not like this. The icy crystals covered everything, giving the world a glittering white, ethereal feel. Cactus caught up to me with ease.

"So now what? We know your father is here, but you aren't going to accuse the queen of lying, are you?"

"I don't know what I'm going to do."

Peta jumped from my shoulder to the ground in front of us. Her body shimmered and she shifted into her snow leopard form, perfect for the environment. "Peta, what do you know of the queen of the Eyrie?"

"I have not been to the Eyrie in many years. But the queen has been on the throne a long time. Longer even than your father." She trotted ahead of us, her big paws leaving imprints in the snow making it easy to follow.

"Yes, I know that much. What else, though? I have not kept up on the political side of things."

"Queen Aria is—from what I understand—very sweet. Kind, merciful. It's why her Enders get bored." Peta bounded up the slope ahead of us, turned and looked back. "This is going to be a hard climb. Why do we not use The Bast—Shazer?"

"Because I have no desire to drop in on the Eyrie. We do not know if we are welcome. At least on the ground, we have a chance at defending ourselves if we need to."

Cactus grunted. "You think it will come to that?"

I stared hard at him. "Are you serious? Have you not been listening to me? The mother goddess is sending me in there to deal with whatever political issues are going on. That is not going to make us popular with at least a few people, and most likely Queen Aria is going to take exception to our presence."

"Well, that's a slope covered in slippery shit, isn't it?" he muttered. I agreed, but said nothing more.

Peta was right about the climb. It was a true test of our abilities, both physical and in our connection to the earth. Snow was a covering on earth; it was water, not earth. So in order to mold handholds, Cactus had to melt the snow, then I made the holds. More than once, we triggered avalanches that sent waves of snow crashing down the slope.

Then there was the fact that we climbed while the night still held tightly to the world. The darkness only added to the degree of difficulty. We had to rely on Peta to find our path.

Without her, I was sure we would not have made the climb. "Almost there," she called down to us, her eyes glowing in the dark.

I kept moving, my legs and back aching from the cold and the fatigue. The night had taken its toll. I could only hope Queen Aria was as Peta had said: kind and merciful.

We pulled ourselves up a ledge, side by side. Cactus's hair was stiff, slicked back from his face. Our sweat froze in droplets as we climbed. "I can check this off my list of things to do before I die."

I stared at him, then laughed. "Only you, Cactus, would think this was a challenge you needed to face."

He grinned. "What can I say? A challenge only makes me want it more. Tells me it's worth the fight."

His words, of course, had nothing to do with the mountain.

My grin slipped and I pulled myself over the ledge, resting on my knees. We'd made it to the gates of the Eyrie.

We were on a flat plain cut deep into the mountain, wide and open. Across the far edge were a pair of tall gates with walls stretching to either side.

Peta sat on her haunches, her ears flicking back and forth. "Lark, the welcoming committee is on its way."

I made myself stand though my legs trembled and my arms felt like boulders. Toward us, the greeter flew. I blinked, surprised at who the queen would send as her emissary.

"First time for everything," I said as the fairy reached me, his sword drawn and pointed at my eye.

First time indeed.

CHAPTER 15

"Hey, you can't damn well be here, you damn stinking dirt brat!" the fairy screamed at me, his face bright red. I raised my eyebrows but didn't move for fear he'd accidently puncture my eye with his miniscule blade.

"Why not?"

"All Terralings are forbidden to enter the Eyrie until further notice," he screeched.

"Do I look like a Terraling?" I asked. That seemed to slow him down. "Does my companion look like a Terraling with his red hair? Would a cat be bound as a familiar to a Terraling?" With each question I asked, he deflated a little more until the sword dropped.

"Well, shit stickers. I never thought of that.

Name's Tom." He floated back from my face, giving me breathing room.

"I'm Larkspur, and this is Cactus, and Peta." I pointed to the others as I named them. "Tom, we'd like to speak with Queen Aria. Where do we petition?"

His sword whipped back up, slicing into my cheek as the scent of berry wine wafted over me. Great. A drunken fairy on a power trip. Just what we needed.

"Wait, she said the only people coming to speak to her would be trouble and I should try and stop them."

"Ahhh," Cactus said. "There's the rub. The word 'try' implies that no matter what you do, you wouldn't be able to stop said trouble."

Tom's mouth dropped open. "Are you sure?"

Peta leapt up and caught him between her big paws so fast she was a white blur. "Yes, quite sure."

"Don't hurt him!" I yelped. I could easily imagine what the queen would say if we killed one of her guards right off the start. Not exactly the introduction I was looking for.

Peta let out a yelp and leapt back, shaking her paw. "Little prick!"

"That's not what the ladies say!" he hollered back as he zipped toward the gates.

"Hurry, we have to make it there ahead of him." I bolted after the fairy, the glitter of his wings making it easy to track his progress. Peta was ahead of me, snarling.

Tom looked over his shoulder, yelped and sped up. Damn it. "Fairy sharts, they're gaining on me! Open the gates, let me in!"

The gates didn't move, though a few faces peered through the tall grills.

I held a hand up and slid to a stop. "Wait, Peta. I think . . . I think he wasn't official."

Cactus panted beside me, leaning over to press his hands onto his legs. "You sure?"

"Yes. If he was, they'd have come running when he yelled for help."

The fairy hit the gates, going so far as to rattle his sword along them as we approached. "Let me in! They said the cat would eat me and pick her teeth with my bones."

One side of the gate opened and a tall, slim figure stepped out. My heart seemed to stutter at the sight of the white leathers the Ender wore and the long white hair braided over one shoulder. He stood easily a foot taller than me, and his cool gray eyes swept us as if we were a mere annoyance. But all that wasn't the reason. It was his resemblance to Wicker, the Sylph who'd helped Cassava take the throne and release the lung burrowers on my people. The Sylph who'd killed my mother and little brother.

He raised one eyebrow. "Who are you, and what do you want?"

Tom flew right up to his eyes. "I told you, you fecking moron! They're here to kill me and assassinate the queen! Now let me in!"

With a casual flick of his wrist, the Ender swatted Tom, sending the fairy flying our way. He tumbled end over end and I caught him mid-air. "That's not very nice. He might be a drunk and out of his mind, but you shouldn't swat fairies. It's bad luck."

The Sylph's lips didn't even twitch. So much for breaking the ice. Tom groaned and I held him carefully. "I wish to speak with the queen."

"Why?"

I made sure to keep eye contact with him. If Tom had been right and Terralings weren't going to be allowed into the Eyrie, it was time to improvise. "We wish to visit the library. We have seen the Pit's few books, and the Rim's. But we have heard the Eyrie boasts the finest knowledge in all four families."

"Scholars?" The Ender pulled back. "Perhaps your story would be more believable if you weren't wearing a Terraling Ender's uniform."

Damn, the cold was making me sloppy. "An Ender cannot also be someone who seeks knowledge?"

"Not when your king is missing. We have sent the information requested, which is more than we had to do." He stepped back.

"Wait. Please take the message to Queen Aria. Tell her I wish to speak with her."

His gray eyes locked onto mine. "She will not see you—and I will take her no message from the lips of a Sylph-killer."

The gate slammed shut and I let out a breath. Apparently my reputation had preceded me.

"What are we going to do if he won't let us in?" Peta asked.

"Well, we have someone to help us, don't we,

Tom?" I held him around the waist and plucked his sword from his hands.

"What?" He slurred the word. I wasn't sure if it was the drink, or the blow from the Ender.

"You want to get into the Eyrie, yes?"

"Yes!" He pushed at my hand. "Hey, let me go."

"Not yet."

Already the plan formed in my head. A secret entrance that Tom would show us; we'd sneak in, find my father and be gone in a flash. Yet that was not how things played out in the least.

The gate opened once more and an old lady peered out. Now, to say an elemental was old was usually a hard thing to determine. We aged . . . well. My father had perhaps a thousand years behind him and he had barely begun to gray.

This woman, though, she was stooped and her white hair trailed to the snow. She wore a pale blue dress dotted with tiny white crystals that caught the light, and a crown rested on her head seemingly made of gossamer silk and spider webs. Milky, unseeing, eyes turned toward me. "Child of the earth. The mother told me you would come. Here, do not mind my Enders, they are protective."

Behind her, the tall Ender glared at us. "My queen, please do not do this. You said your death would come in through the front door. She is the one who killed Wicker."

That was the truth. I'd killed Wicker when I'd ousted Cassava from the Rim. Not that I was going to tell them and confirm the accusation.

"Truly, you were there?" She faced me but her words were for him. "Ender Boreas, please do not spread rumors. I cannot abide by them. And if she was the one who killed Wicker, then so be it. He chose his path and it took him from us. He was banished for a reason."

That was news to me.

His whole face shut down. "As you wish, my queen."

She held a hand out to me. "Come. You three must be cold and hungry."

"What about Tom?" I asked, holding the fairy out to her. "Is he not one of yours?"

Ender Boreas snorted, but the queen held out a trembling hand. "Tom, in trouble again, my old friend? One day you will end up at the ends of our world, I think. Perhaps as far as the Valley of Death."

"Aria, I cannot stay away from the berry wine. It loves me too truly." He gave an awkward bow as I transferred him into her palm.

She put him on her shoulder and went back inside. "Let them pass, and do not molest them."

Peta pressed herself against my leg as we walked through the doors. We said nothing as we followed the queen into the Eyrie. The mountaintop was ringed with a platform at least a mile wide. Seemingly supported by clouds, our footing was anything but certain, and that made me nervous. It would be nothing for any of the Sylphs to take exception to us and toss us into open space. I put a hand to the gem hanging from my neck, remembering it was there for the first time since we'd left the boat on the beach in Greece.

Here and there the wind gusted over us, once with enough force that I had to lean into it to keep from being shoved backward. Peta's fur ruffled in the hard wind. She blinked up at me. "Some of the strongest winds in the world reside here."

I was sure she didn't only mean the natural forces of air.

Ender Boreas kept pace with the queen. Where he was tall and muscled, she was petite and frail. Then again, she was stooped with age. If she stood, she might have been as tall as me. More than once I'd been mistaken as having Sylph blood because of my height.

We were led along open streets paved with nothing but thick clouds, past buildings that hovered, always a few feet above the footing we stood on.

Ahead of us at the mountain's peak was what I could only assume was the palace. Its spires were jagged, like lightning bolts reaching into the sky. Colored a bright gold, they reflected the morning sun so they glowed with its light.

I held my tongue, though to be honest, that was easy. The Eyrie was as stunning as the Deep in its own way. Certainly outstripping the Rim with its grandeur and glittering surfaces.

"Come, there is someone I want you to meet." Aria held her hand out and I looked at Boreas. I pointed at my chest. He nodded, though the look on his face was grim.

"Stop making faces, Boreas. You're much more handsome when you smile."

He blushed and I couldn't help but grin. I put my hand in the queen's and she moved it to the crook of her elbow.

She leaned heavily on me as we walked up the last of the steps to the gates of her inner sanctuary. "Here we can speak without fear of anyone interrupting." Blind though she was, she led without hesitation. The throne room opened to us, and I couldn't help but suck in a breath. Pillars of brilliant white ice reached as high as any redwood to the open sky. A whisper of clouds curled over our heads and snowflakes floated to our feet. A dream . . . it looked as though we walked through a dream made entirely to dazzle the eyes and ease the soul.

Only my soul was anything but calm. The exterior of the Eyrie may have been beautiful, but I knew all too well how beauty could hide the ugly truth.

"Your home is . . . exquisite."

"A home is not the place you live your life, child of the earth." The queen's voice was strong and firm. "Home is the place your life blooms."

I hadn't been expecting advice. She patted my hand. "I think you will understand one day. Rumors have come to us that you did some marvelous work in the Namib Sand Sea."

I blanched. "How?"

"Oh, the usual. Spies. Spies are everywhere. Even mine." She laughed and waved at me. "Fairies mostly, if you must know. Elementals don't notice them, yet they are everywhere. Close your mouth, child of the earth. You will learn soon enough that in our world, very little is as it seems. You have been led on a merry chase, haven't you?"

"The mother goddess," I said before I thought better of it.

Aria blinked up at me. "Well, she *is* a goddess. She sees what we cannot, even the future as it should be. But that is not what I meant. I know you seek your father, but he is not here, child. Whoever told you he was, led you wrong." She stepped away and toward her throne.

I glanced at Cactus. He shook his head and shrugged his shoulders. I dropped a hand to Peta. She flicked one ear, her voice low. "There is no way the Tracker was wrong."

Aria turned and smiled at me. "I see a question in your eyes. Ask it."

"May I look around? It is my father I seek, after all."

"I cannot let you wander on your own. The Eyrie is dangerous for the simple fact that not all the footing is grounded. If you are amenable to a guide, you may stay as long as you wish."

"Take it," Peta whispered, "you will not get better."

"Thank you." I bowed at the waist.

The queen slid onto her throne and let out a sigh. "If you ever have the pleasure of ruling, child, may I suggest a rather comfortable chair? This one bites at my rear no matter how I sit."

I laughed, as did Cactus. "I will keep that in mind, though I doubt the time will ever come."

She picked up a staff beside the throne and tapped it into the rolling clouds at her feet. A high-pitched ringing bell resounded three times, like the tinkling of chimes.

Cactus reached over and touched my hand, then pointed behind us. The doors swung open and three Enders strode in. Two men and a woman. The men were built like most Sylphs: tall and slim, their bodies whip-like in their movement and structure. The woman, on the other hand, was shorter than me. Her body was solid muscle by the way she moved, but she was not the slender shape of the other Sylphs.

"A curvy Sylph? Since when?" Cactus let the questions slip out and I fought not to cringe. The woman's face didn't even twitch, but I saw the hitch in her chest from a breath of air being sucked in too fast.

I stared at him. "And since when have you known a Terraling woman to be my height, Prick? Do you think you have met every kind of woman this world holds?"

Idiot.

"Idiot," Peta spit out.

The female Ender looked at me, and our eyes met. Understanding passed between us. I knew what it was to stand out in your home, to not fit what was considered normal. To say it was a challenge was something of an understatement. The elemental world was not forgiving of those who did not conform.

"Samara, would you be willing to guide Larkspur

through the Eyrie? Take her wherever she wishes and aid her in looking for her father. Nothing is off limits."

Samara made a fist with her right hand and pressed it to her heart. "As you wish, my queen."

"Bah, you wish it too. I see you wanting to know more about her." The queen waved at her, her blind eyes seeing far more than they should have. "Go on now. Take our visitors. Show them a room, and give them some food."

Samara crooked a finger at us. "Come with me." Her voice was as solid as her body; there wasn't a single wavering note in her words. She led us out of the throne room and to the left, down a long hallway that wound around the mountain, like the curve of a woman's hip. "As guests of the queen, you will stay in the heart of the Eyrie. Your rooms are safe, set into the mountain. But the rest of the Eyrie could slip out from under your feet when you least expect it. There will always be a Sylph outside your doors, so if you have need of them, they will help you."

Sounded more like we would have a guard at all times to keep an eye on us. But maybe it was my past experiences in other elemental homes that tainted my view of things.

The halls were wide and tall, with open ceilings like the throne room. Walls with no roof, and the bright blue, cold sky beckoning above us. Of course, the Sylphs could keep the weather constant over their homes. Cactus, Peta, and I, on the other hand, would have no such amenity.

Where the Eyrie was not cloud and drifting fog,

it was set into the mountain, as Samara had said. I couldn't help but reach out and touch those parts, reassuring myself that I could at least still feel the earth here and there.

Samara stopped in front of a door on the left of us, toward the mountain. I let out a sigh of relief. "There is food and drink inside. I will be back in an hour to take you where you wish."

She turned on her heel and strode away, her white leathers blending into the drifting clouds at her feet.

I stepped inside the room and let out a sigh. There was no cloud for footing here, but a solid smooth stone. I bent a knee and pressed my hands against it. Limestone, common to the area. It warmed under my hand and the mountain seemed to strain to reach me.

"Easy, Lark." Cactus put a hand on my shoulder. "I don't think you should connect with the earth here. Neither of us should."

I blinked up at him. "Why not?"

He crouched beside me and lifted my hands from the stone. "Terralings made this place for the Sylphs."

I knew that our family had at one time been close with the Sylphs. "What does that matter?"

"Because, Dirt Girl, what you felt in Giselle applies here too. She had Spirit flowing through her from the things Talan had worked on her; the mountain has had Terralings work through it in detail. It makes the stone eager for your touch."

Frowning, I stood. "That makes no sense. We have helped all the families build their homes in the past.

To one degree or another. Why would touching this particular stone be bad?"

Peta trotted to the large bed that dominated the room and leapt up onto it. She sunk down to her chin in the lush blankets. "Oh, this is nice." She seemed to lose her train of thought for a moment in the physical sensation.

"The Eyrie . . . it is different from the others. The Pit is buried under a mountain close to the fire in the earth. The Deep floats in the ocean, made up of sand and shells. But the Eyrie is built into the mountain, and while it is high within the stratosphere, it is the power of the Terralings that keeps it together. With the connection you have to the earth boosted by Spirit, you are drawn like a magnet to this place. It means you have more power here than anywhere else in this world. It also means the mountain will do as you ask, even if you don't ask."

"Shit, I didn't know that." Cactus tightened his hold on me, and pulled me closer to him. He let go of my hand and wrapped his arm around my waist. "Don't touch anything, Lark. You'll break the mountain in half."

I snorted. "Please, don't be a fool."

Oh, if only that were the truth.

CHAPTER 16

The first day passed in the Eyrie with no clues as to whether my father was there at all. Samara led us around on a tour of the second and third levels. Tiers were built into the mountain with multiple wide stairways leading up and down.

"Night is coming, and I have to go on guard duty." Samara stopped again at the door to our suite.

"Will you come in for a moment? I have a question I'd rather not ask in the open." I stepped through the doorway and waited, looking at her while keeping my face carefully blank. Her pale eyebrows ticked upward, but she stepped through the door.

We hadn't spoken much through the tour, at least not about anything other than the makeup of the

Eyrie and what we were seeing. All interesting, but not what I wanted to know.

I made myself ask the question. "Samara, is there any dissension in the Eyrie? Something a person from outside of your family could exploit?"

If I thought her eyebrows had climbed before, that was nothing to what they did then. "Who exactly would want to exploit my family?" Her words were smooth, but there was a hard bite to them. I saw the way her hand drifted to the pointed short staff strapped to her back.

I held my hands up, palms facing her. "There is one from our family, Cassava. She has . . . caused a great deal of strife not only in the Rim, but has tried to usurp the other families in one way or another too."

Samara's hand dropped away from her staff. "The queen here is well loved, even by her spoiled daughters. The Enders respect her even with her advanced age. There is no reason for anyone to think she will cross the Veil anytime soon. And as I'm sure you've noticed, it is hard to slip anything by her in spite of her eyes."

Tension should have eased off me with her words, but it did not. If there was no dissension here, why was my father hidden away in the Eyrie? Either Samara was lying, or there was more going on than the Ender knew. I hoped it was the latter; I liked Samara.

"Is that the only question?" She looked up at me.

I nodded. "Yes. For now."

She backed out and shut the door behind us with a click. There was no additional click of a lock, though.

Cactus went to the bed and flopped down with his legs and arms spread wide, his fingers reaching for Peta. "Come here, bad luck cat. I know you want to cuddle."

She hissed and swatted at him. I didn't move, didn't take part in their banter as they swapped insults.

"Prick, if I didn't know better, I'd think you had a death wish."

"Well, if I stick close to you, isn't that what will happen?"

"Why, you miserable lizard!"

"Salamander, cat, get it right."

I took a step, then another, moving through the room. I couldn't help but touch the pieces of stone that peered out of the wall. I untied my boots and slipped them off.

The power of the earth curled around me like a pair of strong arms. Peta was right, there was something different here in the Eyrie. Like the earth had more consciousness in this place than anywhere else.

A flick of a tail across my nose made me sneeze. I opened my eyes, not even remembering when I'd closed them or when I'd collapsed to my knees next to the bed. Peta stood in front of me, her eyes crinkled around the edges with worry. "Lark. I think you should wear your boots here. This place calls to you too strongly."

"It was someone like me, Peta. Someone who carried Spirit and Earth. That's why it's like . . . coming home." I choked the words out.

Her lips curled upward. "Then perhaps when this

is done, we come back. Maybe this is where you belong, Lark."

"I would come with you," Cactus said. I looked up at him, expecting him to be teasing me. But the look in his eyes was serious, through and through.

"You would give up the Rim for me? You couldn't; you would have to return there so as to not go mad."

"I would give up anything for you, Lark. I love you and only you. You have held my heart since we were children. How can you not see it?"

The moment was loaded with longing, with the desire to hold him against my skin and feel his lips on mine. To know if he truly was the one I loved. Or if it was Ash who held the key to my heart.

How could I decide between two men so different, each of them calling to parts of me the other didn't?

He held his hand out to me, an invitation I didn't want to turn down. We were here, alone. Together.

Peta put herself between us. "No, I won't let you hurt her." Her words cut the tension like claws shredding silk.

"I'm not the one hurting her, Peta. I would never hurt her." He spoke to her, but his eyes never left mine.

Breathing hard, I made myself stand and put my tall boots on. "We should eat and get some sleep. We have to find my father."

Cactus's jaw tightened to the point I thought he would crack his teeth. He went to the table laden with food and spooned a bowl full of stew for himself. I followed his lead and filled a bowl for Peta, and then one for myself. Heavy with curry, the stew had thick chunks of meat and vegetables that had absorbed the flavor. I dipped flatbread into the liquid. "Peta, do you think you could do some snooping? See if Samara is right about dissension? I can't believe there is nothing out of order here."

She swiped a paw over her face, cleaning off the stew. "You make a good point. I can stay close to the mountain where there is no need for me to have the Sylph guide."

I nodded, trying not to feel bad about what I was doing. "I don't think we have much time here. The queen said we have free rein, but if my father is here and Cassava is with him—"

"Then she might already know we're here," Cactus finished for me. I nodded.

Peta stretched her body out, her eyes on mine. I had to fight not to flush under her gaze. "Let me out then," she said.

I walked her to the door and opened it a crack. She reached back and stuck her claws into my pants. "Lark. He will hurt you. Don't do this."

"I have to know, Peta. Spirit spoke to me when I was with Ash. If it is quiet with Cactus, then—"

A sigh escaped her. "I trust you. I do not trust him."

She stepped out with a flick of her tail and I shut the door.

"Did you get rid of your familiar?" Cactus was right behind me, his hands on my shoulders. He slid them down my arms to my hands, a slow burn flickering in his wake.

I turned my head and stared into his eyes. "I love you both, Cactus."

"I won't share you, Lark."

"Then we can't do this. Because I won't give him up." My own words shocked me, but they came from my heart. I would not give Ash up for Cactus, any more than I would give up Cactus for Ash.

In that moment, I knew I had it in me to love them both, if they would let me.

He tugged me back against his chest and kissed me from behind. His free hands slid under my vest, caressing the skin of my belly. Heat flared where he touched, making me arch against him. I wanted him, wanted his skin on mine and his kisses, his laughter and sweet smile.

I spun in his arms and wrapped myself around him. He stumbled a little under my weight and we both laughed. "Easy, tiger," he murmured against my lips.

"Easy nothing. Love is a harsh taskmistress."

"Then I think I should spank her."

I threw my head back and laughed. He kissed my throat and nipped at the delicate skin, which turned my laugh into a groan.

Stumbling backward, we hit the bed together as we peeled out of our clothes. Every fantasy I'd had about him rushed forward and I took great pleasure as I ran my hands over his bare skin, feeling the way his muscles tensed. He rolled to his side and touched my arm where my tattoo curled. "I should have stopped her sooner."

The wounds had been the result of the lava whip, wielded by the queen of the Pit. I should have died, but was healed first by Blackbird, which still confused me, and then fully healed by the mother goddess. But I was left with the curling vine studded with thorns that marked every place the whip had touched. I barely noticed it.

"What's done is done. Unless you want to kiss it better?" I arched an eyebrow at him, surprising even myself. Playfulness was not something I knew in the bedroom. Yet with Cactus, it seemed natural.

Grinning from ear to ear, he bent his head. "As you wish, princess."

His lips found their way around my body with ease, drawing more than one moan from my own lips.

Cactus lay on top of me, holding himself up on his elbows. "Are you sure? I don't want you to complain I seduced you and you had no idea what you were doing, in the morning."

I rolled my eyes. "Keep talking and I'll change my mind."

He kissed me softly and lowered himself—

The door rattled with the force of a body being tossed against it and Peta screeched, "Lark, Blackbird is here!"

I jerked away from Cactus and ran to the door, scooping only my spear as I went. I flung the door open and Peta—in her leopard form—fell in. Blood splattered her coat and she was breathing hard. "I'm fine, but you can catch him. End of the hall, Samara has him cornered."

I didn't wait for Cactus, or bother with my clothes. My bare feet on the floor energized me in a way I'd never felt when I'd connected with the earth before. I used the power to send me all but flying to where Peta had directed.

At the end of the hall, I slid to a stop as Samara went flying through the air right in front of me. A wild wind whipped down the hallway and held her aloft. She glanced at me, then pointed with her sharpened staff.

I stepped around the corner. Blackbird was indeed cornered, his back to the mountain and no way out.

"Let me guess, you have my father here?"

Blackbird laughed, though there was a nervous edge to it for the first time. "Please, I don't need Father."

"Then why are you here?" I approached him, my spear held across my body.

"You're here, Lark, isn't that enough? You and I are tied, bound together in ways you cannot understand yet."

"Not good enough." I was close enough that I knew I could leap and tackle him.

Samara stepped up beside me. "You know him?"

"One of the problems I've been dealing with."

She grunted.

"You're looking lovely, Lark. Perhaps you and I should be discussing the potential between us. We could produce the most powerful children."

"I'd have to be tied down and unconscious."

He swept his cloak back over one leg and I got a glimpse of dark brown leather pants. Not unlike a Terraling Ender. "That can be arranged."

Revulsion curled through me.

His presence didn't surprise me, but I couldn't figure out what need he had of my father. And then it hit me.

"Your lover is here, isn't she? Cassava has hidden herself away and you're helping her."

He laughed. "Clever girl. Yes, of course I'm helping her. I have been all along. But you're so easy. I know how to make you do what I want."

I swung my spear out and he leapt back, slamming into the wall. Why wasn't he attacking me?

"Samara," he said, and lines of pink slid around him, "kill her."

Worm shit and green sticks.

Samara lunged at me, her eyes filled with his power, tingeing the whites. Her pointed staff swept my legs from under me and I hit the ground hard, the stone biting into my bare back. I rolled as she slammed the point of her spear toward my heart. The tip caught the edge of my back and tore a flap of flesh off. "Samara, fight him!" I yelled, knowing it would do no good. Unless I could get my hands on her skin, the power he held over her would stand.

She came at me again and again, and I deflected each blow. But I knew it was only a matter of time before she got through my guard. Her speed matched mine. I had only one choice. I flung my arms wide. "Kill me then."

With a lunge, she drove her staff toward my middle. At the last possible second, as the tip touched my bare belly, I stepped to the side and slapped my hands on her face. Her momentum carried us forward a few steps before we stumbled to a stop.

"What happened? I dreamed we were fighting." Her words were slurred as if she'd been drinking.

I let her go, watching for signs that the command Blackbird had given her was truly gone from her. I turned, to see if Blackbird remained, already knowing he too would be gone. The hall was empty except for Samara and me.

"Not a dream, my friend." My breath came in gasps, and I touched the spot on my belly that had almost become a new scar. A thin trickle of blood ran down, but it was the injury on my back that was going to give me a good war wound.

Footsteps, and then Cactus was there in nothing but a pair of pants. He stared at me and spoke words that made my blood run cold.

"Blackbird took Peta."

CHAPTER 17

"'m coming with you," Samara said as we ran back to my room. I grabbed my clothes and slid them on with speed, ignoring her. "I said—"

"This is not your fight, Samara." I grabbed my boots and yanked them on. Cactus dressed beside me, not saying a word.

Blackbird had Peta . . . he knew I would come for her, which meant it was a trap I was about to walk into. There was no way I was taking more people into a trap meant for me. The bond between my familiar and me was strong. When I focused on it, I felt the direction she was in. Straight west, toward the Rim.

I wasn't surprised.

"I wasn't asking your permission, Lark," Samara

said, her words cool. "I have every right to pursue an invader of our home."

Damn it, she was right. "Fine, good luck finding him."

"He took your familiar, and you can find her. I will follow you."

Cactus touched my arm. "Lark, wait. Your father is here somewhere. You know that. You know Blackbird is trying to take you away so you don't find him."

I nodded. "Yes. Peta means more to me than my father."

Samara sucked in a sharp breath. "The Terraling king is your father? And you would choose your familiar over him?"

"Do not judge me, Samara," I snapped. "Peta is my heart mate and has been more a part of healing my soul in the short while she has been with me than any other. My father is barely a sperm donor, as far as I'm concerned."

Her face softened. "Believe it or not, I understand." She lifted her hand and from over our heads in the clouds came the shriek of an eagle, the high pitch resonating through the room. The large bird dove out of the sky, banking with his wings so he could land on Samara's shoulder. He preened a moment, but said nothing.

I held my hand out to Samara and she took it. "Then we hunt together, as our families did once."

Her eyes glittered. "I always enjoyed roasted game bird."

Cactus laughed, but I didn't. With Peta's life on the line, nothing was funny to me.

Samara touched my arm. "You have a Traveling band?"

I nodded. "It will take us to the Rim."

Cactus cleared his throat. "You have to say good-bye to the queen, Lark. You can't leave without taking note of the—"

"Do it for me." I took his face in my hands and kissed him. "Get Shazer and fly home as fast as you can, as soon as you can."

His eyes widened as I stepped away from him. Samara nodded and put a hand on my arm. Cactus finally nodded. "I love you, Lark. Don't forget it."

I kept my eyes on his as I reached up and twisted the armband counterclockwise. The world around us sucked us down and I braced myself for the memory I would gain from Samara.

The images were dull, and flickered, unlike the other times I'd Traveled with another.

Samara as a child, beaten and hurt. Her desire to protect others. Her Ender training. The ridicule she endured. How much she loved the queen and how she wanted to protect her family.

So much like me it hurt to see and feel the past played out, even in those flickers and bits. We jerked to a stop, and she let me go. This time, the guards were waiting for us inside the Traveling room.

"You are under arrest—"

I launched myself at the guard who spoke. I didn't know who it was with his visor pulled up, and I didn't care. I slammed the butt of my spear into his head, dropping him before he could finish his sentence. Samara took on a guard while the remaining two surrounded me.

"Lark, don't make us hurt you," Blossom said, her voice distinct even behind the visor.

"It's not me you have to worry about," I snarled.

"Cassava is back," she said.

The guard beside her snapped a fist sideways, catching her in the head. "Shut the hell up, woman."

His distraction was all I needed. I swept his feet, leapt into the air and came down with my fist, driving it into his chest. Ribs cracked under my blow, at least three by the way his body gave under me.

To the side, Samara drove both fists into her opponent's gut, throwing him hard into the wall. He slid down as his eyes rolled upward and he passed out.

I stood and stared at Blossom. "Cassava? Are you sure?"

She slipped off her visor and threw it to the floor. "Yes. As soon as you were gone she showed up, took Vetch under her wing and took the throne. She said . . . she was going to send someone to bring Bella home and deal with her condition." Her voice caught and I put a hand on her shoulder. "She means to kill Bella's baby, doesn't she?"

Just like Bramley. "Has she done it? Has she sent anyone?"

Blossom shook her head. "Not that I know."

I slipped off the Traveling band and put it on Blossom's arm. "Go, protect Bella. You know she is the one who should rule here. She can't be hurt. Tell her to fight for all she's worth and to never forget she holds the necklace. She'll know what I mean."

Slowly Blossom nodded. "What about you, Lark?"

I looked at Samara. "I'm going to kill Cassava. I'll send a message when it's safe to bring Bella home."

Blossom brought the globe around and settled it on the Deep. With a twist of the armband she was gone.

"You should go too." I bent and trussed up the guards, glancing at Samara.

"No. This will affect us too. We know Cassava is a loose cannon. She stole Wicker from us." She helped me tie up the guards. "How do you want to do this?"

I touched my hand to where the smoky diamond lay in my pouch. I opened the leather bag and slipped it out. "Take this. It will boost your power. When you go back to the Eyrie, give it to Aria. It belongs in her hands."

She gasped as I dropped it into her hands. "Mother goddess, the power raging in this . . . is it what I think it is?"

"Yes. Use it carefully. Or maybe in this case, not so carefully." I stood and strode to the door, peeking out. There were no guards waiting for us. But that did not mean it was safe. The bond with Peta tugged at me. She was scared and pissed off as only a cat could be. But she was alive.

I slipped out and Samara followed me, silent. I stopped at the bottom of the steps and tugged off my tall boots. I needed as much connection with the earth as I could get. Wiggling my toes, I pulled the power of the earth below me and let it fill me.

"What can we expect?" Samara asked quietly.

"Blackbird can control all five elements. Cassava is powerful with earth, but nothing else."

She grabbed my arm. "Can you kill her? Are you strong enough?"

"I've been waiting my whole life. I'll kill her or die trying. In which case, you finish the job. All our homes are in danger as long as she is free."

Her face grim, she nodded. I crept up the stairs, all my senses straining. But there was no sound, nothing to indicate there were ever inhabitants in the barracks. A spooky emptiness permeated the air as we slipped into the upper levels. I went to my room and then Ash's. Both were empty, though I hadn't really expected him to be waiting for me there.

Beckoning for Samara to keep close, I crept along the edge of the training room to the main doors of the barracks. I ran a hand over the wooden doors, then pressed an ear to them. There was nothing, not even a buzz of distant talking. I looked at Samara and she shrugged.

There was no other way . . . unless. . . . I spun and we ran back the way we'd come, bolting down the stairs and sliding to a stop in the Traveling room. There was one armband left. I grabbed it and slid it on. "Hang on."

"What are you doing—"

The world dissolved, but the trip was quick. I popped us into the forest at the northern edge of the

Rim. There wasn't even time for a memory to roll over me.

I dropped to a crouch and Samara followed suit. "Where are we?"

"At the outside edge of the Rim."

"Why exactly?"

Slowing for a brief moment, I looked back at her. "Call it a hunch, but there is only one doorway out of the barracks and Cassava knows it. She's not stupid, even if she is deranged. She'll be waiting for us to pop through those doors."

"Great, smart and a psycho." Samara pushed a fern out of her way and caught up to me. We jogged side by side until we reached the first house on the outer edge of the Rim. I ducked down beside the wooden structure. Using the houses for cover, we slipped unnoticed to the center of the Rim where it became apparent things had gotten rather shitty.

By the numbers, it looked as though every single member of my family had been gathered outside the Spiral and the Enders Barracks. In the center of them stood Cassava, with Blackbird at her side. I scanned the crowd looking for Ash, but there was no blond head with his height. My heart clenched. No, she wouldn't have killed him. The bond with Peta thrummed lightly and I felt her eyes sweep toward me. I reached back and touched Samara to bring her forward for a look. Putting my mouth to her ear, I whispered, "Can you sweep everyone away from Cassava?"

She grinned and whispered back, "You got it.

What about Blackbird, though? He could have me pull down on you again."

I reached out and took her hand. "Don't let go of me."

"That's going to get awkward."

"This won't be a fight with weapons."

Her eyes widened and she nodded. I stood and we stepped out together. She lifted her free hand and the trees above us groaned. Everyone looked up, including Cassava and Blackbird.

The wind that swept through the Rim was icy cold, as if it had been pulled from the Wretched Peaks themselves. It slammed into the Terralings surrounding Cassava and swept them away in a gust that sent them flying through the air like a child's ragdolls.

Screams rent the silence and I finally caught a glimpse of Ash. He was on his belly in front of Cassava, stains of red in his golden hair. I dragged Samara forward with me.

I held out a hand and the earth below us rumbled, the plates under our feet shifting as my anger boiled to a fever pitch.

"Ah, Larkspur. So lovely to see you again," Cassava purred. She snapped her fingers and Blackbird picked up Ash. His body was limp. "Don't worry, he isn't dead yet. But if you don't do what I want, he will be."

All the power of the earth couldn't help me. But maybe Spirit could. Samara tugged on my hand. "I can send them flying."

"Do it and I will have Blackbird burn your familiar

SHANNON MAYER

and your lover to a crisp right in front of you," Cassava said.

Blackbird had a hand on Peta's ruff and he shook her hard. "Cooked kitty. I've never had that before."

She hissed at him and swung a paw, but in her housecat form she wasn't much of a threat. I had no doubt he was suppressing her ability to shift.

"What do you want?" I asked. Samara stilled, her hand in mine tightening.

"Don't, Lark. They'll kill all three of you."

"Not if you can get Ash and Peta away." I looked at her and saw a kindred spirit. A child like me who'd been broken and found a way to put herself back together. "I trust you to get them away, Samara."

Her jaw ticked and she nodded. "And what about you?"

The ground under us heaved. From behind us, Vetch laughed his donkey-braying laugh. We landed apart. "Get them!" I yelled at her. She stood and the wind picked her and Ash up. Peta, though, was tangled in Blackbird's hands. My cat twisted and bit him on the wrist and he dropped her with a curse. She ran to me, not to Samara. I caught her up in my arms and clutched her to me. "You have to go."

"No. I will not leave you."

I looked up at Samara and nodded. At least Ash would be safe. Blossom would look after Bella. It was all I could do.

The sound of footsteps, the whistle of a weapon slicing through the air; those were the only sounds of warning I had. A sword pierced my back, right under my heart.

I arched backward as blood bubbled up my throat and trickled out my mouth. Peta let out a screech that turned into a snarl as she shifted into her leopard form. Hanging onto the power of the earth, I pulled a creeping vine forward and wrapped it around her back legs, yanking her out of the circle that tightened around me. I caught a glimpse of Samara and she gave me a nod as she swept Peta away.

"NO, NO!" Peta screamed, her voice breaking on the one word.

The sword was yanked from my back and I slumped forward onto my knees. My siblings, minus Bella and Raven—my only supporters—surrounded me.

There would be no escaping this time. All those who could have saved me were far away; and I wouldn't have wanted them to trade their lives for me. Not even Peta. Maybe most especially not my Peta.

"Little Larkspur. Your time has finally come." Cassava knelt in front of me, cupping my face in her hands. "Do you want to know why I left you alive so long?"

I blinked up at her.
"Yes."

CHAPTER 18

"Y̲ou were to be a part of the new order, Lark." Cassava stroked my face. "Spirit is such a rare element, and to have a child with all five elements . . . is difficult. I'd hoped you would remain biddable enough. But, so be it."

"You wanted a child from me?" I couldn't believe what I was hearing. "Why not keep Bramley alive then?"

"He was named as heir. I couldn't have that. He had to die." She tapped my nose with a finger, and in her eyes I saw the broken mind behind them. "You were nothing to your father even then. I knew I could control you. I promised you to Requiem."

To Requiem . . . "I'd rather die than be your breeding bitch."

"Yes, I realize that now. Which is why I will waste no more time with you. Vetch, take her to the oubliette. I don't want anyone finding her body. Ever."

I caught Briar's eyes as Vetch threw me over his shoulder. "Briar, run away," I whispered.

She blinked back tears and turned her back on me, fear making her biddable. Raven . . . I had to believe he'd at least gotten away. Blackbird fell in behind Vetch as we walked to the barracks and the Traveling room. Vetch set up the globe. I couldn't tell where he was taking me, upside down and dying as I was. Dying. Yes, that was what was happening. I probably should have been more afraid, but there was no strength left in me.

Distantly I recognized that Blackbird could be suppressing my desire to live, using Spirit to control me.

Blackbird faced me, but I had no idea of what was going on with him. "Why did you want Giselle?"

"Even now when you lie on death's cusp you want answers?" He seemed genuinely surprised.

"Yes." Why the hell it mattered to me, I truly did not know. But in this small way, I fought to stay awake, to keep my mind together.

"Giselle would have helped us to be sure of our steps. To be sure it was the right time to kill you and the king. A safety measure. But as you can see, we didn't really need her after all."

The world swirled, and I fell into Vetch's memories.

I struggled at first to understand what I was seeing.

Briar cringed away from Vetch, her hands up, and her clothing torn.

"Mother said we must, so stop your crying."

"I don't want to," she whimpered, clutching her hands around her naked torso.

"Not up to you, Briar. Not up to me." Vetch stripped off his clothes and stalked toward his youngest sister.

A flicker of rage snapped through me as the air popped around us and we were through to somewhere humid and hot. The brush and swirl of a heated wind did nothing to cool the sweat on my brow.

A few seconds later, Blackbird appeared and stepped up beside Vetch as my brother packed me on his shoulder with the indifference of a mindless creature. "Did you break Vetch?"

"Worried about your brother?"

"Tell me. He deserves to be broken." I breathed out, coughed and fought the wave of darkness that flowed over me.

Vetch flipped me off his shoulder. I landed on my back, on the hard ground. The world faded and I fought the desire to close my eyes and let death take me. "Tell me everything."

"So you can die in peace?" There was a thread of sadness to Blackbird's voice I didn't understand.

"Yes." One word, but even one was becoming too much for me.

Blackbird knelt beside me, his cloak spread over my body. It didn't dissolve as Keeda's had.

"Keeda was a tool, as is Cassava. They think they are running the show, but they aren't. I will rule the

Rim through her. As I will rule all the families through their leaders. That is what the mother goddess wants, for her children to all be together."

"Not like that." I stared up at him while I clutched his cloak. "She wouldn't want it done this way."

"You don't know the mother goddess like I do. She and I go way back. She chose me when I was a child. My mother bedded several men while wearing different stones in order to make sure I came into existence." It felt like he was laughing at me and I didn't understand.

"Then why was Cassava scheming with Requiem to create a child like you?"

Blackbird grinned. "Ah, yes. Requiem. Idiot of epic proportion. Mother wanted to see if another child like me could be born naturally and pose a threat. She promised Requiem he could have you for test breeding, over and over." His grin widened. "But it appears he got Bella instead."

A sharp stab of pain shot through my body. I tried to arch away from the wound in my back, but I barely twitched.

"Death is a funny thing. It can help us see more clearly. Or so I'm told. Do you see me clearly yet, Larkspur?" He put his hands to the edge of his hood.

"You are Cassava's lover."

"Yes, I am that," he said. "She is my everything. Lover. Confidante. Partner. And more."

If I could have gagged I would have. I said nothing as he began to peel back the cloak, slowly revealing his dark hair. Coal? No, it couldn't be Coal. I'd killed him.

Dark hair, blue eyes sparkling with mischief.

"Raven."

He ran a hand down my cheek. "Yes, sister. You were to be mine once Requiem was done with you. Mother has a taste for the exotic looks, and I," he leaned in and brushed his lips over mine, "share that with her."

I couldn't move, couldn't even pull away. My brother. He was Cassava's lover, son. The words jumbled up in my head. Twisted was the only thing I could think. She'd twisted him into a monster.

"Vetch, help me put her into the oubliette." He snapped his fingers and Vetch grabbed me under the arms.

There was one last thing I could do, to help Bella and her child survive. I reached toward Vetch with one hand and pushed Spirit into him, driving it deep into his mind. There was nothing of him there, no emotion, no personality. I broke what was left of it apart, and stopped his heart. He stiffened under my hand.

"Lark, that wasn't necessary." Raven chided me as though I'd thrown a temper tantrum. Vetch dropped to the ground, his heart stilled. One less sibling to deal with, and more importantly, my sisters were safe from him. Raven bent and took the armband from Vetch, then leaned over me. "Are you quite done?"

I looked up at him, held his gaze. "No." With the last of my strength, I grabbed him with both hands and pushed Spirit into him. I had to kill him, I had to if Bella and her child were to have a chance at stopping Cassava.

Power raged between us as he fought. Spirit screeched, the sound like a thousand death cries at once, of a hurricane and earthquake, of a tsunami, all rolled into the roar of Spirit doing battle.

I didn't hold back. I was dying, I knew it.

So did he.

"Lark, don't!" His eyes were full of terror as I hammered him with everything I had. He kicked me in the stomach and sent me tumbling backward. I hit the rounded edges of something anything but natural. Smooth, hard, and stinking like rubber.

The oubliette.

"You almost had me there, sis. Almost." Raven stood over the opening of the oubliette and I could do nothing but stare up at him and hate him.

"Almost," I whispered. That had been my life. Almost. Maybe. Nearly. Failure after failure. Tears slipped down my cheeks.

"Don't cry." He crouched beside the opening. "I won't forget you, Lark. Everyone else will, but I will remember you as the one who could have stopped me." He winked and slammed the oubliette's rounded door shut, thrusting me into total darkness.

The oubliette shifted under me, sinking into the ground. Sucking me down into my grave.

"Mother goddess," I whispered. My last hope was that she would hear me. "Please, this can't be the end."

There was no answering whisper, no fleeting touch of comfort. I slumped, my body curled with the curve of my prison. My hand brushed against the leather bag at my waist. Painfully, I lifted the bag and rested it on my belly, spilling the contents onto my chest.

Blinking, I realized I could see them. The white stone I'd taken from the statue in the Pit glowed, flickering with light. I touched my finger to it and a low-grade buzz flickered through my body. The wound in my back throbbed in time with my slowing heart, but the buzz . . . it pushed the pain back. I closed my eyes, and clutched the chunk of stone. Whatever it was doing seemed to be numbing the pain, which was good enough for me. To die without suffering . . . sleep dragged me into its depths. My dreams were strange, distorted images.

Bella hiding in the Deep, her hands around her belly.

Ash and Peta running through the Rim together, Griffin at their side.

Cactus riding Shazer, winging through the skies.

Looking for me, they were looking for me.

My father on his back in a dark hole, an oubliette like mine. His eyes closed in a false sleep.

I jerked awake and groaned. Rolling to my hands and knees, I struggled to sit upright. My head brushed the top of the oubliette when I sat flat on my rear. The silence ate at me, but I refused to acknowledge it by speaking to myself.

A full minute passed before it occurred to me I was not dead, nor did my back hurt. I reached behind myself, twisting my arm so I could feel where the wound had been. A slightly ridged scar under my fingers was the only sign I'd been hurt.

There was no sense of time, no sense of how long I'd been asleep. Except my belly rumbled and my body was healed. I rubbed the white, softly glowing stone. Niah's words rippled through my mind.

"You'll need it, Lark. When you least expect, the stone will save your life, I think."

I broke my own rule and whispered into the darkness. "The Pit holds our greatest healers . . . is it possible this is a part of their power?"

Shifting my weight again, I pressed my hands into the edges of the oubliette. Solid and impenetrable, there was no way I was getting out on my own.

My belly rumbled again. The stone may have healed me, but I was still stuck in the oubliette with no water, and no food. I'd be dead in days.

The small collection of items on my belly from my bag was all I had. I touched the moringa seed and flipped it off me. It tinkled against the sides of the oubliette, settling into the rounded hollow below me. What good was a single seed to me?

I touched the hooked earring. Oubliettes blocked the power of an elemental, keeping them from escaping their punishment. So what good was an earring that would allow me to breathe under water? Useless, just like me.

There was nothing I could do to save myself. No connection to my power. No connection to my bond to Peta.

No way out.

"FUCK!" I screamed and slammed my fists into the oubliette over and over again until the skin broke and the bone ached. The hooked earring hung above my head, jammed into the man-made material. I grabbed at it, but the blood on my hands made it impossible to grip. The tip pierced my finger, drawing a scream out of me. Not pain, not really.

I could do nothing.

I was useless.

I slipped against the inside curve of my prison and fell. Panicked, I couldn't slow my breathing as I struggled to get hold of myself. The light from the stone illuminated my tiny space, showing me how tiny it truly was. How trapped I was.

Trembling, I forced myself to sit quietly and slow my breathing. There had to be a way out. I only needed to calm myself and find the solution.

I closed my eyes and wrapped my hands around the white stone. A faint buzz began again and tickled over my broken-up knuckles, and the flesh slowly knit itself together. But the light dimmed. I dropped the stone and it lay at my feet. My knuckles would heal. I wasn't sure I would be able to keep my sanity if I lost my only light source.

Time passed.

A steady drip of water woke me from the daze I'd fallen into. I blinked several times as I found myself staring up at the hooked earring. From it dripped a steady drizzle of water.

I tipped my head back and slid my mouth under

the water. Drop by drop, my thirst was quenched. So now it was a matter of starving to death.

Time passed.

Above my head a trickle of air wafted over my nose and I looked up. Apparently Blackbird hadn't sunk my oubliette as far down as I'd thought. It had small cuts in it to allow for airflow. The cramped cells were designed to hold someone for a day or two. Three at the most, for a severe punishment. I slid my fingers over the razor-thin openings, feeling the hint of rain on the tiny breeze. Sure enough, a chest-rattling boom of thunder clapped and the patter of rain began around my oubliette. Water dripped in through the openings until I sat in a puddle of dirty water. The rain stopped.

The water shrank away and left behind a tiny pile of sand.

I drank from the hook, which still kept up a steady dripping stream.

Time passed.

The moringa seed took root in the sand that had washed in, sprouted into three trunks and gave me a food source. I ate the leaves sparingly—enough to live. That was all I had. A part of me wanted to stop— to give up and die. But my dreams were full of those who searched for me. For Ash and Peta working together while Shazer and Cactus scoured the land from the sky. Of Bella's growing pregnancy, of the birth of her daughter. The first year of her child's life.

I wondered what Elle would do when she needed help; I knew it wasn't a matter of if she did, but when. Who would help the mouthy Tracker?

Time passed.

Still they looked for me. And so I hung on. I did stomach crunches, and awkward push-ups, miniature squats and stretches as best I could. I had to keep my strength up.

Time passed.

My anger at the mother goddess grew.

Time passed.

I was alone, my thoughts my only companion.

A most dangerous companion indeed.

CHAPTER 19

oices floated to me, on the edges of my dreams. Voices of those I loved, those who had loved me. They comforted me, soothing the edges of panic that reared its head from time to time.

"Peta, you're smelling things again."

"No, this time I'm sure I smell her. She's here, I know it."

I shifted, my body callused in strange places from lying hunched for an amount of time that had no meaning to me.

A soft snuffling, and the sound of dirt trickling down the edge of the oubliette, whispered through one of the cracks.

"Here, she's here! Barely under the surface."

The shifting of the oubliette around me stunned me. They'd found me. They hadn't given up.

And somehow, neither had I.

They pulled the oubliette up, the movement rolling me around.

"Peta, you know she won't be alive. Before I open this, tell me you understand. We do this to lay her to rest."

"You have no faith," she spat out, and I could imagine her back raised in a growing arch. "Do you love her?"

"Do not ask me that. She is—" His voice caught, and I pressed my hands against the door of the oubliette. I couldn't find my voice, couldn't find the words to assure them that I was alive.

I knocked on the plastic with my knuckles.

"Mother goddess," he said, and then the door was ripped open. I fell out and into his arms. Peta let out a shriek and pushed her way between Ash and me. I clung to her with one arm, and to him with the other.

He pushed my hair back from my face, his eyes wide with shock. "How, how could you have lasted this long?"

I blinked, swallowed and spoke the first words since the day I'd been put in the oubliette.

"How long?"

"Two years."

I shivered. "Tell me everything."

"I'll make camp, then . . . then I will tell you." He started a fire and I stood with only a slight tremble, still holding Peta to me. She purred at a rapid, frantic rate I understood because my heart beat in time with hers. "I knew you were alive, Lark. I knew it. Don't you do that to me again, Dirt Girl. I'll kill you myself."

I pressed my face to her body and breathed her in. "I don't plan on it."

I stretched my body, the kinks in my bones and muscles protesting the movement. Peta clung to my shoulder, butting her head into my cheek over and over again as she purred. A droplet of moisture hit my cheek and I turned. "Drooling?"

Her green eyes spilled over with tears and I regretted what I'd said. I took her from my shoulder and sat down with her, stretching out beside the fire. Ash strung a line over the fire and set a pot to boiling. The smell of oatmeal filled the air and my mouth filled with saliva. The thought of eating anything not a green plant made me weep with joy.

I curled Peta into my arms and ran a hand down her back over and over again. "Peta, I'm here."

Ash built the fire up until it blazed, the flames licking at the big black pot. Tasks done, he laid down behind me. His arms went around me and I clung to him, locking the moment in my mind. I would not forget this. That they were the ones to pull me out of the darkness of the oubliette.

"I'm afraid this is a dream, that I will wake up back in . . . there." My words were barely audible over the pop and crackle of the fire. Ash, he knew me though, and he spoke to distract me.

"Cassava rules the Rim, Lark. Raven is her second and Blackbird has gone missing. Your father has never been found. Bella is in exile in the Deep, but her messages are getting frantic. She has been gone too long from the Rim, she needs to come home soon or risk going mad." He paused and his hands stroked up and down my arms. "Cactus and Shazer will be here soon, that horse will have picked up on your bond now that you are out."

"Raven is Blackbird," I said. "And Cassava may rule the Rim right now, but not for much longer." I made a move to sit up and he tugged me back down.

"You need to gain your strength, Lark, before you go after them."

Peta sniffed. "You see, he is the one for you. He knows enough to not try and talk you out of this."

I turned my head so I could look into Ash's eyes. "I do not see this ending well."

He kissed me gently. "I am with you, Lark. From now until whatever the end holds for us."

The warmth from Peta, Ash and the fire lulled me into a fog. Despite the fact that I'd been locked up for two years, I was exhausted. I fell asleep, truly warm in both body and spirit.

Child, welcome home.

I was on my feet in an instant, rage burning hotter than the fire at my back. "You miserable whore! You knew I was locked away and you left me when I needed you most!" My voice cracked, but not with tears.

Ash and Peta stared up at me, their eyes wide. My whole body shook and the earth shook around us, trembling as though it too were afraid of me. Or maybe it felt my anger and agreed with me. Peta shifted into her leopard form and slunk toward my feet.

"Lark, calm yourself. Please."

"No. The mother goddess left me in there to rot as much as Cassava and Raven." I paced in front of the fire. A slow rolling fog misted over the ground, curling up my legs.

I spun and stared into the dark jungle. "You dare show yourself to me now? NOW?"

Distantly, I knew I was out of control. That some little piece of madness had claimed me.

The mother goddess, though, was no fool. In the guise of my mother, she ghosted toward us. "Child, I could not find you any more than Ash or Peta. That is the power of the oubliette. It blocks all from knowing it."

"You saw them put me in. You had to know." I strode toward her, not caring that she was the mother goddess, or that she looked like my mother with her straight white blonde hair and blue eyes. Those eyes flashed.

"You are not my only charge, Larkspur. Others have need of me."

"You said I was your chosen one, and so you'd leave me to fight for my life." All the questions I'd pondered while hidden from the world bubbled up. "Did you feel me dying?"

Her eyes flicked away, so fast I almost missed it. I shoved her hard enough to send her onto her ass in a most un-goddess like sprawl. She gaped up at me, shock written in every line of her face. "How dare you?"

Behind me, Ash let out a moan. "Don't do this, Lark. Please."

Peta stepped beside me, pressing her body tightly to mine. "You felt her dying and you left her to die. Didn't you?"

I dropped a hand to Peta and tears sprang to my eyes. At least there was one I could count on. Blinking, I stared at the mother goddess. "Do you wish my death then? Is that what this is? Some twisted way to see me dead? Perhaps Cassava is the one you wanted on the throne all along."

My words didn't make sense, not even to me. But they were every fear I'd fought for the last two years. Every doubt, every insecurity, every realization and every hope.

The mother goddess folded her legs under her and spread her pale blue gown around her as though she were the center of a flower. "Sit, Larkspur. Sit."

I wanted to take my spear and run her through, but instead I sat and folded my legs. Peta lay to my right, but the tension in her body told me everything. She didn't trust the mother goddess either.

Ash stepped up behind me, but didn't sit. "I will stand with you, Lark. Even against her."

I swallowed hard past the lump that grew in my throat. "No. This . . . this is between her and me."

I tapped my fingers on my knee.

Peta let out a soft growl. "Griffin calls her Viv."

The mother goddess jerked. "That is fine. Call me

Viv." I knew without her saying so that Viv was short for something else. Not that it mattered. Nothing mattered except this moment.

"Well, Viv. What do you want to tell me?"

She closed her eyes and her image shifted to that of a woman I'd met in my testing. Her long brown hair was the color of mineral-rich soil, and her eyes spun with all the colors found in nature. "You have only met one side of me, Lark. There are two sides to nature, and as such, there are two sides to my personality. I cannot dictate when one is in charge."

I leaned back, pressing my body against Ash's legs. "Two."

"Yes. As there is beauty and light in this world, so is there darkness and death. I cannot tell you what the dark side of me is up to. She is completely blocked from me."

"What does it matter that you have two sides?" Ash asked.

"Because without realizing it, she is playing Blackbird and me against one another. Aren't you?" The understanding came hard and fast.

She tipped her head and a tear fell.

"I believe so. I can only guess, because I have no memory of what I do when the darkness takes me. I do what I can to hold up the precepts of light—"

"Cut the goose shit," I snapped. "You are the mother goddess. You may have light and dark, we all do. But I will not sit here and listen to you tell me this isn't your fault. Griffin said it. You're meddling where you shouldn't be."

Her eyes narrowed. "Be careful, Larkspur. A chosen one can fall as easily as she can be raised up."

I stood and stared down at her, my fists clenched at my sides. I had a plan, I just didn't know how smart it was. "Perhaps then I'd be better off to side with your darker half. Perhaps she would see the value in me, the worth I hold."

Viv's eyes widened with understanding a split second before they rolled back. She tipped her head back and laughed, a long, low laugh that sent a chill racing up and down my spine.

"Oh, I like you more and more, little Lark." Her head snapped forward and as she stood, her hair darkened to a blue-black as her eyes lightened. A haunting silver blinked back at me. "You wanted to speak to me."

"You are working with Cassava and Blackbird."

"You mean Raven?"

"No. My brother is dead to me. I mean Blackbird."

Her lips twitched. "Fine. Yes, they are my chosen ones. Chaos, Lark. That is all the world understands. And even while you try to patch up the messes I've created, as you try to put better leaders into the families, you cause chaos. I think you are right. I think you would be better off with me at your back. I would have saved you."

I took a step back, and Peta and Ash moved with me. "Then why didn't you come to save Blackbird? I had him in my hands, his life was draining."

Her eyes narrowed. "How could we save our two chosen ones at the same time?"

Without moving, I reached out with my connection to the earth, the flood of strength buoying me up. The mother goddess raised an eyebrow. "You wish to fight me?"

"No." I raised my left hand and pointed with two fingers at the oubliette. Vines snaked out from the jungle, forking like snake tongues. They grabbed at the opening of the oubliette and wrenched it apart with a violent tear. "Stay away from me. Both of you. I will chose my path from now on."

With a second flick of my hand I sent the vines to her and scooped her up. She laughed. "You think to hurt me?"

I raised an eyebrow. "Ever hear of a slingshot?"

Her eyes widened and she let out a screech as I pulled the vines toward me, then sent them flinging away at a speed my eyes couldn't follow.

"I can't believe you flung the mother goddess through the jungle." Ash put a hand on my arm, turning me to him. "Remind me never to get on your bad side." He smiled and I burst into tears. He caught me against his chest, murmuring into my hair over and over. "Easy, Lark. Easy."

A thump of dirt spun us around and I stared up into the wingspan of the only Pegasus in the world. Shazer stuffed his nose into my chest and breathed me in. "It's about fucking time you showed up."

I held his face for a moment and kissed his nose. "I missed you too." He snorted, but I was already looking past him to the man who slid off his back. Cactus had aged in the two years I'd been gone. His body was harder, his face no longer open as it had been.

Yet in the glimmer of his green eyes, I still saw the boy who'd stolen my heart while we'd played in the forest.

"Cactus."

He caught me up in his arms and I clung to him. Ash put a hand on my back, Peta pressed against my leg, and Shazer hooked his neck around us.

I clung to them all, knowing they would help me fight the darkness that had found me in the oubliette. They had to.

Because without them, I had no doubt I would lose my mind.

CHAPTER 20

The fire crackled hot as the others slept. But I could not close my eyes to the sky above me, the view of the stars and the feel of the earth below me. Touching my power was like opening a conduit I'd never understood.

It was strength and freedom. It was my life.

I stood and crept away from the fire, leaving Peta curled with Ash and Cactus asleep only a few feet from where they lay.

"Sneaking away?" Shazer asked as I reached the edge of the tight clearing. I reached up and ran a hand over his back.

"No."

He was quiet a moment, and the night air lay heavy on my shoulders. Or maybe that was the responsibilities that crashed down around me the second I'd stepped out of the oubliette.

"You know, I never wanted to be tied to an elemental. You're all bastards." He pawed at the earth with a front hoof. "Yet here I am tied to you."

"Still? I thought you came with Cactus out of friendship." I kept my hand on his back, taking comfort in his nearness.

"No. The mother goddess made it clear I am to fly with you until she dictates."

So. He was doing what he had to, too.

We weren't close like Peta and I. Maybe that was why I could open up to him. There was no emotional bond, no worry I'd freak him out.

"I've always held back, Shazer. Always. Fear, for the most part. But also the expectations of being a good girl. Of being what my father wants. Of what is expected of me."

"We all have that moment." He shook his head. "Question is . . . what are you going to do about it?"

"Subtle," I said.

"I'm all about the finer points of dialogue."

I looked into the night sky, as if the answers would be written there, clear for me to see. Variables spun out—Bella, my father, Blackbird, and Cassava. But there were only so many things I could do. And only a few of them were essential.

"Cassava needs to die and my father needs to name his heir. Then I can be free of this."

"Free? Would you not go back to your home?"

I shook my head. Aria's words from so long ago

echoed in my heart. "The Rim is not my home. My home is here, with you and Peta. With Ash and Cactus. That is where I bloom."

He butted me lightly. "Then you have your answer. I will fly you to wherever you wish. Will it be the Eyrie then, to find a trace of your father? Or to the Rim to confront Cassava?"

I closed my eyes and for a moment I felt as though the oubliette was around me. I reached out and grabbed his mane, leaning into him, breathing the scent of sweet grass and horse sweat into my lungs, allowing it to center me. There was a tug on my soul, like a thread tied to me that I could not deny.

I lifted my head and stared into the jungle. I recognized the touch of her ability as she Tracked me.

A part of me knew I shouldn't have been surprised. I'd sensed she would need me before I was stuffed away from the world.

I faced the section of the jungle she approached from. Shazer lowered his head over my shoulder.

"What is it?"

"An old friend calling in a favor, I think," I said. Relief flowed through me. I did not have to decide between my father and Cassava. Whatever help Elle needed I would give her, and hopefully it would take me far from my own problems.

The bushes parted and there she was, her dark hair longer than before, the swirling eyes marking her as a Tracker the same. Her mouth also the same.

"It's about bloody fucking time you showed up

on the radar again," she gasped as she pushed her way through the foliage to me.

My jaw dropped when the firelight touched her. Her belly was swollen, huge with child, but the rest of her was thin, as though food had been a tough thing to find.

Where was the vibrant Tracker I'd first met? What had happened to her in the two years I'd been gone?

"Yeah, I got fat since I saw you last." She grinned, but it was weak. "I've been searching for you the last six months. I knew you weren't dead. Where the fuck have you been hiding?"

"Oubliette," I said. "Someone tried to kill me."

"Looks like we have that in common." She winced and touched her belly. I took her arm and helped her to the fire. Ash was awake, Peta still passed out in the crook of his lap. In the time I'd been away, they'd clearly drawn close.

Elle raised her eyebrows at me. "Two men? Damn, I need lessons. I tried to handle two, almost killed me." Her eyes filled with tears. It was only then I realized she was missing something very much attached to her.

"Where's Bram?" I softened my voice, already knowing the answer would not be good.

"Demons. They've been on our asses the last year. I don't know why, but they've decided I'd make a good kill. He . . . got in the way." Her lips trembled. "You were right, Lark. I can't fucking well do this on my own. I need your help."

Cassava and my father waited for me. My family

waited for me to save them from Cassava. The only one I cared about was Bella, and for the time being she was safe.

"Ash, go to Bella. Get her ready to come home." I didn't look at him. "Cactus, go to the Eyrie and wait for me."

Neither man said anything. I didn't know if they were letting me boss them around, or if they truly trusted me. Or if they were ignoring me. I wanted to believe they trusted me.

Peta let out a pitiful mew. "What about me?"

I scooped her up. "Do you really need to ask, cat? You are with me. You and the horse are mine through and through."

Shazer snorted and fluttered his wings. "I am no horse."

"Manner of speaking." I paused and looked at Elle. "You want me to kill the demons?"

"No, only a Slayer can do that. I want you to protect my daughter when she is born. Put her somewhere the demons won't find her. You can do that, right?"

A dark chill swept through the jungle, dampening the flames and casting an eerie shadow on her face. "Yes, I can do that. But what of you?"

"I will draw them away. I've kept far enough from the nasty shits that they don't know I'm with child. As long as we can keep it that way, the fuckers won't even know she exists."

Cactus cleared his throat. "Lark, your family needs you. You don't have time for this."

I swung my gaze to him, anger making my words

harsh. "My family thinks I'm dead. The only one who needs me is Bella, and I am sending her the man I love to watch over her. Is that not enough?"

He blanched and his jaw ticked. I turned from him, unable to be kind in that moment. "I will no longer explain myself or my actions. I will do what I feel is right. Elle needs me. That is all there is to this."

Cactus jerked to his feet and stomped away into the jungle. Ash wisely said nothing. I stood and helped Elle up. Her hands trembled in mine. "The baby will be here soon. Fuck, Bram left at a rather shitty time." She choked on the words and then broke down. I caught her in my arms, and ran a hand over her head.

"Hush. Your tears won't help you. Trust me on that."

She laughed, but it was a bitter sound, one that resonated in me. "Fuck. You got that right."

She jerked forward and let out a low moan. "Lark, I think . . . the baby is coming sooner than I thought. Eager little monster. I was not planning on this. I'm not due for another few weeks."

I helped her back to the ground as Ash worked to get the fire hotter, and boiled water. "Peta, are there any villages close by?"

"Yes." She bobbed her head. "About three miles to the south."

"Get Cactus and go. See if there is a midwife or wise woman."

I didn't look to see if she did as I asked. I didn't need to. Elle was on her knees panting. "I don't think it's supposed to happen this fast."

her daughter. Around us I felt the twist in the air, the feel of the earth, the calls of the birds and animals. The peace was temporary and soon there would be nothing left.

On the fifth day of my release from the oubliette came the shifting of my world yet again.

lle lifted her head as she finished feeding Rylee. From where I stood, her eyes swirled like whirlpools of color. She Tracked someone.

She swaddled the baby. "Lark, hold her for me."

Before I had a chance to protest, she thrust the child into my arms. I didn't want to hold her. Didn't want to feel the softness of the slowly breathing bundle in my arms and want it for myself.

Elle bent and picked up her sword. "Lark, it's time for you to go. Take her and go."

"What?" I spat the word out as I stood there holding the baby like an idiot. Elle looked at me her swirling eyes serious . . . and full of tears.

"Take her, Lark. Make sure she's safe. If I ever can,

I'll find her. You know that. The demons have found me."

I tapped into the earth and felt the changes there, the shifting of light and dark. I couldn't be sure Elle was right, but the feeling fit. I took two strides and wrapped an arm around her, holding her to me for a breath. A moment that seemed to go on, stretching into the uncertain future.

"Be safe, Elle. I will make sure she makes it, that she survives no matter what I have to do. Even if she hates me," I whispered.

"I know," she whispered back. "That's why it could only be you to protect her. I knew you were special when I met you, but I didn't want to believe it."

I stepped away and mounted Shazer, clutching the baby to me. Ash and Peta leapt up behind me and we launched into the air.

We rose up, Shazer's wings taking us above the trees in a matter of seconds. I strained to see Elle through the thick canopy.

A shout echoed up to us, then a roar of voices that seemed to sweep in from every part of the jungle. I twitched my heels and rested a hand on Shazer.

"We can't go back, not with the baby," Ash said.

I held my hand out, toward our camp. "I can buy her time."

Peta dug her claws into my leg. "Lark. The demons are no fools. They will know you helped her. They will come looking for you. And then they will find the babe."

I tipped my head back in an attempt to breathe

past the lump in my throat. Pain and grief warred with a rage I struggled to control. "She . . . she did not deserve to die."

"You don't know she's dead," Ash said, but his voice was hesitant.

Shazer banked to one side. I clutched the baby close to me and made myself look at her. Thick, dark auburn hair and eyes that were the pale gray of most human children. Yet in them was a spark of gold, chocolate and emerald. The spark of colors that would someday lead her down the same path as her mother. I stroked a finger down her cheek. "Sleep, wee one."

Spirit flickered through me, scaring me until the baby closed her eyes, yawned, fell asleep, and my element retreated.

Below us, Shazer gave a full-body shake. "Where to?"

I made a snap decision. "The Deep."

We flew without trouble all the way to the hidden island. The early morning sun peeked over the edge of the horizon when we landed on the sandy beaches at the edge of the Deep, home of the Undines.

"Are you sure, Lark?" Ash slid from Shazer's back and stared up at me from the ground. I gave him a smile that wobbled at the edges.

"Keep Bella safe. Please. I don't trust anyone else to this." I'd sent Blossom to watch over Bella two years ago, but I had no idea if she'd followed through. If Cassava had come back and taken over, I had no doubt she would have recalled all her guards and Enders.

I bent at the waist and kissed Ash. "Give her

my love. Tell her . . . tell her we'll make this right somehow."

He winked. "Maybe she can come with us for that pedicure."

The laugh that escaped me surprised me. "Yes. It's a deal."

I dug my heels into Shazer and he leapt into the sky with a buck that had Peta gripping my thighs with her claws.

"Stupid horse!" she shrieked, which only made him whinny with laughter.

"Dumb-ass cat!"

The baby woke and I fed her the only bottle I had, the only milk Elle had sent with us. A single bottle was not enough to take us far. "Head to the east coast. We'll stop when I can't console her."

Shazer stretched out. "I have no desire to listen to her scream."

"Nor do I," I said, running my finger down the little girl's face and soothing her back to sleep.

Three hours ticked by and she woke, her hungry cries nothing I could console.

We circled an area of brick houses and tall fences. Midday with the sun high was not the time to be strutting about the human world. But there was no choice. I had to put the girl somewhere safe.

We landed in a green space with the same strange manicured grass and perfectly kept flowers and trees that did not produce anything we'd seen the last time we'd stepped into the human world. I leapt from Shazer's back. "Wait here."

Peta stretched and bounded out ahead of me. I hurried after her, and my walking soothed the baby to a soft whimper. There was no time to be picky about where she went.

"Peta, can I cover her with Spirit? Make her invisible to the supernatural world?"

Peta came to a full stop and craned her head around. "I suppose it would be possible. But it would wear off after a time, I would think."

"How long?"

Her eyes went thoughtful. I jiggled the baby to keep her from fussing. "Peta, think faster."

"Depending on how much you put into it, you might be able to keep her covered for a decade. Maybe longer."

"It will have to be enough." Sweat popped out on my forehead as I thought about what I was about to attempt. Using Spirit had not gone well for me in the past.

Licking my lips, I held the baby close to me and called Spirit up. "Protect her from harm, from those who would hurt her for as long as possible."

A flickering answer beckoned from the baby's Spirit. From what made her mother a Tracker, from what would make the babe a Tracker one day. Spirit flowed through me like a gentle creek curling around us both, tying us together. I went to my knees as my energy was pulled from me. I let it go, knowing it would protect her. Keep her safe.

And even if Elle hadn't asked me, I would have done it. There was something about the child I couldn't quite put my finger on . . . but I knew she was special. The daughter of a Slayer, the daughter of a Tracker, a joining of two powerful blood lines. I opened my eyes and stared into her face. She lifted a hand and touched my nose.

"You . . . I think are going to need all the help you can get, my little friend," I whispered to her.

Peta butted her head against my thigh. "Over there. Two women talking about not being able to have babies."

The scene was too perfect to not have fate's hand in it.

I lifted my head to see a slender young woman with long blonde hair almost as pale as my own. Tears hovered in her eyes as she pressed a hand to her belly and shook her head.

I felt a pull toward her and listened to my instincts. "Peta, we will come back for her. To check on her." I didn't have to say why. We both knew Elle wasn't coming for her daughter. Not in this life.

Peta bobbed her head in agreement. "Of course we will." As though there was no other possible solution.

I strode up to the woman. Her friend had left and she was alone on the bench. "You wish to have a child?"

Her head jerked up. I stared down at her tear-stained face. "What?"

I didn't wait for her to say anything else, just placed the baby into her arms. "She needs a mother. Take her."

The woman's mouth dropped open as I backed away. "You need her too."

She clutched the baby to her. "How . . . why?"

"Because sometimes . . . things have to happen. Good and bad. This is one of the good things. Love her. Protect her. Teach her. Be her mother."

I kept backing away, a part of me feeling as though I'd abandoned the little one.

"Does she have a name?"

Smiling, I nodded. "Her name is Rylee. A warrior's name for a warrior's heart."

The world seemed to still around us, as though the universe had paused to take note of that exact moment. I knew it for what it was; a fork in the road, one I would look back on and wonder if I made the right choice.

I should have been terrified.

Peta and I spun at the same time and ran back the way we'd come.

"She will love her," Peta said. "I saw it in her eyes."

"If she doesn't, it won't matter. We'll be back and if I have to . . . I will raise her myself." The words popped out of me and I realized I meant them.

I would take the girl into my care if the woman proved to be false.

Perhaps the most concerning thing was I almost hoped that would be the case.

CHAPTER 22

The Eyrie was as we'd left it. Chilled by the wind, hidden by clouds and ruled by Queen Aria.

"Where are we landing?" Shazer banked to the right, circling the Eyrie, moving with the air current.

"The throne room." I'd barely said the words and he dropped, tucking his wings and swirling through the clouds in a looping spiral. I clutched his body with my legs, and Peta sank her claws into me. Her hair fluffed up around her body and her green eyes watered.

"I hate this horse. I regret suggesting him." The words were hard, but there was no heat in them.

He laughed and snapped his wings out wide. They caught us only a few feet from the floor of the throne room. With a delicate prance he landed, snorting and blowing.

I slid from his back. By the scene in front of us, we'd interrupted something rather important. There was a row of four women on their knees at the feet of the queen. Her blind eyes came up and somehow seemed to meet mine. To the left of me, Cactus stood between two Sylphs. He gave me the slightest of nods.

"Ah, Larkspur. You made it in time, I see." Aria laughed softly. "I had hoped you would come."

I strode forward, snapping my spear together at my side. "I'm here for my father. Nothing more, nothing less."

Her eyebrows rose. "Child, I told you the truth. He is not here. Both then, and now."

She did speak the truth; I could feel it in her words. I pointed my spear at her and the Sylphs around us shifted. Enders dressed in their white leathers ghosted forward, their long sharpened staffs pointed at me. I should have cared, should have worried.

Yet I felt no fear.

"I know you speak truly. That does not make you right." I lowered my spear, pressed the butt of it into the ground at my feet.

She clapped her hands together once. "Enders, ease off. She means me no harm. Where have you been, Lark? Two years you were missing, everyone thought you dead. Yet now you are here, back searching for your beloved father."

I wanted to rage at her that he was anything but beloved. That he was needed only to fulfill his duty and name a proper heir. But those words would not form.

"An oubliette held me."

A solid gasp went up through the room.

Aria leaned back. "How in the world did you survive?"

Bands of fear tightened over my chest at the mere thought of my prison. "I am here for my father. Either you will allow me to search for him, or I will tear your home apart. It is your choice."

Beside me, Peta sucked in a tiny breath. Surprise filtered through the bond between us. From behind us, Shazer stomped a foot on the tile. "I will catch you if need be, Lark."

The four women on their knees in front of the queen watched us with wide eyes. Except for one. She was on the far left and she stood. "I will not stand for this. I am the heir to the throne. Get back to the ceremony, Mother."

"Noma, calm yourself, my daughter." Aria spoke with a calm tone that brooked no argument.

"Old woman, you have been on the throne too long," Noma snapped, her hand lifting as she turned her back on me. A flash of sapphire blue danced over her fingers and up her arms.

I had no doubt about what I saw. Noma could call water to her aid through the use of the sapphire stone. The fifth and final gem of the elemental world; she carried the Undines' sapphire. She raced up the stairs to her mother's side.

Those thoughts flashed through my mind in less than a single beat of my heart. I connected to the earth and the power rushed into me, filling me. I pushed off the ground in a leap and the stone beneath me buckled, but it didn't slow me. I shot through the air toward Noma who had climbed to her mother and wrapped her hands around her neck. Water surrounded the queen's mouth and nose in a bubble. Too thin perhaps for anyone else to see; but it didn't matter.

I thrust my spear down as I sailed through the air, the blade aimed at the juncture of Noma's neck and head. A perfect kill shot, one she wouldn't even feel, it would happen so fast.

But a snap of wind caught me midair and sent me tumbling sideways into the mountain. The wind was knocked out of me and for a split second I thought it was a Sylph taking my air. I gasped in a breath and used it not for myself. "She is killing your queen!" I screamed.

White Enders leather filled my vision. "Then our queen should not have called her forward as a potential heir."

I blinked up at Samara. She'd changed in the two years. Her eyes were hard, and there was a scar across her chin, jagged and white with age. "She's using water to kill her. Not air."

Samara spun. From where I sat, I threw my spear, drawing from the mountain. The spear shot from my hands and slammed into Noma's lower back. Hardly a clean death, but she jerked away from her mother, a cry escaping her as she fell to the ground.

Aria stumbled backward, and the sound of water splashing to the floor seemed to fill the throne room. "Take her," Aria gasped out.

The Enders were on Noma in a flash. Three pointed spears fell on her at the same time. Boreas, the queen's favored Ender, and two others.

Aria wavered to her feet. Boreas went to her side and helped her stand. "Thank you—"

"My queen, there is no need," he murmured with a smug-ass smile on his lips.

She slapped him, hard enough to leave an imprint on his face. "You would have let her kill me. It was Larkspur who stopped her."

Boreas's face went white; with anger or shock, I wasn't sure.

Aria drew in a breath, bent and took something from Noma's body. "Terraling, you know what this is?" She held it out to me, a stone of blue that swam as though it held the ocean within it.

"Yes."

"Take it to Finley. The girl will need it." Aria threw it to me. I lifted my hand to catch the stone, but my fingers never touched it.

A gust of wind caught the jewel and sent it skittering across the floor at Samara's feet. She bent and picked it up, but that wasn't what drew my attention. From behind her, a figure stepped out of the shadows. The one person I would gladly kill, and whose grave I would gladly dance on. The one who'd stolen my family from me.

"Cassava." I breathed out her name.

"Larkspur, so lovely of you to come. So *predictable.* He would not have done the same for you, I have made sure of it." She reached behind her, grabbed someone and threw him forward.

My father sprawled on his belly, his eyes glazed over as if he were drugged with poppy seeds.

Peta stalked in front of me, her entire body fluffing up as her hair stood on end. "This is the bitch that hurt you. I will tear her throat out."

"No," I said. "She is mine, Peta. Mine alone."

I tore my eyes from my father and looked at Cassava. "I am here, then. You've tried to kill me how many times, yet here I stand." I spread my hands wide. "Perhaps now you want to see if you are stronger than me?"

She grinned. "You don't wonder why I would meet you here?"

Aria answered her. "It has been a long time since elementals openly fought with their power, Cassava. Do not do this."

I knew what Aria meant. Terralings truly battling would cause massive destruction. And the Eyrie would suffer for it.

Cassava sneered at her. "Old woman, will you or your people stop us? Or will you hold to the rules the mother goddess handed down that have slowly strangled our people?"

Aria stiffened. "We will not interfere. That is our way." The Sylphs began to back away.

Cassava pulled a stone from around her neck. The emerald I'd given Bella. The emerald that would give the wearer power over the earth, or in the case of one who already had that connection, would boost it immensely.

Worm shit and green sticks, this was not a good turn.

The reality of what I was seeing set in. If Cassava had the emerald, what had happened to Bella?

It took everything I had not to run forward in a blind rage. "What did you do to her?"

"What makes you think I would hurt my oldest daughter?" Her sweetly laced words were venomous to my ears.

"I think you would destroy anyone who opposed you, even those to whom you gave life. You destroyed Raven."

"You assume she didn't simply hand this lovely gem to me. And Raven and I have a lovely relationship," Cassava countered, her eyes glittering with malice as she licked her lips.

My father lifted himself up to his elbows, his eyes clearing a little. "Bella traded her life and the life of her child for the emerald, Lark."

Cassava stepped up beside him, and kicked him in the side. He grunted, though I doubted her impact was all that hard. More likely he was already hurt. After two years in her care, he probably had his share of injuries.

Behind us, Aria whispered, "This will not go well for my Sylphs."

I had eyes only for Cassava. "We are done with these games then, bitch. It is time you pay for your crimes."

"I agree, at least on being done with the games. You have been in my way since the beginning. I regret not killing you then."

I circled her, drawing the power of the earth to me until I fairly hummed with it. Her eyes flickered and the madness I'd seen in my father was reflected there. Mad. She was out of her mind from using Spirit the way she had; I knew it.

Cassava laughed. "Fool, just like your father. He thought he was strong enough to keep me in line. See him now as he grovels at my feet."

Peta snarled and bared her teeth. "I am here, Lark. We do this together."

She was right. Peta could stand with me, she was a part of me. Cactus made a move and I swung my spear to block him. "No. No matter what happens, do not step in."

"Lark, do not—"

The ground under him bucked, and sent him flying across the throne room.

I whipped my spear around and pointed it at Cassava. She lifted her hands over her head in mock surrender, a smile on her lips. "Little Larkspur. I do believe it is time for you to be with your mother."

Her words rang in my ears. With my mother. But not with Bramley? Her smile widened. "That's right, half-breed. He lives. But not if you do not bow to me."

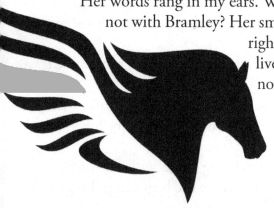

CHAPTER 23

ies, she had to be lying. But it was Aria who snapped me out of the fog of Cassava's words. "She will say anything to stay your hand, child of the earth. She knows you rival her power. Even while she holds the emerald."

My training took over, my instincts and anger driving me. I leapt forward, as I held the spear over my head, snapping it down in a hard thrust toward Cassava's heart.

She screamed, her face contorting as she flung a hand toward me. The lines of power were a brilliant, pulsing green as they wove around her arms and torso. I knew what she was going to do, but in midair I could not avoid the blow. A chunk of the mountain flew toward me, and slammed into my side. As it hit,

I pulled the molecules of the rock apart, breaking it down into a fine dust and circumventing the full power of the impact.

Cassava's eyes widened as I landed right in front of her, the powdered earth floating down around us. No more words. I was done talking.

I lunged at her, driving my spear toward her stomach. She spun backward and flicked her hands at the ground beneath me. Damn, she was fast. The other elementals I faced were slower in how they used their power. They called it up, I saw the intent in the power lines, and then I avoided what they tossed at me.

With Cassava, there was almost no time between her calling the power and what she threw at me. I didn't know if it was the emerald or something else, and it didn't matter.

The ground lurched up beneath me and I fought to smooth it out. Every step I took toward her, she diverted me. I finally dropped my spear. This was not going to be a fight where it would help me.

"Giving up?"

"Just getting started."

We threw our power at one another, pushing back and forth, neither of us truly giving way. The balance between us was too close for either of us to truly get the upper hand. Sweat slid down my face and my legs shook as though I'd been running for miles.

The Eyrie broke apart piece by piece, walls and structures toppling as we tore and hurled the world around us.

Cassava's hand wavered over her opposite arm, but she dropped it and flicked her fingers at me. The tile at my feet broke and the mountain seemed to reach up and take hold of my feet, pinning me in place.

I pushed the rock away from me, and stumbled to the side, ending up next to my father.

"Lark. The Namib Sand Sea," Peta yelled.

She was right, I could use the same tactic here as I'd done on the sand. But I had to get my friends out of the way. "Shazer, fly!" I yelled. The horse gave a grunt followed by the sound of rushing wings.

Cassava laughed. "Still trying to save your friends? I'm going to hunt them down and kill them all, Lark. As soon as you're dead."

I moved to my father's side and pressed my hands against the tile. I broke it apart so I could touch the ground underneath and truly feel the mountain. Within the Wretched Peaks lived intangible pathways that called to me; the elemental who'd created the Eyrie left them behind. I felt them under my hands, under my skin, and in my soul.

Like aqueducts brought water from the rivers, the energy channels that created the mountain and Eyrie flowed to me, and allowed me access to more power than I could ever reach on my own. The ground sucked my hands down in a welcoming embrace.

I felt the mountain sigh, as in relief. *It is time.*

Cassava laughed again, throwing her head back. "You need to touch the earth still to call it up? Goddess, you are weak."

"Peta, Cactus. Stick close."

I didn't have to ask them twice. Peta was at my side in a flash and Cactus was right behind her, crouching with me. The mountain . . . I could feel it as though it were a living creature, breathing slowly. Exactly as my first visit had awakened me to the added power within this part of the earth, again I could feel it waiting for me to call on it.

Cassava's laughter stopped as suddenly as it started. The ground below us sucked Peta, Cactus, and me down so we were trapped up to my waist and Peta's belly.

Vines sprouted between the remaining tiles and wrapped around all three of us, binding us as tightly as any chain. They squeezed until I could barely breathe, but I kept following the paths mountain showed me. Deeper and deeper I reached, Spirit and Earth calling to me in tandem as I sought out what the mountain strove to show me.

"Lark, tell me you've got this," Cactus wheezed out.

"Of course she does," Peta snapped back.

Of course I did . . . the pathways all lit up inside my head and I saw how the two powers interconnected. How Spirit boosted Earth, how the mountain had come alive with so much Spirit poured into it.

The entity welcomed me home. The mountain stirred under us and I called it up, beckoned it to me. The world shook and I closed my eyes. In my mind I saw the earth swallow Cassava, and crush her beneath the mountain, saw the weight of the rocks and the earth end her life.

A roar filled my ears as all around us the ground swelled and ripped apart.

Screams rent the air. Power ripped through me,

and the mountain bellowed, as if a large animal was released from a thousand-year cage.

"Hang on!" I yelled as the ground beneath us dropped. We floated as if we fell for ages. I didn't let go of the power. I funneled it through the mountain. Everything I had, I gave. I opened myself like never before and the mountain crashed around us.

Child, you go too far. This was not what I wanted. The mother goddess spoke to me, her words hard.

"Then you should have let Cassava kill me." I spat the words out. Or I think I did. It was hard to tell with the way the world twisted in on itself. The sounds of elementals crying out, the feel of the mountain turning itself inside out at my command.

The power . . . for all that was holy, it felt as though nothing could stop me. I reached for it with all the strength I had in me. I touched the mountains around us and felt them wake.

Yes, this was the way it should be. To start fresh, wipe out those who used them wrongly. To clean away the interlopers.

Those were not my thoughts.

The mountains spoke through me. Wipe them out, those who see us as nothing. They see us as less because we are of the earth and not the far-reaching skies. I give them life, I give them shelter, I protect them. They do not care. They do not thank me.

Rocks slammed into the ground around us, but none touched my skin. I forced my eyes open, forced myself to truly see what carnage was happening.

The mountain had sunk, dropping out from under

us so we rested in a deep crater. As though a falling rock from the sky had annihilated it.

People were yelling. Peta and Cactus were yelling, but I didn't hear them. I saw their mouths moving, but there was no sound. Cactus slapped me—hard enough to snap my head around. "Stop it, Lark! She's dead, you have to stop this, you're going to kill us all!"

His words hit me harder than his hand. I let go of the power and it receded, slowly, reluctantly. My entire body hummed with energy. Unlike other times, I had not lost anything in using that amount of the earth's power. Instead, it filled me like a cup that overflowed.

My joy was short-lived. Peta trembled beside me, her ears pinned to her head. My father was on his side, his eyes closed, his words thick with the fog of whatever drug Cassava had given him. "Lark . . . you . . . you killed them all."

I spun. "No, I couldn't have."

Cactus ran from my side to where a pile of rubble shifted. He threw the rocks aside, green lines running down his arms as he tapped into the earth and moved the stones. I didn't waste time asking more questions. I fell in beside him, digging out the Sylphs who'd not fled when the fight started. The power in me was different now, normal. As if I were the one controlling it and not the other way around.

Body after body we pulled out, none alive. Cassava was nowhere.

"I saw her go under," Cactus said, as though reading my mind. "She's gone, Lark."

His words should have made me feel better. But nothing could ease the horror flowing through me.

No matter how much rage I carried, this was not what I'd wanted.

I had done the unspeakable, and whatever punishment came to me I would willingly take. Most likely death, and a part of me welcomed the thought of crossing the Veil. My father was safe, and I knew Cactus could get him home. Cassava was dead and the world had no need of me.

Around us, the Sylphs who had fled to the air dropped to the ground. Peta stayed distant from me, as did Cactus. As though they were afraid of me. I refused to consider that I'd truly given them reason to fear me.

We dug for hours until there was nothing left but to face the truth. On my own, I had wiped out nearly half the population of Sylphs. Their bodies lay in front of me broken and twisted by the mountain they had called their home.

Even if their home had hated them.

The Sylphs left stared at me as though I were a monster. And I was. I knew it.

I stumbled away from the mass grave, shaking so hard I could barely keep my feet under me. I fell to my knees and vomited until I had nothing left but dry heaves, and even then my body would not let me stop. This was not happening. This was not happening.

Peta stuck her nose into my face. "Lark."

"Do you not fear me?" I reared back from her, anger, pain and guilt tangling inside my heart. "Do you not want to run from me? Do you not think I will kill you too?"

She looked to the Sylphs identifying those who'd been killed. "You're being selfish, Lark. People have died, lost their lives, and all you are worried about is how you are perceived? I thought you were better than that."

Breathing hard, I stepped back from her. "Selfish?"

"Cat, you are being too hard on her."

We both turned to see the queen walk carefully over the rubble toward us. My throat tightened. "I did not mean to tear down your home, or kill your people. I . . ."

I knew what was coming. She would ask for my surrender and I would give it.

"Those who died," she swept her hand back toward the bodies laid out, "you did not hear them? They cheered for Cassava. They were no longer my Sylphs. You are the bringer of change, child of Earth and Spirit. There are times for change to happen. The slate must be wiped clean."

I wasn't sure I liked the way her words echoed that of the mountain entity.

Aria put a hand to her throat. "For change, you need one who is brave enough to stand the brunt of death. That one . . . is you." She held a hand out to my face and brushed it down my cheek. Her touch undid my control and the tears I'd held at bay since I'd been pulled from the oubliette trickled down my face.

"I do not want this."

"Then the mother goddess has chosen correctly. If you wanted this power, this strength, I would fear you." She cupped my face and turned it upward. "I will name you for what you are, and praise the goddess she has sent you to cleanse our world." She leaned forward and kissed my forehead. "You are the Destroyer. The one who will see our people rise again in glory and strength."

Around us, the world had gone rather quiet. She held tightly to my face, patted my cheeks and turned her back. "I name her the Destroyer. She has done no wrong here in my eyes and as such there will be no recriminations for this act of nature. The Destroyer lives outside our laws, as it should be."

The remaining Sylphs stayed quiet. Except for one. Ender Boreas. "She killed our people and you would let her go? Where is the queen who would fight to the ends of the earth for our survival?" He strode toward her and she flicked a hand at him. The wind that hit him sent him tumbling through the air, but didn't hurt him.

"Ender Boreas, you are young and full of piss and vinegar. Can you see the future? Do you know what would come for our family if we did not have this happen? Do you know that even now, my death creeps closer? We must have change, we must have a new queen. The Destroyer will be the one to name her."

Aria stepped over the rubble as if she were sighted. "Hear me now, those who I love more than my own life. Those who I know have it in them to be all the mother goddess wished for her second-born. By my decree, when the Destroyer shall name my heir, I will step down."

A gasp rippled through the crowd. Several Sylphs burst into tears, covering their faces. She was a beloved queen; why did she need to step down? Her age and lack of sight obviously did not slow her. She'd survived the attack of her own daughter with barely a bruise to show for it.

She held a hand out to me. "Those who are my supplicants, step forward."

The moment was surreal. We stood on the grave of her people I had killed, and now she wanted me to choose an heir to her throne?

I swayed, and a soft warm body pressed against my leg. "Forgive me, Lark. I was wrong."

"Peta," I dropped a hand to her back, "there is nothing to forgive."

Aria waved at me. In front of her stood the three remaining supplicants.

They were tall and slim, and with their hair hanging loosely around them, they looked like angels. If a bit wilted at the edges.

All three stared at me as though I were the devil incarnate. I couldn't disagree with them.

"Hurry, we are running out of time." Aria clutched the diamond I'd given her. "You have your mother's beauty, Larkspur. She was to help me choose my predecessor before she was killed. So now it rests on you."

Spirit. Goddess, every time I used it, another piece of my soul was eaten away. "Peta, I do not want to end up like Cassava."

"You won't. I have . . . someone I think can help you. But we must get through this first." I shot a look to her. My time in the oubliette had given me the opportunity to mull over all that had happened since I'd taken up my Enders leathers.

"You mean Talan, don't you?"

She bobbed her head. "Yes. I didn't know he was alive. If he truly lives, Lark, he can help you. But I can guide you in this in a small way. Touch their hands, use Spirit to discern their hearts."

My fears allayed, at least a little, I stepped up to the first woman. Her blue eyes were the color of a summer sky, brilliant in their purity. "I need to touch your hand."

She held her hand out, palm down. I laid my hand on top of hers. Carefully, calling Spirit with as much softness as I could, I threaded it through her as Peta had said. Colors and images flickered through me. "Kindness, that is your strength. But that is not what is needed now for your people."

I stepped back and Aria nodded. "I concur. Go on."

The next supplicant held her hand out, trembling. I barely touched her and she flinched. "Too much fear, it will stop you from being bold in the decisions you must make."

Again Aria backed my words.

The third supplicant thrust her hand out, fisted. I laid my palm on her, my stomach rolling with the sensation bouncing between us. "Violence and war is your desire. You wish to join with those who see as you do. That the humans should be subjected to our rule."

Around us the Sylphs gasped. It was only then I truly looked at her. The shape of her face, the curve of her lips. She could only be another of the queen's children. She snatched her hand away. "You know nothing."

Aria let out a sigh. "Child of mine, you are not to be queen. Do not fight me on this."

She stormed away, leaving no one else.

I stepped backward, but Spirit pulled me to the side, as if it were a creature I'd leashed and it tugged me in its wake. I followed, curious. I wove between the Sylphs, stopping in front of a group of Enders. They stared at me their eyes hard. Dangerous.

Holding one hand up, I walked in front of them, stopping at the end.

"Samara." My skin itched as though tiny bugs crept along it. "Hold out your hand."

Unlike the others, she held her hand out palm up, the blue stone in it. I took the stone and then placed my hand over hers. A crackle of electricity snapped between our hands, but she did not pull back and neither did I.

"Strength, honor, belief in her people . . . trust in her queen's choices. Love for her home. A razor-sharp intellect."

Lark, I do not wish her to be queen. She is not the one I choose. Well, that made things simpler. I could see Samara and all she held in her heart. She *was* the right choice.

I grinned at Samara. "The mother goddess has chosen you to be the Sylphs' next queen." I bowed from the waist to her and the Enders to either side of her clapped her on the back. Her eyes were locked on mine. She stepped up to me, close enough that our bodies brushed. "Those you wiped out?"

"Yes."

"The queen is right. Most were the ones we knew sought to destroy her. But not all." She drove a finger into my chest so hard it could have been a dull dagger tip.

I glared at her. "You're welcome."

From behind us, a cry broke the air. We spun in tandem.

Queen Aria lay on the ground, her hand clutching the smoky diamond. Her remaining daughter stood over her with a long, narrow staff identical to the Ender weapons. "I will be queen here, not some lowly, dwarf Ender."

Samara stepped around me. "I may be lowly, but I can still kick your ass, Stasha."

For once, I would get to be a spectator and not a participant of a battle.

Yeah, that was what I thought.

Not exactly what happened, though.

CHAPTER 24

amara rushed Stasha. The queen's daughter swung the long crystal staff, catching Samara low on her legs and sweeping them from under her. Not that she was down for long. Springing onto her feet, she launched herself at Stasha and tackled her.

I made my way to the queen's side, going to my knees on the hardened rock. The sound of the battle echoed in the newly made valley, but I kept my eyes locked on Aria. Her chest rose and fell, slowly, but still she breathed. "I can heal you."

"Do not waste your energy on an old woman like me. I have seen too many of my loves cross the Veil. I wish to be with them." Her hand fumbled for mine and I took it.

"Samara said not all of those who died were against you."

A rough cough shook her frame; for a moment, I thought she wasn't able to catch her breath.

Finally, the cough eased and she drew in a long gasp. "Her lover was one of those who fell, I saw him tumble under the rocks. She knows he plotted with Cassava, but she does not want to believe it of him." She tightened her grip on my fingers. "She will hate you, I think. Both for his death and for naming her my heir."

"My life matters not," I said. "If she demands my death I will not fight her."

Aria reached up to my face, her hand trembling. "No, Destroyer. Our families need you yet. You must stay alive, even if you are cast out for doing the things the Glow asked of you."

A scream snapped my head up. Samara had an arm locked around Stasha's neck, but the queen's daughter slipped out at the last second.

I watched them closely, noting something right away. The lines of power I expected to see on their arms as they dueled were missing.

"Are they not allowed to use their element?"

Ender Boreas stepped up beside me. "Not in a battle for the crown."

Peta shook her head, clearly as surprised as me. Though we were not to attack one another using our elements, the right to rule seemed as though it should be all or nothing. Especially after what had happened between Cassava and me.

"Is this the way of Sylphs?" Peta asked.

Boreas looked down at her. "There has not been a new queen in thousands of years. We don't know what our way is."

I stared at the combatants. Stasha's arms lit up as she reached for her element. "Samara, she's going to steal your air!" I yelled.

My words seemed to set off an explosion within the remaining Sylphs. Most turned their faces away, as if they couldn't bear to see what was going to happen. But seven ran toward the two combatants.

Call it a hunch, but I doubted they were going in to help Samara. I couldn't leave her on her own.

"Cactus, with me!" I yelled as I leapt away from the queen toward those who rushed Samara and Stasha. Samara might hate me, and the goddess didn't want her as a queen. But I felt the truth as only Spirit could show me. Samara would be the one to protect and raise the Sylphs like no other.

We ran across the broken rocks, fighting to keep our balance. My spear was somewhere in the mountainous rubble and I had no time to find it.

Hands and fists it was, then.

I caught the first Sylph around the waist in a tackle that took us both to the ground. Our fall knocked the wind out of him, if his gaping, flapping mouth was any indication. "You stay there. This is not your fight." I pointed at him as I scrambled up and ran for the next Sylph closest to me, a woman who stood a few inches taller than me. She spun as I approached, her hands raised and lines of power lighting her pale skin up as she lifted me from the ground.

From her left side, Peta crept along the ground. "Put her down, or I'll turn you into a kitty toy, air bag."

The Sylph startled and her hands lowered. "Samara is the lowest of the low. Her blood is as far from royal as one can get without being a half-breed. She cannot rule."

I closed the distance between us. "I completely understand."

She smiled at me and I slammed my fist into her jaw, dropping her where she stood. "I understand you are as small-minded as the rest of the elementals."

Shazer was right; all of them were assholes.

Cactus took out two of the other Sylphs. Normally I knew it wouldn't be so easy, except we weren't facing Enders. We were facing everyday Sylphs. Which begged the question, why weren't the Enders defending Samara?

I turned to see them standing in a circle around Aria, protecting their dying queen.

A triumphant yell brought my head around. Samara stood over Stasha. The queen's daughter still lived, her chest rose and fell, but her face was a wreck of blood and bits of bone. The shuffle of feet on rock turned me the other way and I swallowed hard. "Cactus, I think we're in trouble."

Peta crept toward me. "What in the world would make you think that, Dirt Girl?"

I grimaced. "Just a guess."

The Enders pulled their weapons as they approached Samara. I stood, putting myself between them. If it was the last thing I did, I would defend her. She was royalty, no matter what the other Sylphs thought.

"Enough," Samara said, her voice raised and full of threat. I held my ground, but the other Enders kept coming.

"Not good." Peta's tail lashed from side to side.

There was a moment where I thought the inevitable was going to slide by.

The Enders leapt as a unit, and I braced for the impact. But it came from a direction I did not expect. A wickedly cold wind snapped down off the remaining peaks and slammed into all of us. The Enders were tossed through the air and Cactus, Peta, and I were hammered into the ground. My cheek hit so hard the skin split and the warmth of my blood shocked the icy cold of my skin. I clung to the rocks as the temperature dropped and my breath misted around my face. Peta somehow managed to get beside me, scraping along the rocks until her fur tickled my face. Her eyes were squinted shut against the blasting wind. I wrapped a hand over her back and buried my face into her thick coat.

Minutes ticked by. I know, I counted each one. If I didn't do something, I was going to freeze in spite of Peta's efforts to keep me warm. Which meant Cactus was in even more trouble.

I rolled with difficulty so I could see behind me. Samara stood with her head thrown back, her short hair rippling in the wind. The lines of power wrapped around her arms, legs and torso, more than I'd ever seen before on another elemental.

Cactus was only a foot away from me. I held my hand out to him, pulling him close. The only person we were missing was my father. Peta picked up on my thoughts, yelling into the wind to me. "He's by the old queen."

As far as I knew, there was only one thing I could do. No one else seemed inclined to try and talk sense into Samara. Angling myself, I faced Samara while still lying on my back. I took a breath and stood, letting the wind catch me and throw me toward her. The speed of the wind slammed me into her so hard we went tumbling through the air three times ass over head before we hit the ground and the wind fell.

Her eyes were glazed and her lips were blue. "Destroyer."

"Yes." I slid off her and sat up in a crouch. "Sorry about that."

She blinked a few times before she put a hand to her head. "I can't let you go without doing something. They will think me weak."

"Do what you must," I said, pushing myself to my feet. "Only let me get my father home."

The Sylphs rushed forward, all of them this time. But there was no malice in them. Apparently her show of force was enough to convince them. They fell at Samara's feet on their knees, their hands raised above their heads and their eyes closed. I pushed through the crowd carefully until I was beside Aria and my father.

His eyes met mine first, and there was a tiny bit of clarity there, a hint of the man he'd been before Cassava had manipulated his mind. Before hope could truly spring forward, his green eyes narrowed and distrust replaced any emotion I might have seen there. Beside him lay the emerald stone, as if it had dropped from the heavens. Yet it had been in Cassava's hand when last I'd seen it. I scooped it up as I crouched down, tucking it into my vest.

"How did you find me?" my father asked.

"I used a Tracker." Exhaustion made my words soft.

His eyes narrowed farther, and his words were heavy with disappointment. "Using a supernatural? We will discuss this when we get back to the Rim."

He shook his head, but unlike the shame I normally felt, there was nothing but fatigue. Ignoring him, I went to my knees beside Aria. Her eyes met mine and she smiled. "Give her the stone. She will need it."

I glanced over my shoulder to where Samara walked through her people, touching them gently on the heads and shoulders. Connecting with them. "She kicked ass without help from anyone else."

"She is the strongest of us. I've always known it. But wild, ah, she is wild like I was when I first took the throne." Aria slipped the smoky diamond from her neck and handed it to me. The stone shook from the trembling in her hand and I folded my fingers over it.

Boreas, the only Ender who hadn't charged Samara, went to his knees beside his queen. Tears trickled down his cheeks as he took her free hand and held it to his chest. "Mother, do not leave us."

"Ah, my boy. How I love you. Protect her. She needs your strength and loyalty. And maybe even your love."

He dropped his head to her chest, his shoulders shaking. His defense of her, his fierce loyalty, it made even more sense. Though her daughters did not love her the way they should have, her son obviously made up for them. To see their bond made the lack of bond with my own remaining parent that much more painful.

I buried my hands into the rocks. One last thing before we left. My mother's spear . . . I wasn't leaving it behind. Using the power of the earth, I searched through the rubble, seeking the weapon and pulling it toward me. The ground bulged and spit up my spear, right into my hand. Peta rolled her eyes. "Shouldn't be able to do that either."

I pushed to my feet and stepped back, unable to stay any longer.

"Larkspur, you have an armband?" my father said, stopping me.

"No."

"You can use one of ours. I want you gone." Samara's voice cut through anything I might have said. She pointed at one of the Enders. He handed her an armband made of pale smoky quartz that mimicked the diamond I held in my hand.

There was no globe to use, though, no way to point ourselves home.

"We need to leave. Now." My father's grip was tight on my forearm, and his fingers dug into me.

"In a minute—"

"You would defy me?" He seemed truly confused.

I shook his hand off. "I need to speak with Samara before we go."

Samara wore no crown; she still wore her Enders leathers . . . yet she was the queen. I could see it in the way she held herself, the tip of her chin. Even the blood splatter on her leathers that spoke of the fight for the throne. I'd made the right choice. Even if the mother goddess didn't like it.

I bent a knee and lowered my head. "I will not fight you."

The Sylphs around us sucked in a collective breath. Cactus let out a single soft word. "No."

Through my bond to Peta, I felt her concern. And her pride in me. That was enough to keep me where I knelt. I no longer cared what my father thought of me. I would follow my heart.

"Look at me," Samara said. I slowly raised my head and lifted my eyes to hers. "Only because Aria spoke your sentence do I not kill you where you kneel. Leave from this place, Destroyer. Never return. Your life will be forfeit if you ever place foot in the Eyrie, wherever it may be."

I stared up at her. "That's it?"

Her eyes narrowed and every muscle in her body seemed to tense at once. "I will not go against her last words. I would like to take your heart from your body and cast it from the highest peak. But I won't. For her."

That was more along the lines of what I'd been expecting. I held the smoky diamond up to her. "A last gift from your queen."

She frowned and took the jewel from me. She knew what it was, but her face gave nothing away.

My father approached from behind, and clamped his hand on my shoulder. "Take us home, Larkspur. The Rim awaits."

Samara handed me the armband and our fingers touched for a brief second. Her eyes met mine and I saw all the emotions I too felt. Anger, fear, relief. She and I were too alike in too many ways.

"Good luck, Samara. You're going to need it."

I looked to Cactus, seeing how much I'd hurt him both in body and spirit. He was bruised and battered, blood trickled from his lip, and yet he stood there, waiting for me. "I'll take my Cactus first, then come back for you, Basileus."

Cactus's eyes softened and he smiled. I'd called him mine.

"No. You will not." My father pushed me down, and the ground softened to squeeze my legs.

"I love him and I am done leaving him behind!" I snapped.

"He is a half-breed who does not belong in the Rim!" my father roared, and I flinched as though he'd hit me. He might as well have.

"Lark, I'll go with Shazer. Wait for me," Cactus

said. His eyes locked on mine, and the smile in them was enough. "It will be okay, Lark. Just go."

With my hand on the armband, I paused for a moment. I felt as though I'd betrayed Cactus . . . again. Peta, once more in her housecat form, put her front paws on my bent knee.

"He will be all right. The Bastard will take him home faster than you realize."

I looked at the armband. "This won't get us home."

My father put his hand over the band and took it from me. "It will tune to me. It is a secret of the bands. They always take a ruler home."

He twisted the armband counterclockwise and the world dissolved around us in a rush of air.

And I was sent hurtling into my father's memories.

"hh, Ulani. My love, my heart. Help me," he whispered. "I can no longer see clearly and my mind . . . it is not my own. I fear what will happen to Lark if I do not write this now." Basileus put both hands on the rough wooden writing desk and lowered his head to the blank piece of paper.

The scent of eucalyptus curled through the room as Fern stepped through the door. Her belly bulged with their child and she cradled it gently. "Basil, what are you still doing up?"

"I am working, Fern." He softened his voice. "Go to bed, I will be there soon."

She smiled and ran a hand over his shoulders, her touch soothing some of the fear in him. Ulani's spirit had been right, Fern had been a good choice. "Come to bed soon, the sickness has only left you. I don't want it to come back."

He nodded and kissed her hand where it lay on his shoulder. "Of course. You are right."

Still smiling, she turned and left the way she'd come in. He waited until he heard the telltale creak of their bed as she lay down.

Picking up the feather to his right, he dipped it into the inkwell and put the tip to the paper.

Dear Larkspur,

The sickness you saw me carry was not a sickness of the body, but of the mind. It was as if Cassava had planted a booby trap in me, and when she could no longer manipulate my actions, she set it off.

I do not know how long I will have where my mind is fully functioning. I pray this will pass, but I fear it never will. I fear the damage done is irrevocable.

He paused and dipped the pen again, the sound of the tip scratching on the thick paper the only noise in the room.

I loved your mother, more than any other woman in my life. You need to know that. I knew she was a child of Spirit. I knew she would give me half-breed children. I didn't care; I wanted both you and your brother. I loved you and your brother for everything you were. Beautiful, sweet babies who were mine in a way Cassava would not allow me with my other children. I tell you this because I remember the things I have done. The words I have said, and I see how they have torn at you. How they have broken you, and it pains me beyond all I can describe.

They were not my words, daughter. Never have I seen you as less than the rest of our family. You have always been the one I pinned my hopes on. Cassava believed Bramley was to be my heir, the one my throne would fall to.

But she does not know the truth.

You were the one, Larkspur. You were always the one with the fire in your heart, and the power in your soul. From the time you took your first breath, you were the warrior Fate decreed would change our world.

I name you as my heir, Larkspur. Should I fall, or should my mind break, you will be the one to see our family through. There is none other who can do this; the mother goddess has made it clear you are the choice for the Rim.

I love you, daughter. No matter what happens, know my love for you is true. You have always been the one I loved the best. The one I pinned all my hopes on.

Again he paused and dipped the feather, but this time he stopped with the tip hanging over the paper. The black liquid dripped off the tip, leaving a blob on the bottom of the page that spread in a shape he knew all too well.

The raven's wings spread wide across the page, and he shook his head. "No. I must finish this. Blackbird, be gone from my mind!"

I wobbled, even though I was on one knee in the Traveling room within the Rim. The memory would have brought me to my knees if I hadn't already been there. Claws dug into my leg. I turned my attention to my familiar. "Peta, did you see—"

"No. I felt things that were not you."

"What are you two talking about?" my father demanded.

The doors burst open and several guards poured in.

Everything jumbled together. The journey, the destruction of the Eyrie, the death of Aria, my father's memory, the oubliette. I slumped forward to my knees.

"Father, Vetch tried to kill Bella and me. The guards *will* corroborate," I said. The guards nodded one by one.

"Why would your brother try to kill you?" His eyes were filled with confusion.

"Because he thought he was the named heir. Because Cassava set him on us." Slowly I pushed myself to my feet, though I was anything but steady. "I need to rest. You need to name an heir."

I walked out of the Traveling room, Peta right with me at my side.

One of the guards, Arbutus, caught up to me. "I will see you to your room, Princess."

I snorted. "Where is Raven?"

"Gone, missing for the last week."

"And Blackbird?"

Arbutus shrugged. "I don't know who that is, but none with the name has been here."

I stopped. "I need a message sent to Bella and Ash. Tell them the queen is dead. And give Bella this." I took the small leather pouch from my side and turned my back to Arbutus. I pulled the emerald stone from my vest and dropped it into the bag. It was the best I could do with what I had at hand.

I gave it over to Arbutus.

He bobbed his head and turned back the way we'd come. "I'll take the message myself."

I should have been happy, but the truth was, I knew Blackbird was far from done. Likely he was licking his wounds and preparing some new trap for me. Then there was my father's memory I'd seen. It tore me up from the inside out. Knowing he *knew* he was losing his mind to the damage Cassava had done.

We reached my room and I slipped inside, closing the door behind me.

I'd lost my father, just as I'd found him within his memories. A rough tongue flicked over my cheek, swiping away a tear. I dropped to the bed, then rolled my head so I could tuck my face against Peta.

"Lark, what did you see?"

Carefully I pieced the words together. "The letter, I'm sure it was the one he sent to me in the Pit. The one Blackbird took. He'll have destroyed it by now."

"Of course." Peta stretched out further, yawning. "He's not a fool."

I closed my eyes, feeling like I was missing something. Something out of reach that if I could put my finger on everything else would make sense.

Peta was right, Blackbird was not a fool. I thought about the final thing my father had said. Even now, with Cassava and Blackbird gone, he couldn't understand how destroyed our family was.

Dysfunction on a royal level.

"You need to sleep, Lark. Close your eyes."

There was no use in arguing. Already the warmth of the bed, the comfort of Peta beside me, and the knowledge that my father was back where he was supposed to be, lulled me into dreamland.

Once there, my dreams were anything but restful. I saw Ash banished, Cactus whipped with the lava whip while Cassava shrieked with laughter, Peta skinned and her hide put on Samara's back. None of the dreams made any sense.

The last was a dream I'd not seen for months. My mother and Bramley killed by Cassava. I held my mother in my arms, sobbing. Her dead eyes stared up at me, empty of soul, empty of anything that made her my mother except the brilliant blue color.

"You have failed me, Lark."

I shot straight up in bed, panting for air, tears streaming down my face. I wanted to believe it was yet another game of the mother goddess . . . but I couldn't be sure. And that doubt hurt me as much as the thought of failing her. I pressed a hand to my eyes and struggled to control my emotions, but the heart pain would not leave me.

Peta slept soundly as I dressed and slipped out of the room into the hall. The night beckoned to me as I walked out of the barracks. The pull of the dark was a visceral sensation that tugged my feet forward until I stood in the center of the blasted field, where everything lay dead around me. Slowly, finally, the dream faded.

My ears caught the shuffle of cloth on cloth, and the faintest snap of a twig underfoot. I held my ground, even as my body tensed. I called the power of the earth to me and held it tightly.

"Blackbird, I'm surprised you would show your face." I kept my back to him.

"Lark, please. Call me Raven."

"You are not my brother." I turned then to stare at him. He wore his cloak, though it did not cover his face for the first time.

His face was drawn in lines of fury. "You think you killed her. You think you're stronger than her?"

"Cassava?" I snorted. "She is nothing without the emerald stone."

"Do not push me, Lark. I could kill you where you stand," he snarled. Lies, they filtered through the air to me. He couldn't reach the earth's power here where the land was dead. I could. And I held the sapphire stone still. I had three elements to his four.

"Then why don't you?" I took a step toward him and he moved back. "That's what I thought. Even with all that power, you are a coward at heart. Every time we've faced each other, you've run. Any time you've been hurt, you flee with your tail tucked between your legs like the incestuous cur you are." I stalked him with every word.

"I will rule the Rim, Lark. I will be named as the heir. Even now Father is writing a new will. Not this piece of dog shit." He shook a piece of paper at me.

The note I'd seen my father writing in his memory. Blackbird truly was a fool to still be carrying it around. Or maybe . . . maybe he couldn't believe what it said. That I was the one Father had loved the best.

"I have no desire to rule, Blackbird, but that doesn't mean I'm going to let you take the throne."

He held out his hand and red lines of power raced up his arm. With a snap of his fingers, fire burst up in a full circle around us.

"Then let us see who is truly stronger once and for all. Does your promise still stand? That you would never hurt me? Or are you a liar now too?"

My jaw ticked as I struggled for words. "A promise predicated on a lie is no promise. We end this now."

A flickering figure to the right of us walked through the flames. The mother goddess glowed with power, her dark hair floating on an unseen and unfelt breeze.

"You are both my chosen ones. I forbid you to fight."

I raised my eyebrows but did not take my eyes off Blackbird. "You are the reason he ran from the other fights, aren't you?"

Blackbird sneered. "I am no coward. I am obedient. To both my mothers." He gave her a bow from the waist.

I took a step back and drew in a breath. "I suppose that makes one of us, then."

His eyes snapped to mine, glittering with a perverse pleasure. "You would fight me still?"

I twitched the fingers on my right hand and the

trees pulled back around us. The fool didn't notice. "I would do more than fight you. I will kill you."

he trees at the edge of the blasted land shot forward, whistling through the air with the velocity of a hurricane. Blackbird dodged the first two, but got caught on one I'd pulled from behind him. I didn't wait to see if he would get up. Bolting forward, I yanked my spear from my side and whipped it around.

"No, Larkspur, I forbid this!" the mother goddess yelled.

I didn't pause. "Then you should never have chosen us both."

I thrust the spear forward and I was jerked backward, vines wrapping around my waist. They tightened and began to heat, bursting into flames.

I threw my head back and screamed, even as I

shattered the remaining vines, breaking apart the molecules into tiny droplets.

Blackbird was on his knees and his blue eyes were wild with fury. There were no words between us. We'd said all we'd needed to say.

Back and forth we fought, flexing our power through the world around us.

Like a game of chess, we were careful in our choices.

I used the sapphire, drawing on its power without knowing what I was doing. I held my hands out and water condensed in front of me into a rolling ball. With a twist, I threw it at Blackbird, changing the molecules, hardening them into a ball of ice. It clipped him on the shoulder, spinning him around. He held a hand up and pointed a single finger at me.

A bolt of lightning snapped out of the sky and shot through my body. The electricity arched my back and sparkling lights danced before me. I couldn't breathe, couldn't think past the pain cascading through me. Blackbird's laughter rolled around me and I fought to find my connection to the earth through the pain. There at the edge of my consciousness it hovered. I reached for it and pulled it to me.

Held to it while Blackbird poured everything he had into me. The lightning stopped, but I was on my knees and his hands were on my head. "This is a battle I did not want, Lark. I do love you."

His words were meaningless as he used Spirit to hammer my mind, as if he were trying to crack a nut.

It felt like he had his fingers inside my brain and

was pulling it apart section by section. The screaming started and I couldn't stop it as I scrabbled to get away from him.

He was stronger than me.

I couldn't stop him.

Were the words mine, or his? A tiny flicker of darkness spun in my mind and black eyes blinked up at me. *Good thing I made sure you kept a piece of me, Elemental.*

Astrid. The darkness swam between Blackbird and me, popping the connection between us like a bubble being burst. I fell back and Blackbird was thrown away from me to the far edge of the blasted field.

My whole body shook, convulsions shuddering through me from head to toe. I wasn't sure I could even stand. I stayed on the ground, my hands buried in the soft, dead earth.

Blackbird stared at me as he stalked forward, his blue eyes full of curiosity. Seeing him jump from one extreme to the other told me all I needed. He was as unstable as Cassava.

"How?"

"Does it matter?" I had to stall, to buy myself time. I didn't dare glance at the mother goddess. To think she would intercede on my behalf was stupid.

Blackbird smiled, and I wondered how I'd missed the lies in him. The deception. My desire to be loved had blinded me to the truth.

With a roar he leapt at me, shifting in midair. Of course he was a shifter. Why was I not surprised?

He landed on four large, black paws as an oversized

bear. He roared a second time, his blue eyes glittering through the heavy pelt around his face.

He swung at my leg with one thick paw, the claws digging deep into my calf as he hauled me toward him. Truth was he could have killed me easily, stealing my air from my lungs. But he was dragging this out.

Making me suffer.

The claws cut into my muscle and tore through it as easily as if it were a razor blade.

I grabbed at his face, driving my fingers into his eye sockets. He roared and pulled back, shaking his head. Stumbling back a few feet, he put distance between us and shifted once more.

"Now you're just showing off." I gasped the words as I fought a sudden wave of nausea followed by a narrowing of my vision. This was not the time to lose consciousness.

Blackbird grinned, blood trickling from his eyes. "Maybe. Maybe I want you to see how puny you are next to me."

"Enough." The mother goddess spoke and her power slammed into us both, dropping us flat. I reached for the strength of the earth and got nothing. By the look on Blackbird's face, he was in the same position.

"Neither of you will fight. I have chosen you both. For different reasons, and while you may never understand fully, I do not expect you to. I expect you to *obey* me." Her words grew in strength with each one until her voice hammered my head with its volume and power. Her hair was dark as the night and

I knew which side of her personality we were dealing with. Yet why then did she save me? Because that was what happened.

Blackbird would have killed me if she hadn't stopped him.

"Yes, Mother." Blackbird bowed his head.

The mother goddess looked at me. I raised an eyebrow. "Get stuffed."

Her lips twitched. "Blackbird. I forbid you from seeking Lark out. You will not fight with your sister." She spoke like a mother scolding small children.

He looked from her to me. "You cannot stop her from coming after me. She is the disobedient one."

I wasn't going to argue with that.

"Then we will make sure she is kept far from you, my boy."

She clapped her hands and a wave of power caught me and threw me backward. I tumbled several times, all the way to the edge of the blasted field. Blackbird and the mother goddess were gone, as if they'd never stood there.

"Did you tell Viv to get stuffed?"

I blinked up at Griffin who stared down at me. "Yeah, I think I did."

"Well, I'll be damned. She finally met her match, yeah?" He grinned as he held a hand out and helped me to stand. I leaned on him, unable to put weight on my mauled leg. He handed me a piece of paper as I stood. I looked down at it, the familiar writing across the parchment and the blob of ink as my father's hand had wavered. This was all I needed to prove that my father should not pick Briar or Raven as heir.

The clearing was battered and bruised from the fight, trees at the edges torn up from the roots, the dirt burnt and charred in places.

Across from us, Peta raced across the blasted field, blending into the dirt. Behind her came Ash and Cactus, weapons drawn.

"Stop doing this to me, Lark!" Peta yelled as she leapt for me. I caught her and placed her on my shoulder.

"It isn't on purpose. Honest."

Ash and Cactus didn't look at one another, only me. I couldn't help the sigh that escaped me.

"Let's go home." Cactus thumbed back toward the Rim. Griffin didn't come with us, but watched us go. I know because I turned twice to see him staring after us. His dark eyes were unfathomable. Yet his stance told me all I needed to know.

The night was not over.

We walked in silence, me leaning on both men, but it was not the silence of comfort. Or of a job well done. The silence tasted of a heavy blow yet to come.

As we approached the Spiral, I was not surprised to see the crowd of people. They parted for us, but not with deference. I did not care. My father stood on the steps of the Spiral. Fern was nowhere to be seen. I put a hand on Ash. "Where is Fern and the baby?"

The words had barely left my lips when I knew. He shook his head and spoke only one word. "Cassava."

My heart thumped hard against my chest. Poor

Fern. Of all the people in our family, she had cared for me in her own way. Had stood up for me against my father.

At least she would be at peace where she was, though it was a small comfort.

The man I called my father raised both hands in the air as we drew close.

"I will name my heir so there will be no dissension in our home."

He paused, saw me, and his shoulders sagged. "Larkspur, I will deal with you in a moment."

Bella was there with him, as was Briar. All my father had left were two girls to choose from.

Bella's eyes met mine and I forced a smile for her. She blinked back tears as she put a hand to her heart. I did the same.

My father spoke. "My people, I have seen the error of my ways. My sons were not worthy of being named heir."

I clutched the paper in my hand, crinkling it. If he named Briar, I would have to say something. I prayed he would name Bella.

"My heir will be my youngest daughter, Briar."

The crowd cheered and it felt as though the weight of the Wretched Peaks had crawled onto my shoulders. There was only one thing I could do.

I held up my hand. "Stop."

A gasp rippled through the crowd, followed closely by my name.

"I have evidence that you are not in your right mind, that Cassava and Blackbird have stripped you of your ability to rule, to make the best choices for this family."

I approached and held the paper out to Bella. "Bella, read this, please."

She did, her voice stumbling until she got to the part about me being named heir. Her eyes shot to mine and she grinned. "By your own hand, Father, you have named Larkspur your heir and rightful ruler to your throne."

By law, there was nothing he could do. The letter pre-dated his naming of Vetch as heir.

His face paled, and from behind him I saw a glimmer of my mother. Whether it was her spirit or the mother goddess come to watch the game, I didn't know and didn't care. She placed a hand on him. I looked around; no one else was looking at her.

Spirit whispered through me, and I knew Spirit was the reason only I could see her.

"I will not recant," my father whispered, his eyes locking on mine. "I . . . name Larkspur as the heir to my throne and the next queen of the Rim."

The crowd went to their knees around me.

How easy would it be to take the throne? I looked at Ash and Cactus. I could have them both.

I glanced at Briar, who looked relieved, and then to Bella. She nodded. "Take it, Lark. I will stand with you in this."

But I was not the best one for the job. I was a half-breed. A Terraling needed to be on the throne of the Rim. A place I no longer belonged.

"I refuse."

My father's eyes widened even as Bella's closed. "Excuse me?"

The mother goddess shook her head and spoke directly to me. "I will let you suffer his madness if you do not accept this. I want you here, on the throne, Larkspur."

Again with the machinations. "Bella is the best choice. She is trained as a diplomat, she is trained as a Princess. I am trained as an Ender, and I would serve her as my queen. It would be my honor to place her life above my own." I went to one knee and bowed my head to Bella.

"You would give up your right to the throne?" My father's voice was incredulous.

A calm surety flowed through me, Spirit calming me. "Yes. Bella is the best choice. If you choose Briar, I will force your hand as your spoken heir."

Again the crowd gasped. I dared to lift my eyes. My father stared at me with little emotion on his face. Fern and his child were gone, killed by Cassava. He had no other heirs awaiting him besides his three daughters.

"Belladonna." He held a hand out to her. "Will you take this responsibility your sister so thoughtlessly casts aside?"

She placed her hand in his, but not before looking at me. Her eyes were troubled. Perhaps she didn't like the thought of being chosen last. Yet I felt the certainty of my choice the same as I'd felt when I'd named Samara as heir. Belladonna was the one who should rule.

Griffin leaned against a tree, watching me dumped like a bag of human garbage. "Kicked out?"

I dusted off my clothes. "You don't seem surprised."

"Not. Seen it coming for a while, yeah? I'm going to come with you for a bit. I got something you should learn."

We walked side by side through the forest, angling to the south. "What's that?"

"Teach you how to make things from the earth. Not with your power, but with your hands. Teach you the ways of a blacksmith. It'll keep you company while you're away. I think you'll have a knack for it."

That was not what I'd been expecting.

The days and nights rolled into each other and we only stopped when fatigue or the pain in my healing leg finally demanded I rest. There was a strange emptiness in my heart I chose not to pay attention to.

The loss of my Peta. Of Ash and Cactus.

Of watching Bella cry as I was dragged away, never having even met my niece.

Of understanding how much the mother goddess had used me.

The edge of the desert beckoned me on the fifth morning. Flat, empty, desolate. The ground was baked so hard it might have been concrete. A hot wind blew across the expanse, kicking up tumbleweeds and dust.

"So this is home."

"Did they give you a time period?" Griffin asked as we stared out over the horizon.

"They didn't. Banishment is forever, you know."

"Only because they don't know you can survive it. Yeah?" Griffin punched me lightly in the arm.

I laughed, but it was bitter-filled. "Yeah, I know." Which was why the punishment didn't scare me. "Griffin, my father banished Cactus too. He won't survive."

"I'll get the boy, take him to a safe place after I show you what I gots to show you. A place outside our world where he can be safe and wait on you. Yeah?" He tipped his chin forward.

"What do you mean, wait on me?"

He burst out laughing. "How long before you decide you're going to leave this desert? How long before the chains that hold you here weaken and you break this rule too?"

My face heated with embarrassment. "I don't try to be disobedient."

"Nah, it comes natural to you. Every Spirit user is like that. It's why you're so much fun." He winked and headed out onto the flats without me. I watched him go, thinking about what my future might hold.

He was right about one thing. I wouldn't stay here forever. Peta needed me, and I needed her. A little more time I could stand apart from her, but not forever.

No, not forever.

I took a step and my bare feet touched the hot, hard ground. The earth shivered as I reached out for my power, feeling its strength.

Above my head the whoosh of wings tugged my gaze heavenward. Shazer flew high above, Peta balanced on his back in her leopard form. Her eyes met mine and I raised a hand to her as they banked away from the desert. I dug into my bag and pulled out the blue sapphire. With a toss, I sent it into the air. Peta caught it in both paws. "Take it to Finley."

I held a hand up to her, the pain of losing her once again tearing at me.

"Wait for me, my friend. This is not forever. A little while and then . . . then we will be together again."

CHAPTER 27

 watched her walk into the desert. The walk of shame was not lost on me; I'd done it more than once. A smile tugged at my lips. The defiance in her stride, the tilt of her head. Every part of her screamed rebellion. I liked her already.

Exiled into the desert . . . she would not have done it if she truly thought it would cause her or her loved ones pain. I had no doubt she went because for the moment, the threats had passed. Or so she thought.

"She thinks she's safe, doesn't she?" Tom whispered from my shoulder. I glanced at the fairy and then to the woman who'd more than captured my attention.

"Yes, she does."

Tom hiccupped. "What you going to do about

that? 'Cause I know you aren't the nice boy everyone thinks you are. Eh?"

I couldn't take my eyes from Larkspur, until the Pegasus flew overhead. I crouched, feeling my heart tug at me. Peta clung to the equine's back, but she never looked my way. Lark lifted a hand and something sparkled in the air between her and Peta.

"I have to let her fall further, Tom. She has to be broken before I can help her. But I want to keep tabs on her. That's where you come in."

"Ahh, Talan. I don't want to stay in the desert! My wings dry up and—"

"I saved you from having your wings removed. Samara was going to rip them from your back, if you recall." I held a hand up to him and he stepped into my palm. "Go and keep an eye on her. I'll check in with you at the edge of the desert twice a year. Summer and winter solstice."

He grunted and lifted off from my hand in a drunken wobble. I put my hands on my knees and rolled my shoulders.

"You need to be shattered, little Larkspur," I 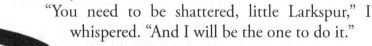 whispered. "And I will be the one to do it."

COMING SOON

COMING SUMMER 2016

ROOTBOUND

THE ELEMENTAL SERIES

BOOK 5

ACKNOWLEDGMENTS

There are always far more people than only a writer behind the making of a book. I am so grateful for the help of my amazing editors, beta readers, proofreaders and formatters. Not in order but: Tina Winograd, Shannon Page, Lysa Lessieur, Jean Faganello (aka Mom) and my ARC Team (too many to list!).

My two amazing boys who tolerate my wacky brain and sometimes absentminded presence as a new story runs throughly mind. They are my heart and the reason I smile every day.

I would be remiss if I did not thank my readers. You trust me with characters you have grown to love, and I hope you continue to enjoy the rides and journeys I take you on.

AUTHORS NOTE

Thanks for reading "Windburn". I truly hope you enjoyed the continuation of Lark and her family's story, and the world I've created for them. If you loved this book, one of the best things you can do is leave a review for it. Amazon.com is where I sell the majority of my work, so if I can only ask for one place for reviews that would be it it – but feel free to spread the word on all retailers.

Again, thank you for coming on this ride with me, I hope we'll take many more together. The rest of The Elemental Series along with my other novels, are available in both ebook and paperback format on all major retailers.

You will find purchase links on my website at www.shannonmayer.com. Enjoy!

ABOUT THE AUTHOR

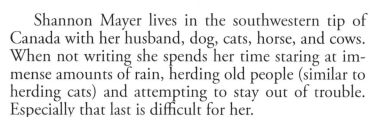

Shannon Mayer lives in the southwestern tip of Canada with her husband, dog, cats, horse, and cows. When not writing she spends her time staring at immense amounts of rain, herding old people (similar to herding cats) and attempting to stay out of trouble. Especially that last is difficult for her.

She is the *USA Today* Bestselling author of the The Rylee Adamson Novels, The Elemental Series, The Nevermore Trilogy, A Celtic Legacy series and several contemporary romances. Please visit her website for more information on her novels.

http://www.shannonmayer.com/

Ms. Mayer's books can be found at these retailers:

Amazon	iTunes
Barnes & Noble	Smashwords
Kobo	Google Play

Made in United States
North Haven, CT
14 June 2024

53602553R10192